STORMS

Gerri Hill

Bella
BOOKS

2011

Bella Books, Inc.
P.O. Box 10543
Tallahassee, FL 32302

Printed in the United States of America on acid-free paper
First published 2011

Editor: Anna Chinappi
Cover Designer: Linda Callaghan

ISBN 13: 978-1-59493-249-6

Other Bella Books By Gerri Hill

CHAPTER ONE

Carson grabbed the phone without looking, knowing it would be Rebecca. She was late—as usual—and she tucked it against her shoulder as she hunted for her keycard.

"I know, I know, I'm late," she said. "Sorry. I'm on my way."

"Then I'm glad I caught you."

She nearly dropped the phone at the sound of the man's voice. She stopped in her tracks, her brain recognizing the voice before her heart allowed her to.

"Chase?" she whispered.

"Hey, sis."

"Oh, my God. How did you find me?" She sat down heavily,

her lunch date with Rebecca forgotten as her mind raced. She hadn't heard her brother's voice in twelve years.

"Well, you know, our lawyer found your lawyer. You really shouldn't have kept your business with Grammy Mae's attorneys if you didn't want to be found."

"I never thought anyone would look," she said, surprised at the bitterness of her words. She'd thought that twelve years was enough to get past it.

"You ran away so fast, we didn't think you wanted us to look."

"Ran away?" She laughed, again the bitterness tasting strange in her mouth.

"What he did to you was wrong, Car, but it didn't reflect what the rest of us felt. At least not me. You know that."

"Whatever," she mumbled childishly, both annoyed and thrilled at the shortening of her name. Chase had rarely called her by her full name.

"You need to come home now."

"What? You call me up after twelve years and tell me to come home? No pleasantries? No *how have you been*? No *where have you been*? Nothing?"

"I know where you've been. Europe mostly. You have a fondness for Italy."

"Well, the women there are really hot."

"No doubt. I imagine now you're back in New York."

"You imagine wrong," she said, glancing out her hotel window at the unobstructed view of Fisherman's Wharf and San Francisco Bay.

"Look, you need to come home. He's dying. He has cancer."

"So? He's been dead to me for a long time."

"Cody and Chance are running the ranch into the ground, and Colt wants to turn it into a dude ranch, of all things," he said. "I need you to come back."

"The old man's too sick to run the place?"

"He's been sick for over a year, in and out of the hospital. He's coming home tomorrow. He's coming home to die. You need to make your peace with him, Car."

She wanted to feel nothing. In fact, she convinced herself that the twinge of guilt she was feeling was for the ranch and not her father. She loved the ranch. She loved everything about it. Up until that final day, however.

"Please, Car. Come back. Come back home."

CHAPTER TWO

"Wow, even by your standards, this is really late," Rebecca said as Carson joined her at their favorite outdoor café.

"Sorry," she said, bending over and kissing her friend quickly on the cheek. "I got a phone call."

Rebecca finally looked at her, her brow furrowed. "What's wrong? You look like you've seen a ghost."

"Aptly put." Carson took a swallow of water before continuing. "My brother."

"Carson Cartwright, you have a brother?"

"Four of them, actually."

Rebecca smiled and leaned her elbows on the table. "Oh, you're always such a woman of mystery. I learn something new about you every time we talk."

"That's because you know nothing about me so any time I let something slip, you're fascinated."

"Of course. Like I said, a woman of mystery." She leaned closer. "Why is that, Carson? Why do you keep yourself so guarded?"

"It's a hard habit to shake," she said, pausing as a waiter placed a bowl in front of her.

"I took the liberty of ordering," Rebecca explained. "Crab salad."

"Thank you," she said, smiling at the waiter. She no longer had an appetite, but she picked up her fork, twisting it in her hand. "He wants me to come home."

"Home?"

"Montana."

"Where is Montana exactly?"

Carson rolled her eyes.

"I'm kidding, of course," Rebecca said. "It's somewhere north, I know that. Cows and snow?"

Carson nodded. "Mountains, forests, huge ranches. Lush green valleys. My family has a ranch there." She sighed, picturing the ranch in the summertime, the bright green meadow against the blue sky almost too beautiful to absorb. How many days did she ride off and lay down on the carpet of green, staring up into the endless blue, thinking there was no better place on earth than right there where she was. And for a while, that was true.

"And? Why does he want you there?"

"My father is dying."

"And she has a father too."

"Look, I know I haven't told you much about my past—"

"Much? Try nothing." Rebecca pushed her salad aside. "When I met you, you were a wide-eyed nineteen-year-old lost in Manhattan. All you told me was you'd run away from home." She shrugged. "Nothing unusual there, except you had a never-ending supply of cash. It took me two years to learn your grandmother was loaded. Now, after knowing you, what, eleven years now, you tell me your estranged family wants you to come home. To Montana." She raised her eyebrows. "So are you going to tell me about it or what?"

Carson looked at her affectionately, the woman who had befriended her all those years ago. Yes, she'd been wide-eyed and scared out of her mind. She didn't recall what had possessed her to flee to New York, she only knew she wanted to be far away from home, and far away from her memories. When her grandmother died—Grammy Mae—she was as surprised as everyone else to learn she'd left her entire estate to Carson. The explanation the attorney gave her was that the ranch would be left to the boys, assuming Carson's father would exclude her from that inheritance. Carson had dropped out of college the next week, leaving Boulder and moving into her grandmother's house in Denver, waiting for it to sell. And it moved so quickly, she hadn't had time to formulate a plan, no time to decide what to do or where to go. Why not New York?

"Why didn't you ever try to sleep with me?"

Rebecca leaned back, surprise showing on her face. "Where did that question come from? I thought we were talking about your family."

"It occurred to me that you never once even hinted that you wanted to sleep with me. Yet you had a parade of women coming and going, but never me."

Rebecca reached across the table and squeezed her hand. "Oh, my beautiful Carson. You were nineteen. I was already thirty-five. Yes, it would have been so easy to seduce you. And I won't lie. The thought did cross my mind." She smiled. "But I didn't want to do that to you. You needed a friend." She waved her hand dismissively. "Besides, I taught you everything you know."

"Yes, how *not* to fall in love."

"Love is so overrated. It's a pain in the ass. Isn't it much more fun to enjoy sex and not have to worry about the emotional turmoil that comes with a relationship?"

"I never understood that about you," Carson said. "You could have had any woman you wanted."

"I did have. Many of them."

"I meant *have* as in love," she clarified. "Yet you never wanted any part of it. Why?"

"We all have our secrets, don't we? And I believe we were discussing yours, not mine."

Carson let it go. At first, she was simply overwhelmed by the number of women Rebecca would bring home. A different one nearly every night. And she took it all in, learning Rebecca's skill of sex without love. Yes, she taught her well. Fortunately, she had enough emotional scars that it didn't take much to dull her to love. No doubt Rebecca had been deeply in love once and had her heart broken. Carson, on the other hand, couldn't relate to that part of things. Her small high school out in the middle of nowhere consisted mostly of kids from other ranches. Mostly boys, and the few girls her own age were straight. Of course, as a teenager with raging hormones, she couldn't be choosy. She found if she kept it quiet and under the table, straight girls were more than willing to experiment. It wasn't until she'd gone to college that she finally slept with another lesbian.

Once in New York, she quickly picked up the social skills required to mimic Rebecca, the woman who took her in and offered a place to live. She wouldn't admit it to her, but she'd long grown weary of that life now. She often exaggerated her sexual trysts just to keep Rebecca amused and thinking that she'd raised a star pupil who followed in her footsteps. She couldn't very well tell her that she spent most of her time alone on her frequent trips to Europe. It was simply too exhausting to keep the pace that Rebecca assumed she kept.

All of which made her question why she had agreed to meet Rebecca in San Francisco in the first place. Despite their age difference, she still couldn't keep up with the older woman. Not when it came to parties and women. Perhaps the excuse of going home—back to Montana—would be her reprieve.

"Would you think I was crazy if I ditched you and took my brother up on his offer?"

"Crazy? Yes. You love San Francisco. You'd leave this to go be with cows?"

"Cows and sheep," she said. "Or that's what the ranch used to raise. And horses." She had an image of the white stallion she used to ride. Windstorm. She purposefully hadn't thought of him—or the ranch—in years.

"Why did you run away? Or is that a subject you still don't want to discuss?"

Over the years, Rebecca had brought it up occasionally. Each time, Carson had chosen to ignore the question. This time was no different. But she was willing to give her something.

"I lived with my grandmother for a few months before I went off to college. She died my second year there." At Rebecca's raised eyebrows, she added, "University of Colorado, Boulder. Anyway, as you know, I was her sole beneficiary." She grinned. "A kid with money. A dangerous combination."

"Yes. Good thing you met me. Some lesser person might have taken you for everything you had."

"That's true." Of course, it helped that Rebecca was a wealthy socialite in her own right. Yes, Rebecca not only showed her how to party with the ladies, she also showed her how to invest wisely. "Thank you."

"You're welcome. So you're going back? To a place you haven't been in eleven, twelve years?"

"Twelve."

"And you've had no contact with them in that time?"

"No. Not until today. Chase—he's my twin—he said—"

"You're a twin? God, woman, what other bombs are you going to drop on me today?" She leaned forward again, elbows braced on the table. "Carson and Chase. Nice Western names. You have three other brothers?"

"Cody, Colt and Chance."

Rebecca laughed. "Are you serious?"

Carson nodded. "Yep. Cartwrights. Circle C Ranch. As you said, very Western."

Rebecca's smile slowly faded. "So? Are you leaving me?"

Carson's gaze left Rebecca as she stared out over the bay. "I shouldn't, should I? I mean, what do I want there? It's been twelve years, right?"

Rebecca again squeezed her hand. "Go if you feel you need to. If for nothing else, closure."

"Closure? I'm not sure that applies to me. I've reconciled everything."

"Have you? I guess since you can so easily talk about your past, then nothing still haunts you. My mistake."

Carson smiled at her friend, knowing she'd hit on the

truth. Yes, her past still haunted her. She could pretend all she wanted that she was happy and content with her life now, but truth was, she wasn't. There was always something missing. She used to think it was the fact that she didn't work, that she had no responsibilities, that she wasn't being a productive member of society that made her feel so empty. But she traveled a lot, she shared special occasions with friends, she never lacked for companionship, so there was little time to dwell on her fate. Maybe that was one reason she constantly kept moving, kept traveling—it kept her from examining her life and questioning her very existence.

"You always could see through my armor, couldn't you?"

"It's funny, Carson, but the older you get the more your pain shows. When you were a brash nineteen-twenty-year-old, you had the world by the balls. You were invincible. The last few years though, you've had such a—I don't know—melancholy look about you. Not really sad, exactly, but more sorrowful, depressed." She smiled, softening her words. "Not to say you've been depressed. That's not what I mean. You just—"

"I know what you mean. You're right. I think maybe I've been more reflective, maybe even judging my life somewhat. It's not always a pretty picture."

"Which is odd. You have everything, Carson. You're a beautiful woman, you have money and the time to spend it. You have connections all over the world. Most people would envy your life."

"Would they? In the end, I'm still alone."

"In the end, we're all alone."

CHAPTER THREE

Kerry Elder stood back, trying politely not to eavesdrop as the brothers argued. It was obvious Colt Cartwright was the only one on board with this. As their voices got louder and more agitated, she thought it was time to intervene before she lost without ever being able to present her case. She blew out an exasperated breath and stepped forward.

"Excuse me," she said, smiling broadly at the four men whose argument with each other strained their handsome features. Four brothers, all tall and dark, each as handsome as the next. And not a one of them wearing a wedding ring. Amazing. Of course, she could use that to her advantage. She wasn't above flirting to get a contract. Irene Randall had taught her that. Besides, it wasn't like she would be cheating on anyone. She hadn't had a date in so long, she had a hard time recalling the last one. She spread her hands out, looking at each one of them. "We're not going to get anywhere like this, guys."

"A dude ranch? Seriously?"

"Please, can we talk about it rationally?" she suggested.

Chance, the oldest of the brothers, glared at her. "The fact that Colt contracted with you without our agreement threw rationale out the window."

Chance and Cody seemed to be the ones most opposed to converting the ranch, Chance more so than Cody. She couldn't decide between the two who would be an easier target for her. "I understand. And as I've stated, the contract is not binding."

"But the deposit is," Cody reminded her.

"Yes, well, I have travel expenses and such to cover if you decide to back out." And maybe that wouldn't be such a bad thing, she reasoned. Starting her own business shouldn't be this difficult. But as Cody watched her, she decided to focus on him instead of Chance. Chance appeared to have his mind made up.

"Let's all sit down and let her explain," Colt said. "If we can't reach a consensus, then we'll go a different route, but we can't continue as we are. We'll be bankrupt in a year."

Finally, a voice of reason. "Yes, please allow me to present my ideas to you as a group. Colt has already heard much of them." She motioned to the leather sofa, smiling as only two of the brothers—Chance and Cody—took her suggestion. Chase, the youngest, chose the fireplace hearth and Colt took the overstuffed chair facing his brothers. Sides had been drawn. Her job was to bring them together.

She picked up the four copies of her portfolio and handed one to each brother, pausing to smile charmingly at Cody. Colt, of course, had already seen it.

"I have worked for Randall Consultants for six years," she started. "And I've been in the consulting field for ten years. I am branching off on my own, but I do have extensive experience."

"We'd be your first client?" Cody asked, a hint of skepticism in his voice.

"Yes." She smiled confidently. "But as I said, I have ten years experience in the consulting business." She pointed to the folders each now held. "As you know, with the downturn in the economy, a lot of the larger ranches have been hit hard. Including yours, I'm told. The photos are from my last project. The Dry Creek Ranch in the Pryor Mountains south of Billings, converted last year."

"Converted?"

"Dude ranch is not really the correct term," Kerry said. "Guest ranch is the term we use now. What we did at Dry Creek, we renovated the bunkhouse to accommodate our guests, along with upgrading the bathroom facilities. They also invested in building three private cabins."

"Wait a minute," Chance said. "During the season, our cowboys live in the bunkhouse."

"Yes, well, your guests will be your new cowboys," she said.

"What the hell?"

"This will allow you to save on payroll. What they did at Dry Creek, they put up temporary housing—one of those room-like tents—for the few they hired. You won't need to hire as many seasonal cowboys to move your herd. Your guests, who will pay you, drive the cattle for you."

"So you expect some guy from Chicago, who has probably never seen a horse before, to just come up here and trail the cattle for us? That's insane."

"And that guy from Chicago will pay you close to two thousand dollars to do just that."

"Two grand?"

"That's the going rate for cattle drives. It's my understanding—and correct me if I'm wrong—but you have two major drives each year. Spring, where you move the cattle and their calves from the winter pasture up to the mountains, and then again in the fall where you move them from their summer location back down to the ranch."

"That's correct," Cody said.

"How long do these drives normally take?"

"Five, six days usually, depending on how many cowboys we hire," he said. "And the weather," he added.

She nodded. "So you hire less, allow your guests to work the cattle, and perhaps take seven days." She held her hands out.

"Let's face it. The horses know what they're doing. They've been trained. You have cattle dogs to help. Just having a couple of seasoned cowboys should be all you'll need."

"And Dry Creek Ranch did this?"

"Yes. And you have an advantage. You have a large lake on your property. When it's not the season for cattle drives, your guests come to enjoy the mountain lake, to ride horses, to get a feel for a real working ranch."

"And for two thousand dollars, what else do they get?" Chase asked.

"Lodging, meals," she said. "Trout fishing. Horseback riding. We'd have to establish some sort of a trail ride into the mountains. We'll have a large campfire and a cookout on the last evening. All depending on how much you want to invest," she said. "Some ranches have turned into resorts, adding large swimming pools and recreation buildings. Others do nothing more than cattle drives. You can do a little or a lot."

"That's just it. We don't have much capital to invest," Chance said.

"Then start out small. Fifteen to twenty guests on a cattle drive will get you thirty to forty thousand dollars. Whatever upgrade you do to the bunkhouse can be paid for on your first drive. After you've added more recreational opportunities for your guests, you can start taking reservations all summer long." She paused, meeting each of their eyes, holding Cody's the longest. "If you build it, they'll come," she said with a smile. "Our cities are congested, our open spaces limited. You'd be surprised at how many people just want to take a break from real life and spend a week without distractions. They can do that out here."

Chance stood up, pacing slowly across the room. "I'll admit, it sounds good. I'm also skeptical that it'll work. What if we do invest in renovating the bunkhouse only to have no guests?"

"Obviously that's a risk," she said. "But my job is to get your name out there, set you up a website and promote this by advertising in outdoor magazines and the like. I'll go over everything you have here at the ranch and assess what changes you need to make. Whereas in the past you hired cowboys, now you'll need to hire a cook who can accommodate a large number of guests. You'll need to hire someone to change and launder linens and towels. Also keep in mind this is seasonal. Will you have enough locals who can work or will you have to advertise for that as well? If you do have to hire from afar, then you'll have to have accommodations for staff too."

"There are enough people in the area looking for work that I don't think that would be a problem," Cody said.

"And I think if we hired someone to cook, Martha would be highly offended," Colt added.

"Martha?" she asked.

"Martha's been our cook here since, well, since our mother died," Chance explained.

"The bunkhouse could stand to be remodeled anyway," Chase said. "It hasn't had any improvements in twenty years."

She watched them, suddenly seeing excitement on their faces as her words began to sink in. Amazing how the mention of money and profits changed their attitudes. She felt her confidence rise, thinking she was close to inking her first real deal.

"Just one thing," Cody said. "What's in this for you?"

"You get six months of my time here at the ranch, plus additional time off-site as warranted. All of which includes my expert analysis and recommendations on improvements, coordination of the renovations, a website that will take reservations and payments, and several varied guest itineraries for you to choose from to implement." She paused. "My salary would be forty thousand."

Silence.

"Seriously?" Chance asked.

"Which is ten thousand less than Randall Consultants was paid by Dry Creek Ranch."

"Unbelievable."

She took a deep breath. She'd made her pitch and they had her portfolio. Now it was up to them. She began gathering her things, a smile still playing across her face. One thing she learned at Randall, always expect to make the deal.

"Well, I'll leave you to discuss it all. Colt has my number in case you have any questions. I can begin as soon as you're ready."

Colt politely guided her out with a light touch on her back. She shook his hand firmly at the door.

"I'll be in touch," he said. "I think this is the best way to save the ranch."

"It certainly is the way a lot of them are going these days. But you must get in at the beginning and establish a reputation. If the market is saturated, then you'll just be another ranch offering a cattle drive," she said. "Our goal is to have a waiting list of guests who are anxious to come here. We just have to offer them what they want."

"I like your enthusiasm. I think my brothers do too. Give us a few days to talk about it. My sister is actually coming soon," he said. "If I remember correctly, she'll most certainly have an opinion. I'd like to get this sorted out before she gets here."

"I didn't know you had a sister."

"She hasn't been around in a number of years."

Kerry nodded. "And with your father so ill—"

"Yeah. But we don't want her involved in this. She has no interest in the ranch."

"Well, I'll wait in Billings for your call. If you decide not to do this, I'd appreciate it if you let me know as soon as possible," she said. "I have another potential client in Idaho to visit."

"Of course. I anticipate only a few days."

She drove away after returning his wave, asking herself for the thousandth time if she'd made the right decision by quitting Randall. She knew in her heart that she had, but it was her bank account which stood to suffer. But really, six years was enough. She'd done the work, she'd secured the contracts, she'd babied the clients, she'd put in the long hours only to see the cash flow go to Irene and David. Yes, it was their company and they'd built it, but she got tired of seeing them jet off to the Bahamas during the winter and then settle into their mountain cabin during the summers, while she toiled away bringing in the cash.

Of course, Randall Consultants did much more than ranch conversions, but it was something she'd found she enjoyed. When she first started with Randall, she did seminars for companies wanting to boost production. The seminars themselves weren't bad, but the research ahead of time bored her to tears. She then moved to on-site consulting, reviewing manufacturers assembly line productivity. That usually meant spending three to four weeks there, feeding data into the software programs that Randall had assembled. Randall Consultants then got involved in higher education, sending two-member teams to observe— and then streamline—office procedures. She enjoyed the travel and found it fascinating how reducing time and energy on certain tasks shifted the workload and freed up hours for other projects. In the end, it was all about money and production. But Randall's higher education goals shifted more toward recruitment and retention and Kerry's enthusiasm shifted as well.

Now, setting out on her own, she wouldn't have the resources at her fingertips like she had at Randall, but she had enough knowledge to manage, especially if she planned to only work with ranches for the time being. But like she'd told Colt, they needed to get in while there was still a market for it. Same with her. There were only so many ranches to convert before the market would become saturated. She hoped by that time she would have established herself—and saved enough money—to start doing more of the varied consulting work she'd learned at Randall.

In the meantime, she'd stay the course. She had little to no expenses, and she'd saved diligently over the years, knowing that she wanted to venture out on her own. The constant travel with Randall meant she could get by without having a permanent residence. Thankfully her parents were willing to store her few possessions and allow her to stay with them whenever she was in Denver. She was thirty-four years old and not in the least embarrassed to say she lived with her parents. They had always had a close relationship, and she never stayed there long enough to wear out her welcome. Which, if this deal didn't work out, she would be heading back there to stay while she courted the ranch owner in Idaho who'd shown an interest in the Dry Creek Ranch conversion.

She shoved thoughts of her future aside and instead mentally listed the changes she thought needed to occur at Circle C Ranch, starting with the old, rundown bunkhouse. The quick tour she'd taken gleaned her enough knowledge of the building to see the potential of possibly fifteen rooms, albeit small. Perhaps a couple of larger rooms, for a higher price, could be worked in.

But it was the lake which held the most interest for her. Not many ranches could offer that, and this one was large enough to accommodate a couple of small piers and perhaps canoes or kayaks for the guests to paddle around in. And of course fishing. She could see that as a big draw in addition to the cattle drives and horseback riding.

Now, if only the brothers could come to an agreement. She was ready and willing to get started. She just needed the go-ahead.

And the money.

CHAPTER FOUR

Carson turned the rental car down the two-lane country road, thinking little had changed in the years she'd been gone. The old Conley ranch house still stood, even though it had been long abandoned. The Conleys had built a new one far back in the valley when she was a kid. Long before her father put a stop to it, she, Chase and Justin Conley had been pals, spending many a lazy summer day riding horses between the ranches. At one time, before she realized she was gay, she thought she and Justin would date. So did he. They were in the eighth grade when they shared their first—and only—kiss. They laughed afterward as it had been as awkward for him as it was for her. They'd grown up together and were as close as brother and sister. In fact, he was the first one she'd told when she was ready to discuss her sexuality.

Well, really, he was the second one. She told her mother first. And as is usually the case, her mother had long suspected so there wasn't any kind of drama. No, not with her mother. Her father was a different story. It was her mother's suggestion that they keep it from him. Of course, getting caught in the hayloft with one of Cody's girlfriends let the cat out of the bag. That essentially ended their relationship.

It was her mother who stood by her—and stood up for her—until the end. But that last day wasn't something she thought about much. She couldn't. It was still too painful. Even now, just thoughts of her mother brought back the memories that were forever etched in her mind—her mother's limp, lifeless body cradled in her arms as she carried her back to the ranch.

She shook her head as if she could shake loose the memories—chase them away—but she never could. So she did what she normally did. She replaced them with happier ones, recalling idyllic days of a carefree childhood, the world—or at least the fifty thousand acres that the ranch had access to—at her fingertips. She rode every day, often with her mother who shared her love of horses. The lush valleys and high mountains had a peaceful, calming effect on her, chasing away whatever paltry, teenage concerns she may have had. Truth was, most of her anxiety came from worrying about what she was going to do when she grew up. She hadn't wanted to leave the ranch. Like her brothers, she loved the place and wanted to spend her life there. But unlike her brothers, she was never allowed to take part in the workings of the ranch, never allowed on the cattle drives or sheep herding. She could only watch from afar as the boys took part in what she considered the fun part. Her father made it clear from early on that she was a girl and was expected to act as such. All of which deepened the chasm between them. The only good was that it gave her and her mother more time together, time that would end up being so short.

It was with both apprehension and anticipation that she turned in at the ranch that encompassed most of Elk Valley. Massive log beams framed the entryway and two iron cutouts of bull elk adorned each side of the road. Hanging on the cross beam was the familiar Circle C logo that she'd grown up with.

The young spruce trees that were planted along the entryway were now larger, more mature. As was she.

She traveled the winding dirt road, her gaze darting from side to side, taking in the greenness of the grass, the clusters of pines and aspens, the high mountains in the distance, still snowcapped as summer was just showing itself. She frowned, though, as something was missing.

Cattle. Surely they hadn't moved them to the summer pastures already. Judging by the snow on the mountain peaks, she wouldn't think the native grasses would be up yet in the high country. Maybe they were rotating winter pastures and had them in another valley. Or maybe their routine had changed in the years she'd been gone, although she found that hard to believe. She remembered well all the stories, first from her grandfather, then from her father, how the cattle were trailed along the same route from mountain to valley and back again for over a hundred years.

It hit her then that she was really back at the ranch. It wasn't an errant phone call from her twin brother. It wasn't just an idea she was still tossing around in her head. And it wasn't a dream. No, she was really here, driving the long road that would take her to the ranch house and her brothers.

And to her dying father.

Had she really bought into Chase's contention that she needed to make her peace, that she needed closure? Or was it his somewhat heartfelt plea that the ranch was falling apart and he needed her to come home? Or maybe it was just time. She'd been wandering the world, searching for a home, searching for someplace where she wanted to settle. So far, that place remained elusive. But here, in the land of her childhood, she felt a little of the wanderlust lift, she felt an unfamiliar contentment take its place. And on the heels of that thought came resentment. That at least was something she was familiar with. Because she didn't want this place to have that effect on her. This place brought her so much joy—and ultimately so much pain. She didn't want to reconcile with her father, she didn't want to be reunited with her brothers.

"Then what the hell am I doing here?"

She slowed the car as a surge of defiance came over her. She didn't *have* to go on. They were expecting her, yes, but that didn't mean she had to go through with it. She could turn around and head right back to Billings and catch the next flight out.

But out to where? Back to San Francisco to resume her getaway with Rebecca? Or back to New York and her Manhattan apartment? An apartment that was as sterile and impersonal as a hotel room. She could always hop a flight to Europe, maybe down to the Mediterranean, maybe stay in a villa in Spain.

She sighed, glancing out at the lush springtime meadow, the deep blue sky, the snowcapped mountains, then back to the road she'd been following. None of the options appealed to her at the moment, not as much as the urge she had to take her shoes off and run wild through the grass. Of course, she wasn't a kid anymore and she controlled that urge. But she drove on, following the road, knowing in her heart that there was no place else she wanted to be than right here at the ranch.

She felt a tinge of excitement as the two-story ranch house came into view. It was larger than it had been, and she assumed her father's plan to add on separate wings for the boys had come to fruition. And despite Chase's declaration, the house at least looked well kept. There was no sign that it was falling apart. She noticed the cluster of blue spruce and aspens her mother had planted in the front had doubled their size since she left. There were no colorful spring annuals, however, and she supposed that tradition had died with her mother.

No less than six trucks were parked haphazardly around the house. Work trucks, all of them, as a coating of dirt and grime hid their true colors. She got out, taking in a deep breath of the freshest air she'd smelled in years. A smile came to her face as she looked skyward, beyond the blue. Home.

And while she had been intentionally evasive on the time of her arrival, she was still surprised to find no welcoming committee. She followed the sidewalk to the wraparound porch, glancing in the windows as she went. She thought it would be appropriate to use the front door. She was a guest after all. However, movement through the windows by the kitchen caught her eye. Chase, his body as long and lanky as she remembered, was leaning casually against the counter watching her. She paused, meeting his eyes through the glass. She matched his smile, then waited, her heart beating wildly as he pushed off the counter and opened the side door.

"Damn, sis, you're even prettier than I remembered."

She felt a blush color her face at his words. "Hey, little brother."

"By two minutes. That hardly counts."

"It'll always count."

He opened his arms, and she didn't hesitate as she went to him. Their hug was hard and tight and she was caught off guard by the tears that formed.

"I missed you, Car," he said into her ear.

"Me too." She squeezed him tighter, then pulled away. "You look good."

He brushed her dark hair away from her face affectionately, then dropped his hand. He motioned inside. "The guys are in with Kerry, the consultant. We voted to do the dude—excuse me, *guest* ranch thing. She ended up being quite persuasive. I think Cody's in love."

"Oh yeah? She cute?"

"Very." He grinned. "But you're not her type, so don't get any ideas. Besides, it would break Cody's heart. He's got a crush."

"Wouldn't be the first time. Remember Angie Bonner?"

He laughed. "I thought Cody was going to shoot you."

"I was only sixteen. I didn't know any better."

"Yeah. But getting caught in the hay barn is classic. I bet Cody still thinks about it when he goes in there."

She elbowed him in the side. "I took Jenny Ramsey in there too," she said with a smile.

His eyes widened. "My prom date? You *slept* with my prom date?"

She shrugged. "What can I say?"

He held open the door for her. "Maybe there's a reason we're all still single," he said. "We should have taken pointers from you."

She stopped. "All still single? Even Chance? Wasn't he dating what's-her-name? From the Evan's Ranch. I thought they were going to get married."

"Marla. We're not quite sure what happened. Just one day they called it off. He wouldn't talk about it. Still hasn't."

She stood in the kitchen, looking around. Some things had changed, but enough remained of her mother's touch to make it feel like home.

"Who cooks?"

"Martha Cox. You probably don't remember her daughter. She was a few years younger than us."

"Beverly?"

"Right. Martha lost her husband and Beverly shortly after you left. Driving in a storm and hit a tree. Anyway, she didn't have anything. They were renting. So we hired her, moved her in here. She does all the household chores now, keeps us in line."

They both looked up as a burst of laughter sounded. She glanced at Chase with raised eyebrows.

"They're in the den. Come on."

She hesitated, her nervousness coming back. It was easy with Chase. It always had been. But the others? She and Chance never really were close. Cody? Cody always had a temper, and she seemed to set it off. The Angie Bonner thing had pretty much done them in. And Colt? Colt was the spitting image of their father—in looks and personality—and their relationship had always been rocky. No matter what, Colt always sided with their father.

"Car? It'll be okay. We're not kids anymore."

She sighed. She and Chase had been so close. When he'd called, they'd just picked up where they left off. But the others? Oh, well. It didn't matter. Her plans were to stay for a week or two, reconnect a bit with the ranch, with Chase. Perhaps have a conversation with her father, maybe try to make amends. Then she'd head back to her life and leave them to theirs.

Carson met his gaze, his hazel eyes identical to her own. She smiled slightly. "Lead the way, little brother."

CHAPTER FIVE

The boisterous laughter came to a sudden halt as they all looked up, Kerry included. The beautiful woman standing beside Chase was obviously their sister. Her dark hair, cut stylishly short and parted on the side, feathered across her forehead, much as Chase's did. Her flawless skin, again like her brothers, made her look younger than her years. Kerry had already learned she was Chase's twin, and she was just as handsome as her brothers, although not nearly as imposing. Her frame was almost slight compared to that of Chance, the oldest.

"Well, well. She returns," Cody said. "I guess I owe Colt twenty bucks."

A charming smile flashed across the woman's face. "I see

you're still losing bets on my account," she said. "Haven't you learned yet?"

Chase stepped forward. "Kerry, this is our sister, Carson. Car, Kerry Elder. She's the consultant I was telling you about."

When Carson turned those hazel eyes on her, Kerry felt an odd familiarity, almost as if she already knew the woman. She returned her smile easily.

"Nice to meet you," she said politely, taking Carson's offered hand. The other woman met her eyes, holding her hand tight for a long moment. Longer, certainly, than was necessary.

"You too," Carson said. "You must have made quite an impression on my brothers. Dude ranch?"

Kerry smiled. "*Guest* ranch," she corrected, thankful that Carson's eyes finally left hers. She didn't know why, but she had a sense that Carson was looking deep within her, finding secrets Kerry didn't even know she had.

"That's right. *Guest* ranch," Carson said.

Chance finally spoke, stepping forward to give Carson a somewhat awkward hug. "Welcome home."

"Chance, you're looking well."

"Thank you."

Carson turned her eyes on Colt, the only one to remain silent. "Hey."

He nodded. "Sis."

Kerry didn't know the circumstances of Carson's departure from the ranch in the first place, but the reception she was getting was downright frosty. All but Chase. His eyes and smile showed nothing but affection for his sister.

"We'll catch up at dinner," Cody said. "We need to get back to this. Kerry's got a trip to Billings this evening."

"Oh, sure. Don't mind me," Carson said.

"I'll give you a tour," Chase offered. "Then get you settled in."

"The old man added on wings for you, huh?" Carson said as Chase guided her out the door.

Kerry looked at the remaining brothers, all showing a bit of shock on their faces. She wasn't sure why. They had been expecting their sister's arrival.

"Can't believe she really showed up," Chance said.

"She came to see him die," Colt said. "Nothing more. And then to try to collect her inheritance. That's just like her."

"She's not in the will, you know that," Cody said. He glanced at Kerry apologetically. "Sorry. Family dirty laundry."

"It's okay. If I'm going to be living here for the next six months, I'm sure I'll hear a lot more family...*laundry*." But curiosity got the better of her. "How long has she been gone?"

"Twelve years."

Her eyes widened. "Oh. I had no idea it was that long."

"Not just gone," Chance said. "But no contact. No phone calls. No letters. Just gone."

"With Grammy Mae's money, let's don't forget," Colt said bitterly. "She didn't offer to share that, did she?"

Oh, yeah, there was a little hostility in the room. Kerry thought it best to steer the conversation back to the ranch and away from the prodigal sister. "Well, do we want to get back to the bunkhouse plans or—"

"You know what. Let's wrap this up for the day," Chance said. "I've got rounds to make. We all do."

Kerry could sense the enthusiasm for the project had waned with the sister's arrival. She looked expectantly at Cody, but he just shrugged as Chance and Colt left abruptly.

"Carson's always been a little different," he said. "She and Chance never saw eye to eye."

More than just Chance, Kerry suspected, but she said nothing. It was obvious the sister was not welcome here. Kerry only hoped her appearance didn't put a kink in their plans and cause them to call the whole thing off. She'd been desperate for a client so she'd accepted their terms. Ten thousand up front with an option to terminate the contract prior to the three-month date with a majority vote. If the contract was terminated, she would see no more money. Colt was in. He's the one who started this project. Chance definitely had his doubts about it. She'd noticed that Cody normally sided with Chance so she'd set her sights on him, so far being able to persuade him with charm and a little flirting. Chase she hadn't quite figured out. He seemed indifferent to the project. Perhaps because he was the youngest and didn't feel he had as much say. Or maybe it was because his sister's impending return had held his attention. Regardless, if she wanted to see this project through, she had to keep at least two of the brothers in her pocket. Colt and Cody.

"Do you think your sister will be involved in the project at all?" she asked.

"Oh, no. She doesn't have anything to do with the ranch. Never did." His smile was almost apologetic. "Our father wouldn't allow it, even though she could ride better than any of us. She always had a thing for horses."

"Why wouldn't he allow it?"

Again, just a shrug. "Long story. Look, maybe we should just call it a day. You said you needed to go to Denver and with the cowboys starting to arrive, we'll be busy getting the cattle ready to head up to their summer pastures. The next couple of weeks we'll all be out and about until we take the week-long trip with the herd. There are a lot of things to get ready."

She knew, of course, that the ranch had to continue working even while the project was starting, but she was afraid if they took a three-week break, then the brothers would be back in familiar territory, trailing the cattle, surrounded by their seasonal cowboys, and the idea of a guest ranch would seem absurd to them then. Cody apparently saw the panic on her face.

"Don't worry. We're not going to scrap the project. A ten-thousand-dollar investment is not something we can throw away just to void the contract. You know enough to know we're losing money each year. We've got to do something other than stay the course."

"Okay. I'll be gone two days. I'm flying out of Billings tonight then I'll drive back with my things. Will anyone be here when I get back?"

"We'll be around. We'll be moving the cattle from the winter place up here to the ranch. There's a lot of prep before we can move them to the mountains. Inoculations, branding and castrations all have to be done before the drive."

She made a face. "I'll definitely stay out of your way for all that."

He laughed. "Yeah, takes some getting used to. Of course,

we've been around it our whole lives. It's just part of it." He pulled her into a quick hug, surprising her. It was the first obvious show of affection he'd given her. "I'll see you in a few days."

She nodded, silently watching him go. Since she didn't protest his hug, she was setting a precedent. She realized she should have stopped him. Despite her innocent—or not so innocent—flirting with him, she didn't want to send the wrong message. She rolled her eyes. Of course she was trying to send him a message. Why else was she flirting with him? She shook her head, wishing she'd never added flirting to her plans to get the contract signed. He was a nice guy—an attractive guy—but there was simply no interest there for her. There never was, it seemed. But she wasn't in the mood to scrutinize her love life just then. She quickly gathered up her drawings and outlines, shoving them into her briefcase without much order. Despite Cody's words that the project would go on, she had a bad feeling about it. Maybe she should have courted the client in Idaho instead. He was an old man with no children living on the ranch. It would be an easy fix. Here? Four opinionated brothers, a dying father she had yet to meet, and now apparently their money-hungry sister had come to stand vigil over the father, expecting an inheritance. It all added up to chaos and uncertainty. What if the father died sooner rather than later, dividing the ranch? What if the father regained strength and put an end to the project? Or what if the sister demanded a say in the ranch? Any or all of those things spelled trouble for her.

But it was too late. She'd signed the contract. Short of her returning the ten thousand dollars—something she was not prepared to do—she was at their mercy.

CHAPTER SIX

"You want to see the old man?"

Carson shook her head. "Not really. Does he know I'm here?"

"I told him you were coming."

"And what did he say?"

Chase grinned. "Hell must have frozen over."

Carson laughed. "I didn't realize he had a sense of humor."

"He doesn't. I think he was serious." Chase opened the fridge. "You want something to drink?"

"What are my choices?"

"Water, lemonade, cola."

"No, thanks."

"Something stronger?"

She glanced at the clock on the wall and nodded. "It's four in New York," she said, as if needing an excuse.

"Let's go into his study. The good stuff is still kept there, despite Chance."

"What do you mean?"

"He's a teetotaler. Won't even drink a beer with us after we've been working all day."

"A teetotaler? In *this* family?"

"Yeah, I know. Weird. They've all gotten weird."

Carson sat down in one of the leather visitor's chairs across from the desk, her eyes darting around the room, a room she was never allowed into as a kid. She remembered standing at the door watching her father sipping whiskey and smoking a cigar, his feet propped up on the edge of the desk, paperwork scattered around.

"Scotch?" he asked, opening a cabinet showing it fully stocked.

She raised her eyebrows. "Not if you expect me to make it until dinner."

"You may need it. Chance cut the session short with the consultant. Apparently your presence here has the guys feeling a bit uneasy."

"Colt is too much like the old man," she said. "And Chance and I never were close."

"True." He handed her a glass half filled with the amber liquid. He lightly touched his glass to hers. "Welcome home."

"Home? It felt like home as I was driving in. But here? Not so much."

He laughed. "I know what you mean. We all have our own suites. It's almost like a hotel now. And since he's been sick, there really hasn't been much direction."

"Where are the cattle? I was expecting the valley to be filled, yet I didn't see a one."

"Not much of a herd left. Less than a thousand. We've had to sell off more than we normally would just to make ends meet."

"Sheep?"

He shook his head. "No. Sold the sheep herd a few years ago.

Wool prices were stagnant and we were losing money. The old man wanted to save the grazing land for the cattle."

"He always said diversity was the key to a successful ranch," she said.

"I've had a little success breeding horses," he said. "In fact, Windstorm turned out to be a great stud. He sired a national barrel racing champion. That's what got us started."

"Oh my God! You still have Windstorm?"

"What the hell were we supposed to do with him? He wouldn't let anyone ride him but you. That never changed. But he was a beauty. I had a fast young filly, so I let them mate."

So her beautiful white stallion was a stud. She'd figured they'd gotten rid of him when she left. Windstorm wouldn't let anyone near him but her. Her father used to say he was as wild as the mountain winds. Maybe so but she named him Windstorm because even on a still day, they would run through the valley so fast—her hanging on to him for dear life—it was like heading into a blustery blue storm as the wind slapped at her face.

"National champion, huh? Good for him. He's fifteen now?"

"Yeah. He's slowed down a little but we still breed him. Some big-time breeders from Kentucky brought four mares up here. I charged them ten grand a pop."

"Damn."

"That's what a national champion will do for you. They're racing them. One's got a chance to win horse of the year. If she does, then we're talking really big bucks for Windstorm. I'll start a sperm bank," he said with a laugh.

"Even though he's low on the temperament scale?"

"That's my selling point. That's what makes him fast."

"The others aren't involved in it?"

Chase shook his head. "No. They have no interest in breeding. I do the legwork, bring in the clients, and then keep the profits. I've got a couple of studs I'm using."

She sipped from her glass, enjoying the smooth taste of the excellent scotch. "So what's with this consultant? She's really cute. I thought you said she wasn't my type."

"Yeah, she's cute. I told you so. But I said you weren't *her* type. She's straight."

Carson shook her head. "The hell she is."

"Of course she is. She and Cody have been flirting back and forth since they met."

"The only puppy dog eyes I saw in that room were Cody's. That woman likes the ladies," she said. "You want me to prove it?"

"I think you're wrong this time, Car. Of course, you always seemed to land your share of straight ones," he said with a laugh.

"There wasn't a whole lot to choose from out here. Plus, you know, I had you guys to compete with." And compete she did. Cody was normally the one she ended up pissing off the most. He had the worst luck with women. Apparently, things hadn't changed if he'd resorted to flirting with lesbians.

"Kerry seems to pay Cody extra attention and he likes it. I thought Colt would be the one, seeing as how he started this whole thing with her, but there hasn't been a spark there at all."

"That's because she's gay," Carson said with a grin. "How much are you paying her?"

"Forty grand."

She nearly spit out the whiskey she'd just taken a swallow of. "Are you serious? For what?"

"Her 'expert' analysis on turning our sleepy little ranch into a vacation destination. That's, of course, on top of the expense of renovating the bunkhouse."

"And you went along with this?"

"I'm kinda torn. We need income. The ranch, as it is, is sinking. She says guests will pay two thousand each for a week's stay. We want to accommodate twenty people a week."

"To do what?"

"Trail the cattle during the two big drives each year. Set up trail rides during the summer. Build some piers on the lake for canoes. Day trips up the mountain for fishing the river." He shrugged. "And the one big campfire cookout each week."

"And the old man's going along with this?"

"Not sure he knows. Unless Colt's told him."

"Chance has legal control?"

"Yeah. In name only and to break a tie. We agreed to vote on everything."

"But it's rarely three against one?" she guessed. Cody always chased after his big brother when they were younger so she would imagine he would defer to Chance now. Colt, on the other hand, followed whatever their father wanted, regardless of his own thoughts. She wasn't sure where Chase's loyalties were.

"I would have bet money that Colt's dude ranch idea would bite the dust but Kerry did a good job selling it. That was a three-to-one vote."

"Chance still holding out?"

"Yeah. But like I said, we need the money."

She studied him for a moment, his flawless face beginning to show signs of maturity. But while the older brothers were ruggedly handsome, Chase kept his youthful appearance, his body still lean and lanky, much like her own. "So why are you all still single?"

"Oh, hell, sis, it's not like there are women beating down our door."

"Hazards of the job?"

"Yeah. We know every eligible female in a three-hundred-mile radius," he said with a laugh. "Colt and Cody get most of the dates and even then, it's few and far between."

"Why's that, little brother? You're cuter and much nicer than both of them."

"And you, my dear," he said, holding up his glass in a silent salute, "are biased."

"Perhaps."

He added more scotch to her glass without asking, topping it off before doing the same to his. "How long will you stay?"

"I don't know. I'm still not sure why I came," she admitted. Rebecca's suggestion of closure didn't really appeal to her. She'd made being angry at her father a staple in her life. If she took that away, what would she have?

"And they're not sure why you left in the first place," he said.

"What the hell does that mean? The old man threw me out," she said, her voice raising.

"Yeah, I know. But that's not what he told them. He said you turned your back on the family at a time when we all needed to stick together. He said you were selfish. He said—"

"Jesus Christ!" She stood up, hands on her hips. "That son of a bitch. He told me to get the hell out of his house. He said he didn't want to ever see my face again."

"I know, Car. But I'm the only one who saw you that day. When the guys came back, you were gone, leaving me to explain. They couldn't believe he would do that to you and he made sure to tell them every chance he got that *you* left us."

"You don't believe that, do you?" It was very important to her to know that Chase didn't think she'd abandoned him.

"No. I saw you that day. I remember your pain, your tears. I know how much you loved it here. You wouldn't leave. You wouldn't just leave me like that."

"Yeah. I loved it here. But...after Mom...well, it wasn't going to be the same for me. Maybe that's why I didn't fight him to stay. Grammy Mae offered me a place, a home. It wasn't the same and I never felt like it was a home to me, but at least I had somebody."

"You could have called. I would have made things right for you," he said.

"I don't think you could have. There was too much hatred, too much resentment. You couldn't have taken that away."

"And now?"

"Time and distance have eased the pain. But anger and resentment? Yeah, I still have plenty of both. I'm sure he does too."

"No. I think he very much regrets what happened. Don't think he didn't look in on you from time to time."

"What do you mean?"

"I mean, I found files on his computer, e-mails from the attorney. He knew where you were and what you were doing. That's how I knew you spent so much time in Europe."

"He was spying on me? That's just like him," she said, sitting down again. "He always was a bastard."

"I wouldn't say spying. I think he was just checking on you, making sure you were okay."

"Okay? He threw me out of the house when I was eighteen. Once Grammy Mae died, I had no family. How the hell did he think I was?" she asked, the bitterness creeping back into her voice.

Chase gave her a crooked smile as he tilted his glass at her. "Good thing he's still alive. You can ask him yourself."

CHAPTER SEVEN

Kerry was on the second day of her long drive from Denver to the ranch. She probably could have made it in one, but she didn't get away early enough. Her mother had insisted she stay for breakfast, which turned into brunch as they'd sat chatting the minutes away. It was noon before she finally left, making it only to Casper in central Wyoming before stopping. Now, as she traveled north to Montana, the beautiful mountain range of Yellowstone to her left, she was starting to feel anxious.

What if this was a mistake?

"Damn these road trips," she murmured.

Hours alone in the car gave her too much time to think. And instead of thinking about the ranch and the possibilities there, she was questioning—yet again—her decision to leave

Randall. She made decent money there. She didn't mind the travel. So what if she felt they were taking advantage of her? They provided insurance and paid her well. But no, she wasn't satisfied with that.

"Let's start our own business," she said to herself sarcastically. She glanced in the mirror and smiled. A road trip from Denver to Santa Fe was to blame for the plan to branch out on her own. Why couldn't she just listen to music like normal people? Why did she like silence while driving?

But it was too late to question it now. She would be at the Circle C Ranch in two hours. And she would be there for at least three months if they didn't change their minds beforehand. Once they got started on the remodeling of the bunkhouse she would feel much better about things. That investment alone would probably be enough to keep them in for the duration. Of course, they couldn't start the remodeling until after the spring's drive when most of the seasonal cowboys headed on to other ranches. Besides the four brothers working the ranch, they only kept three other full-time cowboys on staff, two of whom lived in a nearby town. The other, Johnny Mac, had been with them for years and had his own small cabin not far from the stables. She had only met him once, and he'd been extremely friendly, offering to show her around the property. Cody had quickly stepped in to offer his own services of tour guide though. So far, she hadn't had time for any riding and now that they were starting to work the cattle, she doubted Cody would have time for her.

Well, if the contract went to duration, she had six months to get things in order. Once the plans were set for the bunkhouse renovations, she could focus her attention on the trails and lake. Establishing trails was a given, but adding a couple of fishing piers to the lake hadn't been discussed yet. She'd learned their grandfather had the lake built when a neighbor had purchased the land between them and the national forest, blocking his access to the mountain streams and beaver ponds he liked to fish. The small stream that flowed through their valley made the perfect feed, and he'd spent five years digging out the lake before building the dam to harness the stream. Cody had proudly told her it was one of the largest private lakes in the whole state. The lake would be a big draw for their guests. In fact, she could envision years down the road, building a lodge or even private cabins along the shoreline. Of course, that would severely mar the pristine lake. As it was now—from what she'd seen from a distance—it was an idyllic sight with the lush green grasses growing along the banks, the reflection of the still snowcapped mountains mirroring back to the sky.

She hoped to plan a hike to the lake in the next few days. She would survey the area and see if there was already access. She assumed there was some type of road. If they were to build piers, they would need to get trucks in to haul the lumber and posts. Of course, none of that would matter if the brothers decided they didn't want their guests to have access to the lake. Just having guests on the property would be an adjustment in itself. Cody had already told her that all four brothers were avid fishermen. They may not want to share the lake.

Oh, there was so much to think about. Her head was nearly spinning with all the possibilities. She could make this work. Her very first contract—she'd make sure it went without a hitch. Her portfolio would no longer be exclusively populated with Randall clients. And, if things went smoothly, she could use the brothers for references.

She pushed her worries aside and focused on the scenery as she drove. Having been born and raised in Denver, she was used to the mountain vistas but she never tired of it. After long trips east or to the Midwest, she found she missed the mountain ranges. Of course, living in Denver wasn't exactly living in the mountains. Here at the Circle C Ranch she would spend six months in the lush Elk Valley surrounded by the Rocky Mountains. Despite the stress of her first contract, she was really looking forward to being here.

She slowed as she approached the entrance to the ranch, turning carefully down the long drive. Her apprehension returned as she got closer. She hoped Cody or Colt would be around to welcome her. She didn't feel comfortable yet just making herself at home, even though both brothers had told her to.

The ranch house looked nearly deserted when she pulled up.

All the trucks were gone, meaning the brothers were most likely working the cattle. The car she'd noticed the other day was still there and she assumed it belonged to the sister—she hoped she would be gone by now.

With two of her bags in hand, she made her way to the front door and knocked several times. When no one came, she opened the door and peered in.

"Hello?" she called. "It's Kerry Elder."

Still nothing. "Martha?" she called, thinking maybe the woman who kept the house for them would be about but there was nothing but silence.

"So I'll make myself at home," she murmured as she headed to the stairs. The brothers all lived in separate wings on the first floor, leaving the upstairs bedrooms free. The master suite was in the back facing the lake, and she was told their father was in there, bedridden. His nurse was living in the room next to his.

She opened the door to the bedroom she'd used last week, pleased that Martha had apparently changed the sheets and tidied up. Not that she expected hotel treatment but she wasn't looking forward to changing linens and towels. She tossed her two bags on the bed then went back out for the rest of her things. She paused at her car, taking a minute to survey her surroundings. She could hear the bellowing of cattle in the distance but other than that, all was quiet. A peaceful, calm kind of quiet. She took a deep breath of the cool mountain air, wishing the peacefulness she felt now would stay with her, but she had a feeling it would not.

She turned and glanced up at the house, surprised to find someone watching her from upstairs. She nodded slightly and offered a small smile. The sister—Carson—merely turned away.

CHAPTER EIGHT

Carson turned away from the window, surprised at her rudeness. The consultant couldn't help it if her brothers were idiotic and had agreed to pay her forty thousand for some remodeling suggestions.

"*Guest* ranch," she said with a smirk. But that was their deal, not hers. She'd always known the ranch was theirs, never hers. Her father had made that perfectly clear from the beginning.

Maybe that was one of the things she would talk to him about, if she ever ventured down to his end of the hallway. So far she'd resisted visiting him despite Chase's urging to do so. Chase was doom and gloom, thinking the old man was going to die any day. She'd found out from Martha that he had weeks to a few months at best. She knew her brothers visited him daily although it seemed Chase was not as diligent as the others. She'd detected a bit of underlying bitterness in Chase's voice when they talked about him, and she just assumed it was because of her. Chase had always been her protector growing up. He apparently still resented their father as well.

She listened as the stairs creaked, signaling the consultant's approach. Now was as good a time as any to talk to her. They were as alone in the house as they would ever be. Martha had made a run into town—forty-two miles away—for groceries and wasn't back yet. With the seasonal cowboys starting to show up, her lunchtime meals would become a huge affair as she would fix trays for them all, including the brothers. Her father's nurse—a woman old enough to be their grandmother—was in his room where she stayed most of the day, only slipping away when he napped. She must be a saint to put up with him as long as she did. Carson had heard her in there yesterday reading to him. Other than that, they had the house to themselves.

Her curiosity about the consultant had reached its limit. Carson had joined the brothers for the family dinner both nights and Cody had talked nonstop about her. She'd made eye contact with Chase, grinning at him like they were still in high school. She'd bet Chase a thousand dollars that the beautiful Kerry Elder was gay.

She quietly opened her door, hearing shuffling in the room across the hallway. The door was slightly ajar, and she slowly pushed it open, leaning casually in the doorway. The consultant finally looked up and Carson could tell she was startled.

"Sorry," she said with a smile.

"It's okay. Carson, right?"

Carson nodded and pushed off the wall, going nonchalantly into the room. "So my idiot brothers are paying you forty grand," she said. "What's your deal?"

"Excuse me?"

"Not that it's any of my business," she said. "The ranch is all theirs. It just seems like a lot of money for some renovations."

"They are paying for my analysis of the ranch. They're paying for the website I'm designing, one that will take reservations and credit card payments. They're paying for the initial round of advertising. They're paying me to coordinate the conversion by—"

"*Conversion?*"

"Sorry. Industry term. We're converting this working ranch into a guest ranch. Well, of course it'll still function as a working ranch, but it will now be able to accommodate guests who will pay a surprisingly large sum of money to stay here. Some guest ranches make more income from their vacationers than they do cattle."

"So it's all legitimate?"

"Of course it's legitimate," Kerry said, her brows furrowing. "Why would you think otherwise?"

Carson shrugged. "The whole thing with Cody."

"What thing with Cody?"

"The flirting. He's head over heels already," she said. "Does he know you're gay?"

Kerry Elder's eyes widened and she shook her head. "I don't know what you're talking about."

Carson laughed. "If you're not careful, he's going to propose marriage."

Kerry shook her head again. "Wait. I'm not a lesbian. What gave you that idea?"

"Oh, I don't know. Takes one to know one," she said easily. "Cody is clueless when it comes to women." She dropped her gaze to Kerry's lips. "I'm not."

Kerry straightened her back. "Well, I'm sorry to disappoint you. But I'm not gay."

Carson studied her, wondering if she believed her or not. She could see no reason for her to lie. So she shrugged, turning to leave. "I guess that's a good thing then. Cody hates lesbians."

Kerry raised her eyebrows. "Why's that?"

"He caught me having sex with his girlfriend."

"I thought you haven't been here in twelve years."

"I haven't. I was in high school at the time."

They both looked up as they heard the front door open in a rush. Cody's voice drifted up the stairs.

"Kerry? Is that you?"

Carson looked back at Kerry, meeting her eyes head on. "Your boyfriend's back."

"He's not my boyfriend," she said. "We're just friends. Really."

"Better clue him in on that then. And fast."

Heavy footsteps sounded on the stairs before Cody hurried into the room. He stopped up short when he saw Carson.

"What are you doing in here?"

"Just getting acquainted," she said as she ignored the warning in his eyes. Yeah, he still remembered Angie Bonner and the hayloft. She looked back to Kerry and gave her a subtle wink. "See you later."

Carson went back into her own room, closing the door on Cody's enthusiastic welcome. She caught just a glimpse of an awkward hug between them before her door shut. She shook her head, wondering what kind of game the consultant was playing. Carson was still confused by Kerry Elder. More so now. Not that Kerry *screamed* gay or anything. She didn't. Her dark blond hair reached her shoulders, her bangs hanging low, just begging to be brushed away from her eyes. Her makeup, while subtle, was expertly applied. Small diamond earrings, a silver bracelet, a sterling rope watch—all things a woman would wear. No wonder Cody assumed she was straight. Well, that and the fact that she flirted with him. But it was her hands that drew Carson. Slender fingers, smooth skin, nails filed short and neat, and one ring, its design matching the rope watch. Strong hands, yet feminine. Carson imagined those hands knew their way around a woman's body very well.

She sighed, knowing she couldn't play that game. Not this time. Taking Cody's girlfriends away in high school was one thing. Doing the same now, after a twelve-year absence, would push them even farther apart than they already were. Of course, that's assuming Kerry Elder could be stolen. But maybe she really was straight. She hadn't given even the slightest indication that she found Carson attractive. That, she wasn't used to.

Carson realized she was being a bit arrogant. Not all women were going to fall all over themselves because of her. Although most did. Regardless, Kerry Elder seemed immune, which was probably for the best. Carson had no interest in causing a rift with her brother, no matter how beautiful the consultant was.

Kerry continued putting her clothes away, still somewhat rattled by her encounter with Carson Cartwright. She was surprised by her accusation, but it wasn't the first time someone thought she was gay. Why that was, she had no idea. She had always gravitated toward women, even as a child. To this day, she felt more comfortable in the presence of women than men. But that didn't mean she wanted to sleep with them. She tilted her head, allowing herself a small smile. That's not to say she hadn't thought about it...a time or two.

She turned her thoughts to Carson and those incredibly beautiful hazel eyes. She couldn't remember the last time she'd been around a woman with such powerful magnetism. Carson was positively oozing with it. As handsome and charming as she found the brothers to be, Carson was twice that. No doubt she could have any woman she set her sights on. Kerry paused, wondering if that's what had her so flustered. She found Carson attractive, much more so than her brothers.

She then turned her thoughts to Cody. God, did she lead him on that much that he expected a hug when he saw her? Did he really think their relationship had surpassed friendship just because she'd innocently—or not so innocently—flirted with him?

He was a really nice guy, but she knew she had to speak with him about this. She couldn't continue this charade for much longer. There was not even a tiny hint of sexual attraction there. Of course, if she were smart, she'd wait until the bunkhouse renovations began before opening her mouth. She couldn't risk sending him over to Chance's side.

And if she were really smart, she'd stay away from Carson Cartwright. A certain danger lurked there, she suspected.

CHAPTER NINE

It was still two hours until dinner, and Carson knew the consultant was still holed up in her room. Cody had left the house and if their schedule remained as it had, the guys wouldn't return until an hour before dinner. One thing for sure, the brothers were putting in long hours—they'd leave the house each morning shortly after daybreak, returning only for a quick sandwich for lunch. She'd found out from Martha that breakfast was at five o'clock each morning. Carson decided right then and there that eating cold leftovers at eight suited her just fine.

She hadn't ventured from the ranch house yet, not wanting to go to the stables and stir up those old memories. Not yet, anyway. But she was feeling restless. She did want to see Windstorm.

She hadn't seen him, touched him, since that last day when her mother was alive—and dead.

No, she wasn't ready to travel down that road yet. She was, however, ready to see her father. She went quickly down the hall, hesitating just a second before knocking. She heard the nurse stirring and then the door opened, the old woman frowning at her.

"I'm Carson," she said.

"I know who you are."

When she made no move to allow Carson to enter, Carson looked past her, noting the bedroom furnishings were positioned differently than when her mother had been alive. She looked back to the nurse.

"I'd like to see him."

"He's resting," she said sternly. A loud cough belied her words.

Carson raised an eyebrow. "I won't be long," she said, pushing past the nurse who guarded the door as if it were a prison. She followed the sound of the coughing, finding only a shell of the man who was her father. Chase had tried to prepare her, but she just couldn't match up this frail sack of bones with that of the robust man she'd known.

He turned his head, now totally bald, his eyes cloudy with pain. At first she wasn't sure he recognized her as he seemed to be looking past her.

"I thought I had died there for a minute," he said, his voice gravelly and hoarse. "You look just like your momma."

"I'd ask how you were but...you look like shit," she said bluntly.

He surprised her by laughing which turned into another coughing fit. The nurse hurried over, holding a handkerchief to his lips as blood spewed out. She looked at Carson and shook her head disapprovingly.

"Lung cancer?" she asked the nurse.

"It's affected most organs now, but yes, he has tumors in his lungs." She stood back, glaring at Carson. "You really should be going now."

"In a minute," she said, turning back to her father. "How much longer?" she asked him.

"I'm on borrowed time as it is," he said. "Who the hell knows?"

His gaze left her, moving to the window instead. She followed it, seeing why the bed had been repositioned. He now had a view of the lake and valley. She supposed there were worst things to see from your deathbed.

"Chase seems to think I need to make my peace with you," she finally said. "I think that's impossible. Don't you?"

"Still pissed at me?"

"Pissed? You took away my life. It goes way beyond being pissed," she said, letting her bitterness show in her words.

"Then why did you come back? The ranch was never yours. You think I might have left you a little something in the will?"

"I want nothing from you. Besides, to hear the boys tell it, there's not much left to leave."

"No. I've pretty much ruined that too," he said, his voice barely above a whisper.

She nodded. "Yeah, you were always pretty good at ruining things."

"You did a good job of that all by yourself," he said. "You didn't need my help."

"No. I learned from the best."

"Don't blame me for the way you turned out. I tried my best to make you normal."

"Normal? God, are we going to revisit *that* subject again?"

"You'd rather talk about something else?"

"No. I don't want to talk to you. I don't know why I even came back."

"And I told you not to. Cold day in hell, remember?"

She shook her head. "I see you're the same bastard you always were. I'll just let you die in peace," she said, turning to leave.

He tried to laugh but it turned into a cough. As the nurse went to him, he called to her.

"Come back tomorrow. We should talk."

"Maybe," she said, closing the door on him.

She took a deep breath. Jesus, he looked like hell. She hardly recognized him to be the father she once knew. But a bastard? Yeah. That hadn't changed.

"I told you he looked bad," Chase said as he leaned back in his chair, watching as she added scotch to both their glasses.

"I can't believe he's still alive," she said. "He was coughing blood."

"Yeah. He's been doing that for the last week." He sipped his drink, then put his feet up on their father's desk. "But did you get to talk?"

"Not really. He may be dying, but he's still a bastard," she said.

Chase laughed. "Did he call you queer again?"

"No. He used the word *normal*. As in I'm not." She shrugged. "That's not the issue anyway. That was just a convenient excuse for him at the time. Just like blaming me for her death," she said quietly. "Just an excuse for him."

"I know how much his words hurt you."

"His words, yes. And the look in his eyes. He was just so disgusted with me. I saw hatred. I saw loathing. It was as if he detested my very presence on this earth." She glanced at Chase. "When he told me he never wanted to see me again, when he told me to leave, I knew I had no choice. I could see that in his eyes. He meant those words. It was like I was dead to him."

"It took him years to get over Mom's death. If he ever got over it," he said. "He was never the same after that."

"He was different with you all. He treated you like his sons. Me? I felt like a stepchild who was not allowed to take part in the real family."

"It wasn't always like that," he reminded her.

"Wasn't it? I don't remember a time when it wasn't."

"When we were kids," he said. "Before puberty. I just don't think he knew how to handle having a gay daughter. And having sex with Cody's girlfriends didn't help."

She laughed. "Speaking of, did you see how he hung on her every word at dinner?"

"He held her chair out for her," Chase said with a laugh.

"He's going to get hurt over this one," she said.

"Yeah. Did you see how she nearly cringed every time he touched her?"

"Yes. She looked really uncomfortable with the attention."

To say the least. To her credit, Kerry had done nothing to indicate she viewed Cody as anything more than a friend, but apparently the damage had been done. Cody was like a puppy dog at her heels. He was going to be crushed when he found out she wasn't interested in him.

"She's really cute though, isn't she?"

Chase shook his head. "Don't go there, sis," he warned. "You'll be asking for trouble."

"Oh, I know. And I'm too old to be toying with Cody's girlfriends."

"At least you've learned that much," he said with a laugh.

"Learned what?"

They both turned, finding Chance standing in the doorway, looking at them expectantly.

"Nothing," Chase said.

"He's not even dead yet, Chase. Must you defile his office?"

Chase glanced at Carson and rolled his eyes. "Big brother thinks the old man's study is sacred ground." He held up his glass, leaving his feet propped on the edge of the desk. "Want to join us?"

"I see she's corrupting you already. Don't you have something more productive to do than sit around and drink?"

"Jesus, lighten up man," Carson said. "We have a lot of catching up to do."

"By your own choosing, let's don't forget."

"You sound just like the old man. I always pegged Colt as his clone, not you," she said.

Chance ignored her comment, addressing Chase instead. "I'm heading up the mountain with Johnny Mac at first light. Cody and Colt and the guys will be finishing up inoculations. I need you to meet with the contractor in the morning. Kerry's got the plans but I want one of us there to make sure she doesn't go overboard with this remodeling stuff."

"Shouldn't Cody handle that? I mean, he's sweet on her and all."

"That's exactly why he shouldn't. She's got him wrapped around her finger as it is. Money is—" he paused, glancing at Carson, "well, you know the budget. I just need you to handle this."

It finally made sense to Carson. Kerry needed an ally and Cody fit the bill. Chance wasn't crazy about the idea, that much she could tell. Colt? It was his idea to begin with. That's why she needed Cody. Smart.

"I'll take care of it," he said. "Me and Car," he added. "You and Johnny Mac going up the trail?"

"Yeah. We'll go as far as the first pass. If the snow's gone, we'll head up with the herd in about a week."

He left them without another word and Carson grinned. "Johnny Mac? God, is he still around?"

"Where's he gonna go? He's been working here since he was a boy."

"How old is he?"

"Sixty-two. But nothing's changed. He still keeps to himself in his cabin and comes by for Sunday dinner, that's it. He spends a couple of hours with the old man on Sundays. They've known each other their whole lives."

Carson leaned forward, her voice low. "Chance has changed. He's so serious. Does he ever smile?"

He shook his head. "He's all business now, even before the old man got sick. I think it goes all the way back to when he and Marla broke up."

"So if the ranch is losing money, how are you going to afford to pay the consultant?"

"Don't know. Chance keeps the books."

"And none of you check his work? You don't think he's been embezzling, do you?"

Chase laughed. "God, no. He loves this place. If the ranch failed and we had to sell, then where would we be?"

"True. I sure hope this guest ranch thing works out. That's a lot of money to fork out on *hoping* you get some customers. Is there a plan B?"

"I'm not even sure plan A is finalized," he said. "Maybe if you stick around for a while, you could help with this *conversion*."

"No, no. Chance has made it clear that I'm to have nothing to do with the ranch. Hell, the old man even reminded me of that." She finished her drink and slid the empty glass along the desk top toward him. "This is your deal. I'll just sit back and watch." She grinned. "The view is pretty spectacular," she said with a teasing wiggle of her eyebrows.

"So you're going to amuse yourself by playing with the consultant?"

"Maybe. It could be fun."

"Don't do anything stupid, Car. Cody is already challenged when it comes to the ladies."

"Yeah? Does he still have a complex from high school?"

"Probably."

"And what about you, little brother? You going to live your life alone out here on the ranch?" She was surprised by the light blush that crossed his face. He stared into his glass, his expression thoughtful.

"Being alone is not all bad," he said. He looked up. "Right?"

She shrugged. "I haven't known anything else."

"There's no one special in your life?"

"I have a handful of close friends. There's a woman who took me in all those years ago. She's been my family."

"Lover?"

Carson smiled and shook her head. "No. Rebecca and I have never been lovers. Big sister." She met his eyes. "I've had a lot of lovers. But love?" She shook her head. "Love is painful. I wanted no part of that."

"You can't equate your pain from your childhood to that of a lover, Car. Two different things."

"Love is love. I had my heart ripped out just the same."

CHAPTER TEN

Kerry paced, her hands clasped together behind her back, her patience running thin as she waited for one of the brothers to show up. She let out an impatient breath.

"Let's start without them," she finally said. She held up the printout of the new bunkhouse plans and showed them to the contractor. "I'm assuming you'll want this electronically, but I thought it'd be easier to walk through the plans this way."

"Now we're not some fancy construction company from the city, miss. Old-fashioned blueprints will do the trick," he said.

She smiled. "Not exactly blueprints," she said. "The structure will remain intact. We're just gutting the inside and remodeling. There will be some plumbing involved, of course, but it's nothing too elaborate."

"My guys can do pretty much anything. Work is hard to come by these days. Not going to turn down a job."

Kerry looked up at the approaching truck, surprised that Chase Cartwright was accompanied by his sister this morning. Kerry made a point of looking at her watch as they walked over. They were twenty minutes late.

"Sorry. We got tied up," Carson said.

"Yes, I imagine traffic was heavy during this morning's rush hour," she said without thinking, but Carson laughed good-naturedly.

"I'm not used to keeping such early hours," she said. "At least, not at this end of the clock," she added with a wink.

Kerry wanted to ignore her but a smile lit her face before she could stop it. She glanced at Chase. "So you're in charge of the bunkhouse?"

"Apparently so. Chance is checking out the trail to the summer pastures. The guys are still working the herd," he said.

"Well, you've already seen the plans. I was just telling Mr. Burris here that we don't want anything extravagant. I would like to stick to a more rustic look. If your guests want fancy, they could stay in the city at a five-star hotel. What they're looking for is authentic ranch life. They want to be taken away to another time, where the pace is slow." She paused, knowing she was giving a sales pitch. "Besides, when you're on a budget, rustic is easier to do." She glanced at Mr. Burris. "Right?"

"Oh, sure. We can do rough, unfinished lumber. You said you wanted the interior to look like logs. We can also put planks down for flooring. That'd really be rustic," he said.

"Planks? Seriously?" Carson said. She glanced at Chase. "You've got to draw the line at planks."

Kerry nodded. "I agree. We'll discuss flooring later." She pointed to the now sparingly used bunkhouse. The few seasonal cowboys they'd hired this year would be moving out with the herd. "Shall we take a tour?"

"After you, ma'am."

The four of them went into the bunkhouse, the original construction having taken place some seventy years prior. It had been added on to over time but the central room—a lounge of sorts—dominated. There was a large kitchen adjacent to it, and she'd been told the cowboys usually fended for themselves at dinner. Lunch was provided by Martha. Back in the day, when the ranch housed ten or more cowboys for most of the year, they hired a cook to oversee the meals. Now, since the brothers did most of the day-to-day work, they hired mostly seasonal. Cody said they stock the pantry and fridge each year and leave the cooking to the boys themselves.

"I'd forgotten how massive this fireplace was," Carson said as she moved closer to inspect it.

"It'll look great in promotional photos," Kerry said. "And quite functional for the fall cattle drive. Imagine coming back inside to a roaring fire after being out in the cold," she mused.

"I'm still trying to wrap my brain around the fact that you're going to have untested laymen trailing the cattle," Carson said.

Kerry glanced at Chase, hoping for a little support. She and the brothers had been over this countless times, and it seemed to be the biggest hang-up for them.

"With the four of us, Johnny Mac, Greg and Lucas," he said, "we're going to try to get by with only a couple of seasonals. We may find we won't need to hire any."

"The horses are trained. They can take a newbie rider," Kerry said. "Dry Creek Ranch did a one-day tutorial before the drive, letting the guests know what they expected and what *not* to do. I think we should put something together like that for us." She smiled at Mr. Burris. "Sorry. We got off topic." She held her hand out to the great room. "We won't do anything in here other than strip-walls and re-stain," she said. The main room was the only one made from logs and they'd held up nicely. A fresh coat of varnish was all they needed.

He stomped hard on the floor, the smooth polished wood not showing any signs of wear. "Solid," he said.

"There are two small bathrooms now. We need at least four," she said. "I'd originally thought we could get fifteen rooms out of it, but I think we should scale down to twelve."

"We have twenty now," Chase said.

"And they're nothing more than boxes," she countered.

"You can't offer something that small to guests shelling out two thousand bucks. Bathrooms will obviously have to be shared."

Carson moved into the kitchen, eyeing the ancient appliances. "Plans for this?" she asked.

"There will be no need for a full kitchen since meals will be built into the price. However, a refrigerator, microwave and coffeepots will be provided. Not all guests enjoy big group meals." She pointed down the hallway. "Shall we go into the living quarters?"

As she showed Mr. Burris which walls she wanted removed— practically all of them—she sensed the apprehension growing in Chase as they talked of gutting the inside. She chanced a glance at Carson, trying to gauge her reaction, but she looked almost bored. And why wouldn't she? She wasn't really a part of this, not a part of the ranch and certainly not a part of the renovations. She wondered if it were true, what Cody and Colt had said, that she was only here for her inheritance. Kerry certainly didn't know the woman but for some reason, she got the impression that Carson Cartwright could care less about the inheritance. There was such an indifference about her, as if she couldn't be bothered with any of it.

All of which made her more curious, not less. Even though Carson Cartwright made her slightly uncomfortable in her presence—that invisible aura she possessed—Kerry decided she would confront her head on. Even though it was absolutely none of her business, she had a lot of questions, namely, what was she doing here and why the animosity with the brothers. All but Chase. There was genuine affection between them that you would have to be blind not to see.

Kerry made her way through the silent house, finally finding Martha in the kitchen cleaning up after lunch. She always made platters of sandwiches, along with deviled eggs or some other side dish. She delivered them promptly at noon to wherever the guys were working. She'd then spend the afternoon cleaning up and preparing the family dinner which was served at seven sharp. Kerry had joined them each evening she'd been here. She imagined that wouldn't change.

"Hi Martha," she greeted, getting a smile from the older woman. From what Kerry had observed, Martha worked tirelessly and seemed to enjoy every minute of taking care of the Cartwright clan.

"Oh, Miss Kerry. Hi. I saved you a sandwich," she said, going to the fridge and taking out a plate covered with a napkin. "I couldn't find you when I left earlier."

"I went back out to the bunkhouse to measure the fireplace," she said. She lifted the napkin, finding a thick chicken salad sandwich waiting. "Thanks. This looks great."

"I've got a big roast planned for dinner so I thought something light for lunch was in order," she said, smiling as Kerry took a big bite.

Kerry closed her eyes, the creamy taste simply delicious. "This is so good," she murmured. She wiped the corner of her mouth with the napkin. "Have you seen Carson?" she asked casually.

"The last I saw, she was heading out the back. Maybe to the lake," she suggested with a shrug. "She didn't stay around for lunch."

No, Kerry suspected that Carson felt uncomfortable here alone without Chase, so naturally she tried to make herself scarce. Again, she wondered why she was here in the first place. Kerry finished off the first half of the sandwich, wrapping the other in the napkin.

"Thanks, Martha. I'm going to save this for later," she said, slipping it back into the fridge.

"See you at dinner," she said as she went back to wiping down the countertops.

Kerry hadn't been down to the lake yet. This was a perfect excuse to go and hopefully find Carson in the process. Getting lost on fifty-thousand acres probably wouldn't be too hard to do if Carson wanted to.

She found a path at the back of the ranch house and followed it, assuming it went to the lake. It wasn't exactly well worn, but it was traveled enough to keep the weeds down. There was only a scattering of trees along the way—aspen and spruce—as the lush valley impinged on the trail. It was a pleasant walk, the day warming nicely after the cool morning. She could envision guests at the ranch making this same trek to the lake, fishing gear in tow. Of course, they would have to maintain the path somewhat.

She spotted Carson standing near the shore, her hands shoved casually in the pockets of her jeans. She appeared to be staring at the water or perhaps she was staring at nothing, just absorbing the lake, the mountains, the air. Kerry almost decided to turn around and give Carson her space—and solitude—but Carson must have sensed her presence as she turned slowly, eyebrows raised.

"Sorry," Kerry called. "Do you mind company?"

"As long as you don't bring up bunkhouse renovations," she said.

Kerry smiled as she walked closer. "I knew you were bored with it."

"Out of my mind."

"As was Chase."

"He was just following big brother's orders," Carson said. She turned her gaze back to the lake. "This is gorgeous, isn't it?"

"Yes, beautiful. It's one unique asset that this ranch has that most others can't offer."

Carson looked at her. "Does everything have to tie in to the *conversion*?" she asked. "Can't you just enjoy the beauty of it without seeing dollar signs?"

"Sorry, but your brothers are paying me to see dollar signs. Lots of them."

Carson moved slowly along the shore and Kerry followed, the spring grasses and flowers hiding the many rocks Carson used as a footpath. They were silent as they walked, and again Kerry was amazed at the absolute quiet. A few bird calls, nothing more.

"It's so peaceful," she murmured, giving voice to her thoughts.

"I've missed this," Carson said. "More than I realized."

It was the opening Kerry had been waiting for.

"Why have you been away so long?"

"You mean, in all of your little intimate talks, Cody hasn't shared the family's dirty secrets?"

Kerry shook her head. "There is nothing intimate between Cody and me." She dared to meet her eyes. "As you well know."

Carson arched an eyebrow. "Coming clean with the whole flirting thing?"

Kerry was taking a chance by confiding in her, she knew, but somehow she sensed that Carson could really care less about the contract the brothers had signed.

"I quit my job at a consulting firm, wanting to start my own business," she said. "Your brothers were divided, and I needed a contract," she said.

Carson laughed. "So you preyed on poor innocent Cody? God, he's got the worst luck with women."

"I may have...flirted with him a little, trying to persuade him," she admitted. "It was foolish. I had no idea he would take it so seriously."

"Four bachelors starved for female company, how could you think otherwise?"

"I know. But I was desperate." She studied her, wondering if she could trust Carson. "You think I'm scamming them, don't you?"

Carson shrugged. "Are you?"

"No. This really is a viable option to their financial woes," she said. "And I do know what I'm doing. Dry Creek Ranch has been very successful, and they don't even have a lake," she said, motioning to the water.

"Well, as I said before, it's their deal. My interest in the ranch is purely nostalgic," Carson said, and Kerry noticed the sadness in her voice.

"Why did you stay away?" she asked again.

Carson glanced at her, then turned back to the water, her profile giving Kerry an opportunity to observe her openly. With the sun shining on her face, it gave her naturally dark skin a lovely amber glow. Kerry was hesitant to use the word beautiful to describe someone as it was so overused, but Carson was breathtakingly so. She was very handsome in a fresh and natural way. She blinked several times, turning her gaze to the lake and away from Carson—she was startled by her thoughts.

"It's a long, complicated story," Carson finally said. She turned, her gaze finding Kerry's. "Have you been introduced to my father yet?"

"No. Cody says he's very ill."

"Yes. I saw him briefly. Long enough for us to quarrel, something we used to be quite good at," Carson said.

"He sent you away?" Kerry guessed. "Surely not because you were gay," she said.

"It was an excuse, but no, that's not the reason." She started walking again. "But it's a long story."

"I have time," she offered.

"Maybe another day," Carson said. "Why ruin a lovely afternoon?"

And it was, Kerry admitted. Blue skies, the sun warming the air around them, a gentle breeze carrying the enticing smells of the high mountains. A truly lovely afternoon.

"Are you afraid I'm going to ruin things for you with Cody?" Carson asked after a few moments of silence.

"Yes," she answered truthfully.

"Well don't be. It's none of my business. But I wasn't joking about him proposing marriage. You might want to ease back a bit," she said.

"I know. I just don't want to turn this into some big drama."

"And you don't want to lose the contract," Carson added.

"You know about the three-month rule?"

"Yes. Crazy. Why did you agree to that?"

"Like I said, I was desperate for a contract." She stopped. "I know you say it's none of your business, but what do you think about the lake? I mean, for guests. Do you think the guys will allow a pier or two to be built?"

"Do they have a choice?"

"I've mentioned the lake several times but they never give a concrete answer," she said.

"That's because they don't want to, but they know they have to," Carson said.

They stopped again, both gazing at the water. The light breeze made ripples on the surface, distorting the image of the mountain reflection. Kerry again found herself observing Carson, watching a hint of a smile play across her face. Kerry wondered what memory she was recalling. Her curiosity escalated once again, but she refrained from asking questions, not wanting to disturb Carson as she was obviously traveling down an old road.

She was still staring at her when Carson turned, capturing her eyes. Kerry couldn't pull away and was surprised by the intensity of Carson's gaze. She swallowed hard when that gaze dropped to her lips before meeting her eyes again.

"I used to swim in the summer," Carson said, her voice quiet. "The guys would all be out with the herd. I wasn't allowed to go," she said. "So I'd sneak off down here, strip naked and swim with my imaginary friends."

Kerry was shocked that her mind conjured up not the young girl Carson must have been at the time but an image of a very adult Carson Cartwright swimming naked in the lake. She shook it away, wondering what was wrong with her. She swallowed once again.

"And was it cold?" she asked when she finally found her voice.

"I was a kid. I don't think I knew what cold was," Carson said with a smile. "Now? July or August would probably be bearable. Other than that, yeah, cold."

"Why weren't you allowed to go with the guys?" she asked.

Carson took a deep breath and turned away from the lake, heading back the way they'd come.

"My father wanted me to be a *proper* young lady," she said. "He was grooming me to marry one of the other ranch owner's sons."

"You're joking."

"Sadly, I'm not. I was allowed to barrel race, as that was considered appropriate for young girls."

"What about your mother?" she asked. She'd learned that their mother had died but knew nothing of the circumstances.

As soon as she asked the question, she wished she could take it back. Carson's eyes took on a nearly haunted look.

"A story for another time," Carson said, her voice thick with emotion.

"I'm sorry," Kerry said immediately. "I have no right to pry."

"She died when I was eighteen."

Kerry mentally calculated back, wondering if that was when Carson had left the ranch. She knew the brothers' ages, all separated by two years. Chase, the youngest, was thirty. She knew she should stop with her questions, but she couldn't resist.

"Why did he send you away?"

Carson turned sad eyes her way. "He blamed me for my mother's death."

Kerry barely knew this woman, but she had a strong urge to hold her at that moment to offer comfort. She was certain she'd never seen such profound sadness in someone's eyes before. Certainly not someone as young as Carson. She managed to curb the urge to hug her, but she couldn't resist some form of physical contact. She reached over, wrapping her fingers around Carson's forearm, squeezing her gently.

"We don't really know each other and we're not exactly friends, but if you'd like to talk, I'm a good listener," she offered. She suspected *talking* wasn't Carson's strong suit. She seemed the type to keep things inside, letting it eat at her.

Carson's gaze drifted from her face down to the hand that was still wrapped around her arm. Kerry knew she should release her but she didn't. In fact, she squeezed tighter, letting Carson know her offer was genuine.

"Thank you." Her gaze returned to Kerry's face and Kerry was pleased to see some of the sadness leave her eyes. "I'm not certain why I even came back. Chase wants me to make my peace with our father before he dies." She shrugged. "Get closure, but I'm not sure how that's going to work out."

Kerry finally let her fingers slip away as they continued walking, but Carson had nothing else to say and Kerry didn't push her with more questions. It wasn't an uncomfortable silence as they walked side by side, their arms brushing occasionally, their eyes meeting.

When they made it back to the house, Kerry found she wasn't ready to part company, but she could think of nothing to say to prolong their encounter. They climbed the stairs together, both stopping in the hallway that separated their bedrooms.

"I enjoyed the company," Carson said. "Thank you."

Kerry nodded. "Me too." She felt embarrassed by her reluctance to leave, but knew she must. She motioned to her door. "Well, I've got some work to do. I'm just getting started on the website," she said.

"Sounds exciting," Carson said with a smile. "See you at dinner."

Kerry slipped into her room and closed the door, pausing to lean against it as she reflected on their conversation. She felt drawn to Carson on so many levels, and she didn't understand it. Was it simply compassion for the teenaged girl who was forced from her home? Maybe it was the haunted look in her eyes that drew her. Or maybe she simply felt a connection to her, one that couldn't be explained.

She took a deep breath then shoved off the door, wondering why it was so easy with Carson, yet so trying with her brothers... with Cody. Maybe because it was their signatures at the bottom of the contract, not Carson's, she thought wryly.

CHAPTER ELEVEN

Carson stood at the window, looking over the valley, Kerry's words still tumbling around in her head. Her offer to talk, to listen, touched Carson in a way she couldn't explain. Over the years, none of the women she'd met or been with had ever asked about her past. Perhaps they just weren't interested. She had money, that's all they cared about. And Rebecca, her questions were mostly out of curiosity, nothing more. Yet Kerry, practically a stranger to her, had offered an ear, had offered to talk. If Carson was so inclined, she knew the offer was sincere.

But as was always the case, she wasn't inclined to discuss her past. There were just too many memories. Memories she'd kept locked up and hidden away all these years. She was afraid of what would happen if she let them out.

She turned away from the window, a slight smile on her face as she recalled the gentle touch on her arm. She shook her head. Damn shame Kerry Elder preferred her brother's gender over her. Such a waste. But it was probably for the best. She wasn't sure she had the energy to pursue anything. Besides, she sort of liked her. It had been a very long time since she'd added a friend to her life.

She sighed, again feeling a restlessness inside her. She glanced at the clock, still a couple of hours before the guys would return for dinner. All but Chance. He and Johnny Mac would camp out on the trail. The first mountain pass was a day's ride. And if the snow cleared, they'd take the herd up next week. The renovations on the bunkhouse were also starting next week. Things were rolling along, and she didn't know how much longer she'd be here. After the old man died, was there any reason to hang around? She wasn't really welcome here, that much was obvious.

She sighed again, moving to the door. She walked purposefully down the hallway before she could change her mind. She stood in his doorway, hearing the incessant coughing. She knocked quickly on the doorjam, then went inside, not waiting on the nurse to greet her. She was met with a cold stare.

"He's resting."

"He'll have plenty of time for resting, don't you think?" she said as she walked closer to the bed. Her father turned his head and for a moment his eyes lit up. But not for her, she realized. She'd always favored her mother. They all got their dark complexion, their dark hair from her.

"You came back," he said, his voice raspy from coughing.

She nodded, noting how pale he looked today. He glanced at the nurse, motioning her away with a weak wave of his hand.

"My time is short," he said. "I think they know."

"The guys?"

He nodded. "They don't come around so much anymore. I think dying is women's work. Men aren't strong enough."

"No. Men aren't strong enough for a lot of things," she said. She moved to the window, staring out at the lake.

"Who was that woman you were with?"

She turned, a question in her eyes. Ah. He saw them at the

lake. She cleared her throat. "Kerry Elder, the consultant your sons have hired."

"The dude ranch thing," he said, coughing again. "They're trying to save the ranch."

"What happened? Why is it losing money?"

He coughed again, turning his head into his pillow. When he turned back around, Carson saw sadness in his eyes. "My father—and his father before him—ran a tight ship here. They built this ranch. They had business sense. So did my brother," he said, pausing to cough again. "If only he'd lived. He was meant to run the place, not me. The boys, for all their hard work, got my brains for business, not my father's." His breathing was shallow, and she wondered if he had the strength to continue. "Bad decisions over the years. Can't change that now."

"Well, this might work out. Bring in some cash anyway."

She watched him, his eyes looking far away. There wasn't a lot of life left in them, she could see that. It was as if he was ready to die, but his body wouldn't let him. Not yet.

"Do you know why I sent you away?" he asked, surprising her.

"You hated me?"

"I looked at you and I saw her," he said. "And I wished it was you that had died that day. Not her."

"Don't you think I wished the same? I would have gladly taken her place."

"I needed to blame someone. I needed answers. I was hurting so much," he said, his voice cracking. "I died that day too."

"Don't you think I was hurting too?" she asked as she moved closer to his bed. "I'm the one who had to bring her back here. I'm the one who had to see it happen. Yet no one seemed to care that I was hurting," she said loudly, tapping her chest. "Everyone was so goddamned concerned about you." She stood beside him, meeting his eyes. "I was hurting too. But I didn't get any comfort. I got accused. I got blamed. I got ostracized from the family. I got sent away."

"There was nothing else I could do."

"Bullshit," she said loudly. "You could have been a man and accepted it. I had to. It was an accident. That's all it was. An accident. Not my fault. Not anyone's fault. Yet you couldn't handle it. You blamed an eighteen-year-old kid. You blamed your only daughter." She paused, her voice thick with unshed tears. "And then you sent her away from her family."

While her tears remained hidden, his did not. They streamed down his face, and she very nearly felt sorry for him. The nurse briskly pushed her aside.

"You should leave. I think you've done enough damage for one day," she said as she held a cloth to her father's face as he coughed.

Carson felt a stab of guilt as she watched her father cry, but she turned away without another word. As she walked back down the hall, Kerry stood in the doorway to her bedroom, her eyes filled with concern. No doubt she'd heard it all. Carson shook her head at Kerry's unspoken question, moving on to her own room, but Kerry followed.

"Carson?"

"I'm okay," she said. "Just working on that closure I thought I needed." She went immediately to the window, keeping her back to Kerry as her tears threatened. She had cried so much after her mother died, after she got sent away, that she didn't think she'd have any tears left to shed. And certainly none for him. But she'd been alone—and lonely—for so long, it just all hit her at once. He didn't love her. Not then. Certainly not now. He blamed her. He wished her dead.

The gentle, tentative touch on her back only compounded her loneliness. She ducked her head, willing her tears to stop. They didn't.

"Come here," Kerry said, slowly turning her around.

It was absurd, this stranger offering her comfort, but she took it anyway. Her eyes squeezed closed as surprisingly strong arms held her.

"God, I'm sorry," she whispered as she buried her face in Kerry's shoulder. She'd never broken down before in front of anyone, not even Rebecca. Yet here she was, practically sobbing as she clung to Kerry.

"Shhh. No. I heard everything. You don't have to be sorry."

For the first time in years, Carson didn't feel so terribly

alone. She unburdened her soul, letting the years wash away along with her tears. Kerry held her while she cried, murmuring incoherent sounds as her hands moved soothingly against her back. Carson—as was completely natural for her—let her body sink against Kerry, not caring that their embrace was far more intimate than it should be. It felt too good to be held and comforted that she had no desire to pull away. But the slamming of truck doors broke the moment. Soon, male voices filled the downstairs, and she stepped out of Kerry's arms, now feeling embarrassed for having clung to her so.

She cleared her throat, then went to the dresser and grabbed a handful of tissues, quietly blowing her nose and attempting to dry her eyes. She didn't want her brothers to see her like this.

"Thank you," she finally said. "I don't know what to say."

"You don't have to say anything."

Carson pointed to the wet spot on her shirt. "I—"

"It's okay. I don't mind." She met her eyes. "When you're ready to talk, I'll be here."

When, Carson noted. Not *if*, but *when*. She nodded, accepting the invitation. They both glanced at the closed door as they heard heavy footsteps on the stairs.

"You don't want Cody to catch you in here," Carson said. "I wasn't joking earlier when I mentioned he hates lesbians," she said, trying to lighten the mood. "The fact that I'm his sister doesn't matter in the least."

"Then I better run," she said, matching Carson's smile. "See you at dinner."

Carson turned back to the window when Kerry opened her door. She knew Cody would be in the hallway, and she didn't want to see his accusing eyes on her. She'd had enough accusations for one day.

"What were you doing in there?" Carson tilted her head when she heard her brother's voice.

"Talking," Kerry answered.

"I need to tell you something about my sister."

Oh, wow. Gonna drop the "she's gay" bombshell now? She rolled her eyes.

"Too late."

"You need to stay away from her."

Kerry frowned. "Whatever for?"

"She's...she's gay," he said as he twisted his hands nervously together.

Kerry smiled at him. "I know she's gay. It's not a contagious disease, Cody."

"You can't trust her, that's all I'm saying. She doesn't care if you're not just like her. She'll force herself on you."

Kerry couldn't believe she was hearing this. Or maybe she could. Cody was obviously insecure, but it definitely wasn't her place to reassure him.

"I'll take your concern under advisement, but I'm certainly not going to avoid her," she said.

He stared at her, his eyes finding the wet spot on her shirt. "Why are you wet?"

"I...I spilled water," she said evasively.

"Look, I don't mean to sound so paranoid, but if she does anything, *says* anything, you let me know."

"Cody, I can take care of myself. I'm not afraid of your sister," she said. She pointed to her laptop. "Now, if you'll excuse me, I need to get back to work. I believe you are paying me to produce a website," she said with a smile, trying to soften her words. Unfortunately, he didn't take her hint to leave.

"You know, we're going to be gone with the herd in about a week," he said.

"Yes. We'll be starting on the bunkhouse then."

"Well, before we go, I thought you might want to take a trip into town. We could, maybe, get dinner...catch a movie," he said hopefully.

"Cody, as much as I enjoy spending time with you, I really can't afford to go out," she said, choosing her words carefully. "Six months may seem like a long time, but it'll go by so fast. There is so much preparation to do to get us ready for guests." She went to the door and held it open. "Now, let me get back to work. I'll see you at dinner."

She let out an exasperated breath when he finally left her, puzzled by the possessiveness he seemed to be showing. Why, oh why, did she ever flirt with him in the first place?

To get the contract, remember? "Oh, yeah," she murmured. "The contract."

She went toward the bed where she'd tossed her laptop earlier when she'd heard Carson's loud voice. She caught sight of her reflection in the mirror, her gaze drawn to her shirt, still damp with Carson's tears. She touched it, running her fingers over it. When Carson had come out of her father's room, she had a look of pure agony on her face. Kerry didn't care that they didn't know each other very well, she simply couldn't bear seeing the pain in her eyes.

She hadn't met the father and knew nothing of the circumstances of their mother's death—or Carson's leaving, for that matter—but no one should have to suffer through the emotional abandonment that Carson obviously had. Emotional *and* physical. It seemed the most natural thing in the world to offer comfort and a shoulder to cry on. She'd been afraid Carson would resist but she didn't pull away. Quite the opposite. She clung to her as if they were...*lovers.*

Kerry met her eyes in the mirror, wondering at the faint hum in her body, wondering at her fascination with Carson Cartwright.

CHAPTER TWELVE

"You sure were quiet at dinner," Chase said as they strolled along the road. Carson skipped their after-dinner drink in their father's office and opted for a walk instead.

"I saw the old man," she said. "After he told me he wished I'd died instead of her, he broke down in tears. I felt like an ass," she admitted.

"Jesus. He *cried*? I haven't seen him cry since, well, since we buried her."

"Yeah. Some closure I'm getting, huh," she said.

"You want to talk about it?"

She shook her head. "No. I'm tired of thinking about it."

"Why the walk then?"

"Cody was giving me the stare down all during dinner. I needed to get out of the house."

"I thought he was acting weird. What's going on?"

She laughed. "He caught Kerry in my room."

"Whoa, sis. What's up with that?" He playfully nudged her arm. "You're not thinking of—"

"No. She heard me talking to the old man and I was upset. So she was just—" Carson glanced at Chase, deciding not to tell him that she had broken down and cried in Kerry's arms. "She was just checking on me, that's all. Cody, of course, ran up the stairs as soon as he came in the house. I can't believe the way he's acting with her."

Chase laughed. "It's got to be déjà vu with him. Whenever Angie would be here at the ranch, all she wanted to do was follow you around, not him. He's probably afraid Kerry will do the same."

"No. All Angie wanted to do was get naked with me so I could give her what Cody couldn't. An orgasm."

"So they *were* sleeping together? I thought he was so upset because she was putting out for you but not him."

"No. He was upset because he watched us and saw how... passionate she was," Carson said with a grin. "He knew then that she'd been faking it with him."

"Oh. Low blow," Chase said.

"Yeah. His sixteen-year-old sister could get her off but he couldn't."

"Okay, okay. Let's stop talking about Cody's sex life," he said.

"Does he have a sex life? Do *any* of you?"

"Like I said, there aren't—"

"That's just crap, Chase. It's not normal for the four of you to be bachelors. Hell, meet someone online, if nothing else," she said.

"I think Colt has tried that."

"And?"

"Some chick from Billings. One date. That's it. But even in high school, he didn't really date."

"And you?"

"And me what?"

"Damn Chase. You're cute as hell. You should have women all over you."

He stopped walking and turned to her, their eyes meeting as darkness settled around them.

"What if I don't want them?" he asked quietly.

She stared at him. "What does that mean?"

He shook his head and turned to go, but she stopped him with a touch on his arm. "Chase?"

"I don't...I don't date women, Car."

"Okay, baby brother, what are you saying?"

"Do I have to spell it out for you?"

She stared at him, still frowning, then her eyes widened. "Oh, my God!" She slapped her thigh, nearly roaring with laughter. "You're *gay*?"

"Will you keep it down?" He tugged her arm, leading them farther from the house.

"They don't know?"

"Of course not. After what he did to you, you think I was going to come out to him?"

"Oh, man. How long?"

"Always."

"Always? Then why didn't you tell me? I told you."

"I was scared." He laughed quietly. "Actually, I was hoping it would just go away."

"Yeah. Funny that it doesn't, huh?"

"Yeah."

They stared at each other, smiles playing on both their faces. Then she grabbed him, pulling him into a tight hug.

"God, my baby brother is a queen," she teased. She leaned back, grinning. "That would send him to his grave for sure."

"It's funny, you know. When I saw how well mom handled things with you, I wanted to tell her too. I'd finally worked up the nerve to talk to her. But..." he said, his voice trailing away.

"Yeah. There were a lot of things I didn't get to tell her either," Carson said. She shook her head. "I just can't believe you never told *me*."

"It all happened so fast there at the end, there was never a good time. And then you were gone, and I was left here with my secret."

She stopped walking as full dark was upon them. She looked

to the sky, seeing a million stars overhead. Oh, how she missed the night sky. Cool and quiet, nothing but stars.

"So what do you do?" she asked. "I mean, for entertainment."

"When it's slow here at the ranch, I take off for long weekends," he said.

"You don't cruise the bars, do you?"

"I used to. But I've met a handful of guys online. It's been enough years that we've become friends."

"Friends with benefits?"

"Oh yeah," he said.

"But no one special? No one you're in love with?"

He shook his head. "I only get off the ranch four or five times a year. You can't fall in love like that," he said. "Maybe someday," he said wistfully. "What about you?"

"No. There's been no one."

"Why not? You have the looks and money."

"Yeah. That's why. The crowd I hang with, money is all that matters." Of course, it was her choice to *hang* with them. Rebecca taught her well. Sex, fun...no complications.

"Maybe you need a new crowd," he suggested.

"Oh, I don't know. It's what I'm used to, I guess. I never had any intention of settling down. Love hurts."

"Yeah. But that's what makes it real. I don't want to shun love. I just haven't found it yet."

They turned, heading back to the ranch house, the lights on the lower floor beckoning.

"So what do you guys do at night? You just retire to your own suites?"

"Pretty much. We split up after dinner and meet up again at breakfast."

"Strange."

"Not really. We work together. We see each other all day long. I look forward to my alone time," he said.

"And that big ass TV." She bumped his shoulder when they reached the porch. "So, you ever going to tell them?"

"Maybe when I leave."

"You have plans? I thought you loved it here," she said.

"I do. For the most part. But I feel stagnant. I've been saving. You know the old man gives us a salary, right? Crazy money considering we live for free, but he always has."

"Maybe that's why the ranch is going under."

"No. It's not like we're operating in the red," he said. "At least not according to Chance. But I've saved up quite a bit. I think I'd like to breed horses full time. What with Windstorm and all, I've made a lot of contacts."

"Buy you a little ranch somewhere?"

He nodded. "Idaho, just across the border. I've got my eye on some land there. Just gorgeous." He smiled. "I can see calling that home."

"You need some money? Because I can—"

"No, sis. I got the money. But they're asking above going rate. I love it, but I'm not willing to pay that much. He'll come down eventually."

"I think that's great. I'm shocked though. It never occurred to me that you'd want to leave here."

"Oh, hell, Car. You've been around a week. There's not a whole lot of fun happening here. And once the old man dies, well, there's nothing to hold the place together."

"Then why are you doing this *conversion*?" she asked. "Why not just sell?"

"I mentioned it once and Chance nearly had a coronary. It's been in the family a hundred and fifty years."

"Yeah, but none of you are married. There are no sons to pass it on to. What the hell are you working for?"

"I imagine one of them will get married one day."

"So you leave? What? They buy you out?"

"Yeah. That's always been the deal." He stepped up on the porch, the light casting shadows around them. "But I'm not in any hurry. It'll happen when the time's right." He paused at the door. "You want a nightcap?"

"No. I'll pass. I think I just want to sit out here and enjoy the stars," she said.

"Okay. See you tomorrow."

"Good night."

She went to the side of the house and sat down in one of the rockers. It creaked beneath her weight as she put it in motion. It was her mother's favorite place to sit. After dinner, she'd sneak out here alone and just sit. Carson often wondered what she thought about while she was out here.

Maybe nothing. Maybe she just liked to sit and watch the stars.

CHAPTER THIRTEEN

Kerry turned a corner in the bunkhouse, scribbling down her latest measurements when she ran smack into Carson. Startled, she let out a scream as she stumbled backward. Carson grabbed her arms, steadying her.

"Didn't mean to sneak up on you. Sorry."

Kerry touched her chest as if feigning a heart attack. "You scared the crap out of me," she said.

"Well, knowing my brother, he's already warned you to be afraid of me," Carson said with a slight smile.

Kerry squeezed her hand quickly. "I'm not afraid of you and you know it," she said, moving into the large living room. "But yes, he did warn me." She put her pad down, smiling at Carson. "In fact, he was quite firm that I needed to stay clear of you."

"And will you heed his warning?"

"Do I need to?" For a second, Kerry saw a glimmer of a challenge in Carson's eyes, then it was gone.

"You're perfectly safe. I believe you're the one who's into *converting* things, not me."

Kerry laughed. "So you didn't convert Cody's girlfriend? You said you were sixteen. How old was she?"

"She was eighteen. A senior."

"Cody is thirty-four, my age," she said. "So four years older than you. He would have been twenty then." She shook her head. "I imagine it did throw him for a loop that his kid sister was stealing his girlfriend."

"Not stealing. And no, I didn't convert her. At least, I don't think so." She shrugged. "Angie preferred my...*oral* skills, I believe."

Kerry's face turned red as she felt herself blushing profusely which only caused Carson to laugh.

"I'm sorry. Did I embarrass you?"

"Yes." But she smiled good-naturedly. "Yes," she said again.

"Then let's stop talking about sex."

Kerry met her eyes. "Were we talking about sex?"

Carson arched an eyebrow. "Weren't we?"

With Carson standing close, watching her, Kerry felt that hum in her body again. On some level, she knew she should be afraid of it. Very afraid. Surprisingly, she wasn't.

"What are you doing here, anyway?"

"Looking for you," Carson said. "I was bored."

"And I'm your amusement?" Kerry asked.

Carson went to the giant fireplace, running her hand across the smooth stone. "I thought you might need help with something." She turned. "I haven't really been out and about yet," she said. "The lake the other day, that's it."

"I noticed you and Chase have taken walks the last two evenings." She'd noticed, yes, mainly because she'd been curious. After dinner, they usually retired to their father's study for a drink, something she knew irritated the other brothers. What she found really odd about the whole thing is that after dinner, the four brothers would go their separate ways, having their own suites. Oh, Cody would hang around and want to talk, even sharing wine with her on a couple of occasions, but even he would eventually leave her to fend for herself.

"Chase and I were always close," Carson said. "We have a lot of catching up to do."

"And the others?"

"I'm sure you've been able to tell that there's not a lot of affection there."

"Why? Because you stole their girlfriends?"

"No. It started before that." Carson sat down on the hearth, her legs stretched out in front of her. "It's hard to explain. It's like I was kept separate from them," she said. "They were a part of the ranch. I was not. By the time puberty hit and I realized I preferred the company of girls, there was already a gap between us."

"Who was he grooming you to marry?"

"At first, I thought it was Justin Conley. They have the neighboring ranch. Justin, Chase and I were pals growing up. We used to ride horses when we were younger, before Chase had to work. And before our father put a stop to it," Carson said. "But he and Kenneth Conley had a falling out so Justin was off the hook," she said with a laugh.

Kerry was about to ask about her mother, but she sensed that Carson wasn't in the mood to talk. Not about that. The sadness she'd seen in her eyes that day was gone and she didn't want to bring it back. So, she turned the conversation to the bunkhouse.

"What do you think for the bedrooms? Carpet or tile?"

"Carpet."

"It doesn't wear as well."

"If you have tile, you'll have to have rugs."

"Rugs can be washed."

Carson grinned. "I see you've made up your mind."

"Not really. I'm just arguing both sides. I actually prefer carpet. I was thinking of maintenance."

"So, do you think things will be up and running in time for the fall drive?"

"In September? No, I don't think they should start then. Any help they need, they'll have to hire as seasonal. You don't want to bring in someone for a few weeks, then lay them off until spring."

"Who do they have to hire?"

"Someone to do laundry, clean the rooms. Maybe a cook to help Martha."

"And where will they live?"

"They thought they could hire someone locally so they wouldn't have to supply housing."

"The ranch house is plenty big, especially when the old man dies," Carson said.

Kerry watched her, seeing that the statement was said without any remorse or regret. "How much time does he have?"

"I'd say any day now, but Chase said the doctor has been saying that for a month. He's very frail, weak."

"But not so weak that he couldn't have a loud conversation with you," she said gently.

"Conversation? Is that what you'd call it?"

"Will you see him again?"

Carson stood up, moving to one of the windows. "I don't really see the point. I mean, I doubt I'll get any sort of closure by visiting with him again. And he certainly doesn't seem to want to make things right." She turned slowly, her eyes again showing signs of sadness. "He thinks I'm her. When he sees me, his eyes light up as if he's seeing her. Then he realizes it's me, and I just see hatred there."

"I'm sorry."

Carson shrugged, her gaze again going to the window. "It doesn't matter anymore."

"But it does. You're still hurting over it," she stated

Carson turned back toward her and leaned against the wall, her hands shoved casually in her pockets. "And I probably always will. Nothing's going to change that. That's why I told you I wasn't certain why I came back."

"But despite your father, aren't you glad you did?"

"Yeah. Chase and I have reconnected. When I leave here, we'll continue to have a relationship." She shoved off the wall, coming closer. "So what are you working on?" Carson asked, motioning to the tape measure in her hand.

"Just trying to get a feel for the size of the new bedrooms. It's not working so well. I just need to wait until the walls are down."

"And they start on Monday?"

"First thing," she said, then laughed. "Although their first thing is probably much earlier than yours," she teased.

Carson held the door open for her as they walked out into the sunshine. "My body has actually adjusted somewhat," Carson said. "I've always been a bit of a night owl. Living in New York will do that. But I've switched my clock around, I think."

Kerry stopped and faced her, knowing she needed to go inside and work on the website, but she wasn't ready to leave Carson's company just yet. She didn't stop to consider why that was. She knew she wouldn't have a reason for the pull she felt.

"What do you have planned for the rest of the afternoon?" she asked.

Carson studied her, finally raising an eyebrow. "What do *you* have planned?" she asked instead.

"I need to work on the website, but it's just so beautiful out today. I could possibly be persuaded to work on it tonight," she said.

"And what activity would you have to be tempted with?"

It was an innocent question, Kerry was sure, but Carson's low voice sent a shiver right through her. Cody's words of warning echoed in her ear, and she realized she was possibly playing with fire.

"Riding?"

Carson shook her head. "For one thing, I've not been riding since the day I left here. And two, you don't want to go down to the stables while the guys are there." Carson leaned closer to her. "Cody would go berserk if we showed up together."

Kerry swallowed. "The stables are next to the hay barn?" she asked.

Carson's smile nearly melted her on the spot. "Yes. Attached. Perhaps when we go I'll show you my...*favorite* high school spot. We'll have to wait until the guys are gone with the herd though. Like I said, Cody would most likely get a shotgun after me."

Kerry again felt a blush cross her face and was thankful

when Carson moved away from her, her eyes twinkling with amusement.

"I'm just teasing you," Carson said with a smile. "Please don't go tell Cody I was flirting with you," she said as she playfully bumped her arm.

Again, Kerry's body simply hummed with life in this woman's presence. They walked back to the ranch house in a comfortable silence.

"Cody asked me out," she finally said.

"Oh, yeah? Like a real date?"

"Yes. Dinner and the movies."

"That's my brother. But in all fairness, there aren't a lot of options out here." Carson arched an eyebrow. "So? You going?"

Kerry shook her head. "No. I mean, for one, I don't want to encourage him. And really, I'm getting paid to work, not socialize." She didn't add that she never seriously considered the offer. Cody Cartwright stirred absolutely zero interest in her.

"Did you let him down easy?"

"I'm not sure. He wanted to do something before they head out with the herd. They'll be gone a week, he said."

"Yeah. And I hope the old man doesn't die while they're gone. I don't want to be the one to have to deal with it all."

"I'm sure arrangements have been made," Kerry said. Surely, as sick as he's been, the brothers haven't left it up in the air.

As if reading her thoughts, Carson smirked. "They're guys," she said. "It probably hasn't occurred to them."

CHAPTER FOURTEEN

Chase poured the amber liquid in her glass then slid it along the desk. She leaned back in the leather chair, using the edge of the desk to prop up her feet.

"You're quiet this evening," Chase said. "Did you see the old man again?"

"No. Have you? He mentioned you guys don't see him as much any more."

"I usually pop in there in the mornings before we head out," he said. "Chance visits him before dinner. Colt and Cody after."

"Every day?"

"I think so. He probably thinks we don't because she's got him on so much morphine."

"You think he'll make it the week? I mean, you guys are heading out in two days."

He laughed. "And you don't want to be left here alone? Don't worry, sis. Chance has it all worked out. Everything's taken care of."

"Will you get cell service when you're out with the herd?"

"No. We barely have it here at the ranch. You'll be on your own."

"Because I don't think he's going to hang on much longer," she said.

"No. But we can't delay it and wait on him to die. We've got to get the herd moved and established out there." He leaned back in their father's chair, the leather creaking. "That sounds crass and uncaring, doesn't it?"

"It is what it is," Carson said with a shrug.

He sat up, resting his elbows on the desk as he looked at her. "So, what's up with you, sis?"

"What do you mean?"

"Something's on your mind," he said. "What's up?"

She glanced over her shoulder to the empty doorway, making sure they were still alone. She smiled at him and wiggled her eyebrows.

"Oh, no," he said, shaking his head. "You're not serious."

She grinned. "I like her."

"Come on, Car. You said yourself, she's straight."

"No. I said she was gay. *She* said she was straight," she reminded him. "But there's something going on. There's this vibe between us."

"What kind of a vibe?"

"Just...something," she said. And there was. She suspected Kerry felt it too. Whenever they were alone together, there was an underlying intimacy, which was crazy, seeing how they *hadn't* been intimate. And Carson's not-so-subtle flirting was met with amusement, not disdain. She enjoyed Kerry's company, enjoyed their talks. They had become friends in a short period of time, something Carson never did. But just under the surface lingered a sexual attraction that Carson was having a hard time ignoring. Because frankly, she wasn't *used* to ignoring it.

"Does she know there's a vibe?"

Carson flicked her eyes his way. "Probably not," she lied.

"Then you need to let it go," he said. "Cody will kill you."

"Cody's only claim on her is imaginary," she said.

"He's—"

"Can we join you?"

They both turned at the sound of Cody's voice. Kerry stood behind him, a smile on her face as she met Carson's eyes.

"Sure. Pull up a chair," Chase said.

"Kerry was interested in seeing where you two ran off to." He glared at Carson in an unspoken challenge. "I told her you were probably in here swiping our father's expensive scotch," he said.

"I don't think he'll be drinking any more of it," she said without thinking.

"He's not even dead and you're already staking your claim?" Cody shook his head as Chase offered him a glass.

"I'm just having a drink with my brother. No crime in that."

Kerry nodded when Chase held up an empty glass. Cody's eyes narrowed as Chase filled it. Jesus, Chase was right. They had turned into a bunch of uptight teetotalers. Well, that's one thing they didn't get from their father. The old man liked his scotch. Apparently that was the only thing she and Chase got from him, Carson thought.

"How's the website coming?" she asked. She knew Kerry had spent the afternoon working on it.

"I probably shouldn't admit this in front of your brothers, but web design is not my strong suit." She smiled at Cody. "I do know what I'm doing," she assured him. "I just have to tinker with all the settings."

"I have no doubt it'll turn out great," he said.

Carson and Chase exchanged amused glances, glances that Kerry saw and added her own quick smile to.

"So? Bunkhouse starts Monday?"

"Yes," she said. "He promised he'd be here at eight sharp."

"I think Chance wants to head out with the herd on Sunday," Cody said, directing his statement to Chase. "A storm's coming on Wednesday, and he wants to be in the next valley by then," he explained.

"Lightning," Chase supplied when Kerry raised a questioning eyebrow. "Spring storms can be brutal."

"Spring storms can also have you holed up in the valley for a few days," Carson added, blatantly baiting Cody. "Your one-week trip might turn into ten days or more," she said.

"I doubt that will happen," he said. "But really, why are you still hanging around here? I thought you'd be ready to head back to the big city by now."

"I am *so* enjoying my time here," she said with a smile. "Besides, I wouldn't miss the big event."

"I don't believe the reading of the will is gonna be all that exciting for you," he said with a smirk. "I don't believe you're mentioned."

"The will?" She looked at Kerry, smiling. "Actually, I was talking about Kerry's conversion project," she said.

"Wow. You plan on sticking around here for six months?"

"Maybe. Summer in the mountains sounds pretty good," she said, her gaze landing on Kerry.

"Great," Kerry said. "Then maybe I could get you to show me around the property. I'll need to start planning the route for the trail rides."

"Sure. I'd be happy to," she said easily as she waited for Cody's eruption.

Cody's jaw clenched as he took a protective step closer to Kerry. "I can do that for you. There's no need to involve Carson. No need at all."

"You already told me you would be out a lot during the summer," Kerry said. "I know it's a busy time for you all."

"Then I'll do it when we come in. There's plenty of daylight in the summer," he said. "I'll have time."

But Kerry shook her head. "We'll manage. I told you all up front that I would do most of the legwork, and you guys didn't have to worry about it."

When Cody opened his mouth to protest, Kerry held up her hand, indicating the conversation was over.

"Now, if you'll excuse me, I have a little work to do tonight."

She set her empty glass on the desk. "Thank you, Chase. That was excellent."

He nodded. "Good night, Kerry."

"Good night," Carson murmured, watching her go.

Cody turned on her as soon as Kerry was out of earshot. He bent lower, pointing his finger at her.

"You stay away from her," he hissed. "She's not like that. She's a nice person."

Carson simply couldn't help herself. She smiled wickedly. "Oh, she's *very* nice."

"I swear, if you lay a hand on her—"

"You'll what?"

He squared his shoulders. "This isn't high school any longer, Carson," he said. "Those same rules no longer apply."

"I wasn't aware there were any rules." She glanced at Chase, seeing the warning in his eyes, so she relented. "Relax, Cody. I'm too old to be chasing after straight women. I'm just messing with you."

"Yeah, right," he snorted. "You suddenly got scruples or what?"

"Well, we all grow up someday," she said. "Can't I just come back and visit the old home place?" she asked.

"Yeah. Just don't wear out your welcome."

After he left, Carson held her glass out to Chase. "Hit me," she said. He did, adding more scotch to her glass.

"Did you enjoy that?" Chase asked.

She grinned. "Yeah. Didn't you?"

CHAPTER FIFTEEN

Kerry could pretend she was out on a stroll, but she'd made it a habit not to lie to herself. She was out looking for Carson and didn't try to analyze it—she knew why. Of course, she could make excuses. And if she found her she undoubtedly would. But lie to herself? No. She simply wanted to see her, wanted to *be* with her.

She found her in much the same spot as the last time they had met up at the lake—standing near the shore, staring across the water. But unlike before, when Kerry had nearly made a hasty retreat, she walked up beside her. Carson didn't turn and Kerry didn't speak. She didn't want to disturb the silence.

"How did you escape?" Carson asked quietly, finally turning toward her.

"They're packing their gear," she said. She smiled at Carson, then turned her gaze back to the lake. "Did you enjoy baiting Cody last night?"

Carson laughed. "Sorry. It was just too easy. I couldn't resist. He's so uptight."

"Yes, he is."

"But I think you did your share of baiting."

Kerry nodded. "He caught up with me on the stairs. He said I needed to *seriously* reconsider having you show me around."

"And will you?"

Kerry shook her head. "Should I?"

"No. I'm harmless."

Kerry tilted her head and smiled. "Are you really?"

"Of course. As I told Cody, I'm too old to chase after straight women." She shrugged. "Besides, we're friends."

Kerry looked at her, getting lost in her eyes. "Are we?"

Carson shifted, plunging her hands into her pockets. "I think we are," she said, her voice quiet. "It's been a long time since I've added a new friend to my life. Besides, it feels good."

"Yeah. Yeah it does."

Carson grinned and took a step away from her. "See how easy that was? Now we're friends. No worries."

"Do you think I'm worried?"

"I think Cody's constant reminders of how bad I am have put some doubt in your mind, yes."

Yes, it should have, Kerry thought. But no, it hadn't. Quite the opposite. She felt completely safe in Carson's presence. And why wouldn't she? She'd spent much more time with Carson than she had Cody. Carson hardly felt like a woman she'd only met a few weeks ago.

"I've heard them mention more than once that you're only here for the inheritance. Is that true?"

Carson laughed. "God, no. I don't have any claim to the ranch. Our father made that perfectly clear. The ranch goes to the boys. As for money, it seems like that's running a little thin anyway." Carson started walking again, much like she had the first time. And as before, Kerry followed. "I guess they feel threatened. I haven't been around in twelve years. Suddenly, the old man is dying and I show up."

"So you don't talk at all? I mean, I know you and Chase do. But the others?"

"No. The conversations we have at dinner are it. And really, it was always that way. Chance is six years older. We just never bonded." She stopped. "What about you? Any siblings?"

Kerry shook her head. "No. My parents wanted a big family, but there were complications with her pregnancy. She had surgery, so, it was just me."

"Where are you from?"

"Denver," she said. "My parents still live there. Actually, I still have a room there. I traveled so much with Randall that there wasn't really any point to get my own place."

"Randall?"

"Randall Consultants," she said. "My previous employer."

"Oh, yes. Before selling your soul and signing a contract with the Cartwrights," she said with a smile.

"Yes. Thanks for reminding me. I guess I should get back to it."

"It's Saturday. You don't get a break?"

"No. That's how I got out of having a date with Cody. I told him I couldn't possibly spare an evening away from work. I should at least make good on that."

She turned to go but Carson called her back.

"I'll show you around the ranch on Monday, if you'd like."

She nodded. "That would be great. Thanks."

"Of course, it may be you teaching me to ride," Carson said. "I haven't been on a horse in twelve years."

"I'm sure we'll manage."

She left Carson standing near the shore as she headed back to the ranch house. She wished she had an explanation for the way she felt. Her encounters with Carson always left her feeling a bit refreshed. And content in some way. She felt completely at ease with her. It was the feeling she had the very first time she met her. That familiarity she felt whenever she was around her. She wondered why she didn't feel that with Cody, or with anyone else, for that matter.

And speaking of Cody, he greeted her at the back door and she was surprised to see a bit of suspicion in his eyes.

"Where have you been?"

The question, while not accusatory, had an edge to it. And unlike her rule to never lie to herself, it didn't apply to clients. So she smiled pleasantly as she stopped beside him.

"I was making the drawings of the lake and decided to check it out again to see where we might put the piers. I know you guys want to keep part of it private so it'll have to be a group decision," she said.

His eyes slid past her and narrowed. No doubt he spotted Carson.

"Did she follow you down there?"

This time, the question was accusatory. Kerry turned, following his gaze, seeing Carson as she made her way up the trail. She shook her head. "No, she was already there."

"I told you, you need to stay away from her. She's—"

"Cody, why are you so adamant about this? She's never done or said anything inappropriate. In fact, I find her to be very pleasant," she said honestly.

"Pleasant? There's nothing pleasant about her. She's selfish and is only concerned about what *she* wants."

"Well, you obviously have a history with her. I don't. So my view of her is only what I see today."

He took a deep breath. "Look, I don't have any right to say this, but maybe you should consider leaving while we're gone. There'll be no one here but Martha. You'd be safer if—"

"You're correct, Cody. You have no right," she said briskly, cutting him off. "Now I need to get back to work."

CHAPTER SIXTEEN

Kerry was leaning casually against a post, her camera held ready, and Carson sat on the top railing of the corral while they watched the guys get ready to head out. The air was filled with the sounds of bellowing cattle and the short, quick barks of the two cattle dogs who tried to keep them together. Kerry had been busy trying to capture the scene for the website.

It was a sight Carson had seen many, many years ago and it brought on a rush of memories. Especially seeing Johnny Mac, now twelve years older, sitting astride the big, black mare, his sharp whistles as familiar to her today as they were back then. His greeting had been warm, even though she knew he had sided with her father when it came to her.

"There's so many," Kerry said. "How big is the herd?"

"Not sure. Chase said they've had to sell off quite a few. I'd say close to a thousand," she said.

"The mules carry the supplies?" Kerry asked.

"Yes. Food, water for cooking, pots and pans. They each carry their own bedrolls and tents, but one mule carries the mess tent," she explained.

Carson and Kerry watched in silence as they headed out, moving the herd slowly. They would spread them out, making a trail, as they got closer to the mountains. Chase said to expect them back in six days unless the predicted storm on Wednesday delayed them.

Carson kept catching the jealous glances of Cody as they worked the cattle. She refused to get into a battle with him and simply ignored his stares. Much as she'd ignored the last warning he'd given her early that morning.

"I swear Carson, if you lay a hand on her, I'll kill you."

"What's up with you? Are you in love with her or something?"

"I like her," he said.

"So do I. She's very nice."

"Exactly. She's nice. She doesn't need you to taint her."

"Jesus, Cody, possessive or what? It's not like you're dating or anything. She works for you guys."

"As soon as I get back, I'm going to tell her how I feel. So you leave her alone." His stare was intense. "I'm not joking this time, Carson."

She had turned away then, not wanting to get into a contest with him, but she couldn't believe how naive he was. But then again, why wouldn't he be. He had no experience in life. Like all them, he'd never left the ranch, never left the valley. Their high school was forty miles away. After graduation, they came back to the ranch to work and had never left. Of course their social skills would be lacking.

Except Chase. He got away. She wondered if his involvement in breeding Windstorm, in meeting breeders and making contacts had helped him break away from the bubble they lived in out here.

"Why so quiet?" Kerry asked.

Carson looked down at her, mesmerized by her soft features, the early morning sun warming her face. She was absolutely lovely. She realized she was staring, and she smiled quickly, looking back to the herd.

"I was just thinking about my brothers," she said. "Do you know they've never left here."

"What do you mean?"

"I mean, other than Chase, they've not traveled out of this valley. Oh, maybe a trip to Billings for something, but other than that, nothing."

"Are you serious?"

"I was considering Cody's...social skills," she said. "I mean, after his little talk with me this morning, I—"

"What little talk?"

"The *I'll kill you if you touch her* talk," she said. "It's really not his fault that he never learned how to interact with women. Their life is out here."

"I've never met a more possessive man," Kerry said. "Especially one I haven't even slept with."

"Oh, he's just marking his territory," she said.

"Well, I'm neither his territory nor his possession. In fact, I'm very tired of it. I thought he was going to kiss me this morning when he was telling me goodbye."

Carson was surprised by the anger she heard in Kerry's voice. "Sorry to say, but you probably should get prepared for a marriage proposal when he gets back."

Kerry laughed, then stopped when Carson didn't join in.

"You're being serious," she stated.

"Yes."

"Oh, God. How did this happen?"

At this, Carson did laugh. "I believe you said something about desperately needing a contract," she said.

Kerry sighed. "This is going to get ugly, isn't it?"

"Probably." Carson jumped off the railing, standing beside her. "Come on. Let's go meet Windstorm."

"He was your childhood horse?"

"No. I was in high school when we got him," she said as they made their way to the stables. "He took a liking to me for some reason. Wouldn't let anyone else get near him. He hasn't been ridden since the day I left."

"I'm surprised they kept him then," Kerry said.

"Me too. But Chase said they breed him."

"Will you ride him?"

Carson laughed. "You trying to get me killed? I haven't been on a horse in twelve years. Windstorm is huge."

The stables were as well-kept as she remembered. The stalls were enclosed, all opening up to the large fenced area to allow the horses room to roam. She spotted him off by himself, kept separate from the mares and foals.

"God, look at him. Isn't he handsome?"

"Yes. And you're right. He's huge."

Carson stared at the beautiful animal, her heart racing. She hadn't said goodbye to him. It was as if she were blaming him for what happened, much like her father had blamed her. She took a deep breath, then whistled, the tone coming out as clear as a bell. His head jerked up and he stared at her. Amazingly, she felt tears threaten. Windstorm apparently remembered her call.

"Stay here," she said as she climbed the fence and jumped into the pasture. She walked closer, staring in his big eyes. "Hey, boy," she said softly. "You remember me?"

He snorted and pawed the dirt, never taking his eyes off of her. She stopped walking, but couldn't keep the smile off her face. "Windstorm, come here," she said and whistled again.

To her amazement, he came forward, albeit a bit warily. She stood still, holding out one hand to him. He stopped, then stretched his neck out, sniffing her hand. He snorted again and shook his head, his long white mane bouncing along his neck.

"Come on, boy. Don't play hard to get," she murmured. She stood perfectly still as he walked around her. She kept her back to him, then let her tears fall as she felt him nuzzle her hips, sniffing her back pockets. *Oh God, he remembered.* He was looking for a carrot. She always stuffed them in her back pockets, and he'd learn to steal them from her.

She turned to Kerry, not caring that she was crying. She had a big grin on her face. "He remembers," she said. She then took a step toward the big horse, not afraid in the least as she hugged his neck. He stood still and allowed her affection. She imagined she felt him tremble and wondered if anyone had bothered touching him at all. Most had been afraid of him. He'd tossed his share of cowboys on their asses. He simply refused to be ridden. She, however, could climb on his back without a saddle, and he was the gentlest creature in the world.

"Come on in," she called to Kerry. "Come meet Windstorm."

Kerry was a bit hesitant as she came closer. She stared at Carson, seeing her tears, Carson knew. She seemed to know that the tears were just an emotional release and made no mention of them.

"He's gorgeous," she said quietly. She reached out a tentative hand, lightly rubbing his face.

He stood still and allowed this inspection of him. Carson suspected he was enjoying the attention.

"I used to put carrots in my back pockets," Carson explained. "So when he walked behind me just then, that's what he was looking for."

Kerry smiled. "Were you afraid he wouldn't remember you?"

"Yes. That would have broken my heart."

She gave him one last scratch then turned, guiding Kerry back to the stables. Windstorm, however, hadn't had enough and he followed close behind.

"He's so big," Kerry said.

"Don't be afraid of him. He's really gentle." She turned, rubbing his nose again. "Aren't you, boy?"

"I was never really around horses," Kerry said. "Vacations and ponies, mainly."

"Yeah? But you rode at Dry Creek Ranch?"

"Yes. That was my first time to actually ride without it being an old mare taking a guided tour," Kerry said. "I really enjoyed it. It's so...freeing," she said with a smile.

"We'll go out tomorrow," Carson said, suddenly looking forward to the outing and no longer dreading it...and dreading whatever memories it might evoke.

"That'll be fun. But we start on the bunkhouse in the morning," Kerry reminded her.

"And you'll get in the way. Mr. Burris will be happy I've taken you away."

Kerry flicked her eyes at her and smirked. "You think I'm going to be the annoying *anal* female?"

"Aren't you?"

Kerry laughed. "I just like things done my way. I don't think that's anal."

They climbed back over the fence, Windstorm still at their heels. Carson felt bad about leaving him and again scratched behind his ears.

"I need to bring him something," she said. "Carrots or sugar cubes. Something."

"Let's raid Martha's fridge," Kerry suggested.

Carson cocked an eyebrow. "You're just dying to get into trouble, aren't you?"

CHAPTER SEVENTEEN

"You know, you didn't have to go to all this trouble," Carson said as Martha placed a plate in front of her.

Kerry smiled, watching as Martha put an identical plate in front of her. It was laden with a chicken breast, a broccoli and cauliflower medley, and scalloped potatoes.

"With your brothers gone," Martha said, addressing Carson, "it gave me a chance to cook chicken. They think they have to have beef at every meal," she said. "Now, I have a lot of chicken recipes. I'll try them this week. I hope you won't mind."

Carson laughed. "Sounds good, Martha. Whatever you'd like."

"I prefer chicken," Kerry added as she cut into the tender breast.

"Then we'll get along fine this week," Martha said. "Enjoy," she added as she left them alone.

Kerry took a sip of her water, then rolled her shoulders, trying to get the kinks out. She'd spent the entire afternoon holed up in her room with her laptop. And while she accomplished much on the new website, she had to constantly remind herself that she was here working and not vacationing. Her mind kept wandering to Carson and on more than one occasion, she had to talk herself out of going to find her. It was different, somehow, with the brothers gone. With Cody gone, she clarified. They were alone. There were no barriers or obstacles. It was as if things had changed between them. The looks they shared were unguarded now, open. Kerry wasn't so naive that she didn't recognize what was happening between them. She did. She didn't, however, have a clue as to how to stop it. She wasn't altogether certain she wanted to stop it, despite the uncharted territory she was heading into. Gravitating toward women, enjoying their presence was one thing. Being attracted—sexually attracted—to a lesbian was something quite different.

"Did you get a lot of work done?" Carson asked, pulling her from her musings.

"I did. Although I admit, I would have much rather been outside enjoying the beautiful weather," she said as she took a bite of chicken.

"Bring your laptop out with you," Carson suggested.

"I don't work well that way. Too many things would distract me." She met her eyes for a moment, then looked away. "Like you," she added.

"Me? Afraid I'll steal you away and go exploring or something."

Kerry smiled. "That's what I'd *want* to do, yes. Which is why I'm glad you're taking me riding tomorrow," she said. "I can still call it working."

"Not working. Just a tour," Carson said as she sampled the potatoes. "God, these are good," she murmured.

"Yes, they're excellent," she said. "So, how much of it do you remember? I mean, if we're going to offer trail rides, we'll need a route. Are there trails into the mountains already, or will we have to make some?"

"There are some, but I don't know if it's what you're looking for. You know, as a kid, I used to ride all over out there, trail or not. Then there's a trail that goes through the valley and onto the next ranch, the Conleys' place," she said. "My boyfriend," she added with a smirk.

"The would-be groom?"

Carson nodded. "We were in the eighth grade when we kissed. And it was as romantic as kissing my brother would have been," she said. "I already knew I liked girls but that just confirmed it."

"That must have been hard," she said. "You're so removed from everything out here. It's so remote. I imagine it must have been difficult."

"It was. Why do you think I had to resort to my brothers' girlfriends?"

Kerry laughed. "That's not what I meant. I mean, you were alone. There couldn't have been a lot of support. Not as if you were in a big city school," she said.

"My mother was supportive. Of course she already knew by the time I told her. And the two of us kept it a secret from my father." She smiled. "That is, until the day Cody caught me with Angie Bonner."

"So he just walked in on you? In the hayloft?" she asked. She had been curious about the whole incident since Carson had first mentioned it.

"Not exactly. He watched first," Carson said.

"You're kidding? Why would he watch?" As soon as the words were out, she blushed and added, "Don't answer that."

Carson laughed. "Cody was twenty. His girlfriend—eighteen and a senior in high school. And I'm this skinny tomboy, sixteen, and she was begging for me to...well, you know, do something Cody would never do."

Again Kerry blushed, not needing for Carson to say the words. Still, her mind conjured up an image she couldn't shake. "Then what?" she asked, despite her embarrassment.

"Then we got into one of many fights and he threw me from

the loft and I broke my arm," she said matter-of-factly. "That's when my father found out I was gay. That's really when everyone found out."

"At school?"

"Most already knew. Small school. Not much escaped notice," Carson said. "Chase was the only one of my brothers who knew. Or at least they pretended not to know. They were all shocked and everything."

Kerry stared at her, eyebrows raised. "You broke your arm?"

Carson grinned. "And *that* pissed me off." She pushed her plate aside, sipping from her own water. "Enough about all that. Where do you go from here?"

"You mean, providing I make the six months?" she teased.

"I'm sure you will. There's only one thing that would make Cody turn on you," she said as she smiled, amusement dancing in her eyes.

The logical thing to say was that she shouldn't have anything to worry about then, but she didn't speak the words. For some reason, they seemed inappropriate. So she simply matched Carson's easy smile with one of her own. She was about to answer her earlier question when Martha popped into the dining room.

"You ladies all done?"

"That was excellent, Martha," Carson said. "The best potatoes I've ever had."

Kerry wasn't surprised to find that Carson's charm worked on the older woman as well. She blushed as she busied herself with their plates.

"Why, thank you, Miss Carson. It's an old family recipe. I swear, your brothers could eat plain old mashed potatoes at every meal if I let them," she said.

"Well, you can serve all the chicken you want," Kerry added. "It's a nice change."

"Thank you. You may be sorry you requested that. I, for one, am sick to death of beef." She shook her head when they both attempted to help her clear the table. "You'll leave that right where you found it," she said. "I tend to that around here. Why don't you two go to the study? A little girl talk must be nice what with the guys finally gone."

Her movements were fluid as she cleared the table and Kerry and Carson exchanged an amused glance as she ushered them out of the room.

"Well, I suppose I could put in another hour or so on the website," Kerry said.

"Or you could join me for a nightcap," Carson suggested. "I think I saw a nice bottle of brandy in there."

Kerry paused. Common sense told her she should decline. She'd spent enough time with Carson as it was. But common sense didn't win out as she found herself following Carson into the study.

"Or scotch?" Carson offered.

"Brandy is fine," she said as she settled into a plush leather chair. "Thank you," she murmured as Carson handed her a glass.

"My father came in here every night after dinner for exactly two glasses of scotch and one cigar," Carson said as she sat across from her. "My mother joined him only on Friday nights. No one else was allowed inside," she said. "Ever."

"Did he have secrets?"

"No. I think he was just keeping this for himself. You know, a place where he could come and not be interrupted by kids." Carson's gaze landed on her and Kerry raised her eyebrows questioningly. "You're curious about our family yet you haven't shared much about you."

"Nothing exciting, trust me. An only child with two doting parents, I didn't want for anything, yet we were hardly what you'd call wealthy," she said. "Then I worked for a small consulting firm after college, before I joined Randall. It was lots of travel, especially at first. I got the jobs no one wanted."

"Ever married?"

Kerry shook her head. "No. Not even close."

"You're thirty-four?"

"Yes." She smiled.

"Do you want kids?"

"I'm not sure," she said honestly. "I always just assumed I

would have kids, but I don't miss not having them." She shrugged. "I don't really think about it, I guess. I've been focused on my career." She looked at her briefly. "You?"

"God, no. I never wanted kids," Carson said. "It was never even a consideration."

Kerry sipped her brandy, wondering if Carson's childhood—her father—was the reason she was so adamant about not having kids. But then, some women never craved motherhood, regardless of their upbringing. So she changed the subject, back to something less personal.

"Where will you take me tomorrow?"

Carson gave her a saucy look. "I can take you places you've never been before." Their eyes met, then Carson laughed. "God, that was so lame," she said.

Kerry laughed too. For a second there, she thought Carson was serious. "You haven't really used that line before, have you?"

"No. I was just teasing you." Carson added a bit more brandy to both their glasses. "Actually, I'm really looking forward to getting out there," she said. "I just hope Windstorm is up for it. Chase said he hasn't been ridden. I hope he doesn't toss me on my ass."

"I don't think he will," she said. "But what about me? Got some nice, slow mare I can ride?"

"Yeah. Chase told me which one would be best for you. She's young but gentle." Carson watched her. "Are you nervous?"

"To be on a horse? Not really."

"We should be fine," Carson said. "It's just quiet around the ranch with the guys and the cattle gone."

"Yes. Nice and quiet," she said. "I feel no pressure. I don't feel like I have to watch everything I say," she admitted.

"You mean with Cody?"

"Yes. I don't want him to misconstrue something I've said. I tend to talk less around him for that very reason."

"I've noticed."

"It's different with you," Kerry said, wondering why she felt the need to explain. "Everything feels familiar. It's so easy, this friendship we've developed. Don't you think?"

Carson held her eyes for a moment although the look in hers was veiled. She smiled easily and nodded.

"Yes, it is familiar. You've known me all of three weeks and you already know more about me than anyone else. I haven't shared much of my past with any of my current...friends," Carson said.

"Where do you live?"

"I have an apartment in Manhattan. That's officially home, I suppose. I travel a lot," she said evasively.

That declaration brought a whole new series of questions to the surface, but Kerry saw the guarded look that Carson now sported. She wouldn't ruin the pleasant evening with more questions.

"I've found the more I travel, the more I'm ready to settle down," Kerry said. "Unfortunately, starting my own business, especially one like this, will require continued travel." She stood then, signaling an end to the evening. "Thank you for the brandy," she said. "It was nice to sit and talk, but I have a busy day tomorrow."

"Yes. And I'll let you get started on the bunkhouse before we head out. I'll come find you."

"I just need one last run-through with Mr. Burris. Don't want him to take out the wrong wall." She bowed slightly. "Good night, Carson."

"Good night."

CHAPTER EIGHTEEN

Carson heard the banging of hammers and the clanking of boards as she approached the bunkhouse. It was after ten, and she thought she'd given them enough time to get started on it. As she suspected, Kerry was underfoot, watching the demolition with an attentive eye.

"Making progress?" she asked as she ducked under a two-by-four.

Kerry smiled at her. "Good morning. Yeah, they got to work right away." She tugged Carson away, leading her back outside. "I think they're sick of me already," she said with a laugh.

"Time for me to steal you away then?"

"Yes. He said it would take them through tomorrow to get all the walls down and hauled away. I'm all yours."

There were so many things Carson could say to that, but she let it go with only a slight twitch of her lips. Kerry bumped her shoulder.

"Not touching that one, huh?"

"I'm behaving myself," she said. She held up a canvas bag. "Martha packed us lunch."

"Oh, that was sweet of her."

"Yes. She's very thoughtful. The guys are lucky to have her."

They walked on to the stables, their boots crunching on the gravel path. For some reason, Carson was nervous. She wasn't sure if it was the fact that she was about to saddle Windstorm or that she would be completely alone with Kerry. As Kerry had said last night, their friendship was easy, natural. And it was evolving. She wondered if Kerry realized the path they were taking or the swiftness at which they traveled it. In her younger days—another time, another place—Carson would have already tested the waters. Hell, she would have dived in headfirst. But there was something about Kerry that made her want to take it slow, if not change direction altogether. It had nothing to do with the ranch or Cody or even Kerry's supposed orientation. It was on a deeper level, one she couldn't quite reach, couldn't quite explain. She wasn't certain she wanted to delve into it further, but on some level she was afraid. She was afraid of her growing attachment to this woman.

"You're being quiet," Kerry said. "Everything okay?"

"Oh...yeah, sorry. I was thinking about riding again after all this time," she lied. "I hope I remember how to saddle a horse."

Kerry tilted her head, studying her, and Carson had a sense that Kerry knew she was lying.

"Did you see your father?"

"No. Well, I went to his room this morning, but she had given him a dose of morphine and he was out."

"It must be terrible to spend your last days like that," Kerry said.

"Yes. In his heart, in his mind, he's already died, I think. It's just his body hasn't let him go yet." She held the door open to the barn, letting Kerry go first. "She says he's in a lot of pain."

"I imagine so. But Carson, isn't it a little strange? I mean, your father is dying yet your brothers just rode off as if nothing is wrong."

"Yeah, but they've got to get the herd moved. I'm guessing they all said their goodbyes to him before they left."

"I suppose. But if it were me, I wouldn't leave his side."

"And that's where things are very different," she said. "The ranch comes first. It always has." She went to the rack where the bridles were kept, choosing one without a bit for Windstorm—he'd always hated them—and another with a bit for the young mare Kerry would ride. "Here we go," she said.

Back out in the sunshine, she easily hopped the fence and stood still, whistling for Windstorm. His ears perked up, eyeing her. Then he trotted over, sniffing her.

"See if you can find it," she whispered, holding still as he moved behind her. She grinned as she felt him pushing at her from behind. Soon, the loud crunching of a carrot was heard. She turned triumphantly to Kerry. "Awesome," she said.

Kerry nodded and Carson felt her eyes following her as she walked closer to Windstorm, gently rubbing his neck.

"You want to ride, big fella?" she murmured, touching him as she used to. He stood still when she slipped the bridle onto his face and over his ears. Once secured, he shook his head several times but didn't shy away. "Good boy." She took the reins, leading him toward the stable. She glanced at Kerry. "I think he's going to be fine."

And he was. He stood still as Carson lifted the saddle onto his back, and she wondered if perhaps he wasn't anxious to get out on the trails and out of the stables. Surprisingly, the art of saddling a horse came back to her—she had the mare and Windstorm ready to go in no time. She held the mare steady as Kerry climbed onto the saddle, then handed her the reins.

She patted Windstorm's neck before putting her foot in the stirrup. "Don't toss me on my ass, please," she said as she grabbed the horn of the saddle and pulled herself up. He danced sideways, shaking his neck but didn't attempt to throw her. She bent low in the saddle, again rubbing his neck. "Good boy," she said again, feeling nearly like the teenager she'd been when she left. She shifted the reins, guiding him to the gate and out into the valley.

She could sense the excitement in the powerful animal and let him run, leaning down low over his mane, the wind whistling around her. It was just like old times...she and Windstorm chasing the wind through the valley. She was laughing heartily by the time she reined him in. She glanced behind her, finding Kerry not far behind, the mare sporting an easy gait.

"Oh, *God*, that was fabulous," Carson said as she patted his neck. He was still dancing, anxious to run again, but she held him tight.

"I'll say. We couldn't keep up and I let her go."

"I've missed this," she said. "I just feel so...free out here."

"Is this what you did as a kid?"

She nodded. "Yeah. This was my escape." She turned Windstorm, heading up higher into the valley. "Come on, let's tour."

Carson led them through the valley and up into the foothills, taking familiar routes, surprised that she still remembered. She stopped occasionally, pointing out features to Kerry, pausing as they enjoyed the view of the lake now far below them. They rode amongst the trees—spruce and aspen—taking a trail into a small, grassy canyon.

Carson pulled Windstorm to a sudden halt when she realized where she was. Had she subconsciously come here? Or was it just by chance they'd ended up here in the canyon.

She slid from the saddle, dropping the reins as her eyes darted across the rocks, then farther up the trail before coming back to the rocks, her eyes finding the spot.

"Carson? What's wrong?" Kerry, too, got off her horse and came closer, standing beside her. When Carson didn't answer, she touched her arm. "What is it?"

"This is where it happened."

"This is where what happened?" Kerry asked quietly.

Carson took a deep breath, turning to Kerry. "My mother. This is where she died." She saw the immediate softening in Kerry's eyes, felt a warm hand move across her skin to clasp her forearm tightly.

"Tell me."

Carson shook her head, not wanting to relive it, but Kerry's hand slid lower, their fingers entwining.

"It's not always good to keep things inside. Sometimes it's better to open up, to let things escape."

Carson shuddered as the whole scene came back to her—the bear, the screaming, the fear in the horse's eyes. It happened so quickly, there was nothing she could have done. Back then, she'd convinced herself that she could have—*should* have—done something to stop it.

She met Kerry's eyes, seeing compassion there. Not sympathy really, but concern. She looked away, pointing to the pile of rocks just off the trail. "There," she said. "We rode up on a grizzly bear and her cubs. We stopped to let them run off, but once the cubs went to the trees, the momma bear turned and charged us. My mother's horse reared up and threw her. She landed on the rocks there," she said. She turned away, unable to look at the spot as her mind flashed all-too real images. "Her horse ran, trampled her. Her skull was crushed," she finished in a whisper.

She knew she would feel Kerry's hands on her and she did. Kerry walked up behind her, both hands rubbing lightly across her tense shoulders, up to her neck, squeezing gently. She said nothing, waiting for Carson to continue.

"I could barely hold Windstorm. He wanted to follow the other horse. The bear...the bear ran off finally," she said. "And I carried her down on Windstorm." She swallowed. "She was already dead."

Kerry squeezed her shoulders hard, then continued to rub her back but didn't say anything. Carson was glad she didn't. She stood there, letting Kerry soothe her until finally her hands stilled and moved away. Carson closed her eyes, wishing for her touch again but it didn't come. Carson turned to her then, their eyes meeting. She wasn't really surprised at what she saw in Kerry's. She wondered if Kerry could see what Carson was still trying to hide.

"I always thought that the trauma I felt, the pain and guilt I've carried with me all these years, was because of her death. Now that I've been back, I realize that it wasn't. I've accepted her death," she said. "It was an accident. That's all. I've accepted that." She moved away, going back to the rocks. "The trauma I felt was because of him. When I brought her back to the ranch, a scared eighteen-year-old kid, nearly hysterical, he looked at me and said 'My, God, what have you done?'. That's what he said to me. Nothing consoling. Just accusing." She took a deep breath, turning back to Kerry. "They took her. Chance was there, Johnny Mac too. And I'm crying. I was in shock. I couldn't even complete a sentence. It was the next day before I could even tell them what happened. And that's when he started blaming me. I should have seen the bear. I should have controlled the horse. I should have done this, I should have done that," she said. "It was all my fault. That's all I heard until the day we buried her. By that time, I think I believed his words."

"That's when he sent you away?" Kerry asked, her words nearly a whisper.

"After the funeral, he called me into his study and...well, we had our last big fight. And yes, he sent me away."

CHAPTER NINETEEN

Kerry paced in her room, listening for signs of Carson. The unopened laptop held no interest for her. Dinner had been a quiet affair, mainly because Carson never showed up. When it became obvious Carson was skipping, Kerry had hurried through the meal, apologizing to Martha for not savoring the food she'd prepared.

"Is Miss Carson all right?" Martha had asked.

"I'm not sure," Kerry said.

And she still wasn't. After their ride, after the horses had been brushed down, Kerry had headed to the bunkhouse to check the contractors' progress and Carson went to the house. That was the last Kerry had seen of her. She found evidence she'd been in the study as the bottle of scotch and one lone glass was out on the desk. She'd gone in search of her, looking everywhere except her father's room. She wouldn't intrude in there, but she doubted Carson had sought him out for solace. He was the cause of her pain. She wouldn't go to him for comfort.

No. That is what Kerry tried to offer earlier. And Carson had accepted it, the light touch upon her back as she told her story. Kerry couldn't imagine the pain she felt, the grief she carried, or how alone she must have felt. Even now, Kerry could see it in her eyes—loneliness. Kerry had wanted to gather Carson in her arms and hold her close, to chase away her loneliness. But she hadn't dared. Not then. Not at that moment.

She wouldn't lie to herself though. She knew she was changing, that her feelings were changing. Every day she felt the connection grow stronger, and she wasn't frightened by it any longer. Not really. Even Carson, with all her gentle flirting, though she said she was teasing, underneath it all, Kerry knows there's some truth to it. They'd both been flirting with each other in some way, because the attraction was strong. So strong that she thought she should try to fight it, but it felt right somehow. It felt too right, too good. She didn't want to fight it.

Had that been what she'd been doing all along? All these years? Fighting subtle attractions to women? Sure, she could admit that she had, on occasion, thought about sleeping with a woman. She'd always enjoyed the company of women. She felt much more relaxed with women than men. She assumed all women felt that way. But was that it? Was it an attraction? Was that why she never could find fulfillment with a man? Was that why Cody held no interest for her? Why none of the handsome Cartwright brothers did? All single, all eligible, yet none of them stirred any interest in her.

Carson, on the other hand, made her feel like a ticking time bomb, ready to explode.

Was it disconcerting? Confusing? Yes. But frightening? No. She could feel the change in herself and she wasn't afraid of it.

So she paced, wondering at what point she should become worried. At what point should she think about going to look for Carson. *Should* she go look for her?

Probably not. Carson obviously wanted to be alone. Kerry decided she wouldn't intrude on her. But sleep eluded her and nearly two hours later as she lay wide awake in bed, she heard quiet footsteps in the hallway. She sighed with relief, listening as those steps stopped outside her door. Her heart beat just a little faster as she imagined Carson standing there, debating whether to knock or not. She didn't. Kerry heard her leave, then heard the quiet click of Carson's door.

Kerry rolled over, away from the door, ignoring her instinct to go check on her. She had to remind herself that, essentially, they were new friends. And new friends didn't just rush across the hall to make sure things were okay. She punched her pillow and closed her eyes, content to at least know that Carson was back and apparently safe.

Carson turned on the lone lamp in the room, then quickly shed her clothes. She had showered before dinner, as had become her routine, but she hadn't planned on an evening hike. It just... everything hit her at once. Her mother's death, being shunned by her father, being sent away, being alone...and lonely.

She hadn't wanted dinner, and she wasn't in the mood to talk, wasn't in the mood for questions, so she hid in the study with her father's scotch. But she couldn't shut her mind down, couldn't stop old memories, old conversations from replaying over and over like a skip in a record. She'd bolted from the house, taking the long, winding road away from the ranch, walking until past dark. When she returned, lights were still on so she escaped to the stables, finding Windstorm. She brushed him while she talked, and he was patient and listened.

She smiled and shook her head. Good thing no one was around to witness that. But she felt better, more in control again. She hated that her memories and her father's words still had such a hold on her. It was that hold that she was trying to break free of, she realized. Maybe that's the real reason she'd come back home. To finally sever the ties to the past.

The house was dark when she'd come inside, except for the one light at the back door that was left on for her. Martha's doing, most likely. Or Kerry.

She knew Kerry was probably worried about her. Their bond had grown strong in a few short weeks. That was something else that surprised her. It was simply effortless with Kerry. An invisible cord linked them, pulled at them, pushed them together. Kerry felt it too, she knew that now. She could see that when Kerry looked at her, that sense of awe in her eyes at the attraction that had sprung up between them. Was Kerry frightened by it? If so, she didn't shy away from Carson. But Carson suspected that on some level Kerry must be terrified.

Which was one reason Carson hadn't knocked on her door to let her know she was back.

She slipped on her robe and went out to the bathroom, wanting to clean up before bed. She was suddenly very tired.

CHAPTER TWENTY

Kerry closed her door quietly, not wanting to wake Carson. Downstairs, she found Martha in the kitchen kneading bread dough.

"Homemade bread?" she asked as she poured a cup of coffee.

"I'm making a stew for dinner," she said. "I thought it would go good with that."

"Sounds wonderful."

Martha formed the dough into a ball, then placed it in a bowl and covered it with a cloth. "To rise," she explained as she washed her hands. "What would you like for breakfast?"

"I'm not really hungry right this moment," Kerry said. "Maybe I'll sneak back down in an hour or so."

"That's fine, dear." Martha helped herself to a cup of coffee and joined Kerry at the bar. "Did Miss Carson come in finally?"

"I heard her come up about eleven, but we didn't talk," she said.

"Well, I hope she's okay. Her brothers don't appear too fond of her. Well, Chase, of course, but not the others."

"Yes, I know."

"Do you know why she left all those years ago?"

"What do you mean?"

"Well, they've never said outright, but I've heard bits and pieces over the years. They said she just abandoned them after their mother died. Just up and left and they never heard from her again."

Kerry shook her head. "No, he kicked her out. He made her leave."

"Mr. Cartwright? But why?"

"I think he blamed her for his wife's death," Kerry said, wondering how much she should be sharing with Martha. Some of the things Carson told her, well, she knew they were private.

"She was thrown by a horse. What did Miss Carson have to do with that?"

"I don't know, Martha. People, when they grieve, they say things, do things that don't make sense." She paused. "What's he like?"

"Well, he's...he took me in after my husband and daughter were killed. Gave me a home. Now the brothers, they're always so nice, so thoughtful. But him?" She shook her head. "He's a cold man, a hard man. I don't know if he was always that way or if he turned that way after his wife died."

Kerry suspected he was always that way.

"Is it true about Miss Carson? Is she a gay?"

Kerry smiled but was able to contain her laughter. *A gay?* "Yes, she's a lesbian," she said, thinking how much fun she was going to have when she shared this conversation with Carson.

Martha smiled shyly and patted her hand. "You like her, don't you."

"Well, sure, I like her. We get along fine." Then her eyes

widened. "Oh, you mean *like* her? In that way?" She shook her head. "No, no, no. It's not like that. We're friends."

"Oh, that's right. It's Cody you fancy," she said with a chuckle as she went into the laundry room.

Kerry stared after her. "What? What just happened here?" But she got no answer as she heard the dryer turn on. *My, but isn't Martha perceptive.* She topped off her coffee cup again. "I'm going to the bunkhouse," she called as she slipped out the back door. Today she would drive the half-mile instead of walk it.

Carson slept in, only waking when the sun hit her face. She'd taken to sleeping with the window open, the curtains pulled back. She enjoyed watching the night sky. Unfortunately, the morning sun wasn't quite as kind as the midnight moon had been.

She listened, hearing the banging of wood again in the distance. No doubt Mr. Burris and his crew were already at it. As was Kerry.

She stood and stretched, yawning around a moan as her backed popped. She stumbled sleepily to the bathroom, wanting a shower. She didn't linger, feeling a bit anxious to start her day. She smiled at herself in the mirror. To see Kerry, she admitted.

When she went back to her room, she was surprised to find her pile of dirty laundry had been removed as well as the sheets stripped. She dressed in clean jeans and a T-shirt, but took a sweatshirt with her. She still wasn't used to the cool mornings.

She met Martha coming out of the laundry room and she raised her eyebrows. "You steal my clothes?"

"Oh, I was washing a load of Miss Kerry's things, and it was just as easy to include your jeans and stuff. I hope you don't mind."

Carson grinned. "Don't mind at all. But you don't have to do that. I'm perfectly capable."

"I'm sure you are. I, however, am particular about my laundry room," she said with a smile. "Now, what would you like for breakfast?"

"I'm actually starving," Carson admitted as she eyed the coffeepot.

"I should say so, what with you missing dinner," she said, her tone indicating she should not do it again.

"I'm sorry. I'm sure it was delicious. Maybe I could just have some of that for breakfast," Carson said, adding sugar to her coffee.

"How about a breakfast sandwich? I'll make two. Miss Kerry left without eating."

"Yeah, I heard all the banging down at the bunkhouse. I'm sure Mr. Burris is happy to have his supervisor back," she said.

Martha smiled. "She takes it very seriously. I only hope this works out."

"Yeah, me too." She watched as Martha cracked two eggs into a pan. "What kind of sandwich?"

"Egg and ham on toast," she said.

"Sounds good." Carson rubbed her flat stomach, wondering how many pounds she'd gained since eating Martha's cooking.

She finished her coffee, watching Martha's easy, efficient movements. In no time at all she'd produced two sandwiches and placed them side-by-side on a platter and covered it with foil.

"Now, you run and take this to her before it gets cold."

"Yes, ma'am," she said. She grabbed two water bottles and dutifully went to find Kerry.

No one was about when she got there so she went inside, leaving the plate and water on the kitchen counter. She followed the sound of the hammering, finding herself in a huge open area where once twenty small bedrooms had been. Kerry was talking to Mr. Burris—talking and pointing—so Carson didn't interrupt. Kerry noticed her soon enough, excusing herself and walking over, a smile on her face as she approached.

"Hey. Are you okay?" she asked quietly.

"Yeah. I'm sorry I bailed on you last night."

"It's okay."

They stood together, only a few feet apart, then Kerry surprised her by wrapping her arms around her and giving her a tight, albeit brief, hug.

"What's that for?"

"Because I wanted to do that yesterday and I didn't," she said.

Carson nodded, her eyes never leaving Kerry's. "I'm okay. I just wasn't going to be very good company, so I took a walk."

"You don't have to explain."

Carson finally looked away. "So, how's it going in here?"

"Oh, we're making progress. They should have it all cleaned out today and ready to start tomorrow."

"Good." She pointed back down the hall. "Listen, I brought breakfast. Martha said you'd left without eating."

Kerry smiled and took her arm, leading her back toward the kitchen. "What'd you bring?"

"A sandwich. Egg and ham," she said, watching as Kerry lifted the foil, inspecting her treat.

"Mmm," she said. She grabbed the plate and motioned for Carson to follow her. "Come on. Let's get out of here."

They stepped back out into the sunshine and went to the three old pines that shaded one corner of the bunkhouse. Kerry sat down and leaned against a tree and Carson did the same, sitting opposite her and crossing her legs. Kerry handed her one of the sandwiches and accepted the water bottle Carson held out for her.

"What do you think about adding a small porch?" Kerry asked as she took a bite. "Oh, God, this is good. I'm getting very spoiled by Martha's cooking."

"Anything would taste good right now," Carson said. "I'm starving." She, too, took a bite, savoring the thick, smoky ham. She smiled as she chewed. "Good," she mumbled around a mouthful.

"That's what happens when you skip dinner."

Carson smiled, then looked back to the bunkhouse. "Where do you want this porch?"

"Well, the only thing there now is just the little concrete slab at the front door. I was thinking we could enlarge that, say to twenty-by-twenty, maybe put a railing up or something. You know, make it a sitting area."

"The view's not great. You're looking at the barn and stables," Carson said.

"True. But we need something. We're offering the great outdoors, yet we don't have a place for them to sit and enjoy it."

"Then make a specific area," Carson suggested. "Put a nice deck in, big enough for patio furniture. Have it face the valley. Or put it on the back corner and you can get a view of the lake and the valley," she said.

"And we could establish some sort of walkway to it, like out of stone or something," she said. "I like it."

"Yes, but you'll need to get the guys to like it as well," Carson reminded her.

"I know. They've put me on a very tight budget. If we do that, we'll have to kill one of the piers. Those aren't cheap."

"I imagine not." Carson ate the last of her sandwich, then wiped her mouth with her hand. "So, how's the website coming along?"

"I'm pretty close to finishing the setup and the internal links. I need to get some pictures of the valley and the lake," she said. "And of course, the bunkhouse, once it's finished and furnished."

"You really think people will shell out two grand for this?"

"Yes. If we give them enough to choose from. The lake, horses, fishing, hiking, all right here at their fingertips. For people who are stuck in a city, being able to spend a week out here would be heaven," Kerry said. She eyed her. "Don't you think so? Haven't you enjoyed the peace and quiet after coming from New York?"

Carson nodded. "I actually came from San Francisco, but yeah."

Kerry frowned. "I thought you lived in Manhattan."

"I have an apartment there, but I met a friend in San Francisco. We were going to spend a couple of weeks there."

"A special friend?"

"Special? You mean a lover?"

Kerry nodded, and Carson was fascinated at the way Kerry's expression changed, as if just saying the word put a charge in the air around them.

"I don't have a lover," Carson said. "Rebecca is the woman

who took me in when I first landed in New York way back when. We've remained good friends."

She expected Kerry to ask her why she didn't have a lover, but she didn't. Kerry's gaze was suddenly shy as she occupied her hands by folding the foil neatly and placing it on the empty plate. Carson tried to read her expression, curious as to what thoughts were running through her mind, but Kerry kept them masked. She felt a need to ease the tension somewhat, but she doubted her next question would do it.

"Do *you* have a lover?"

Kerry's eyes flew to hers as a blush lit her face. "No, I...no," she said simply. "I'm...I don't."

The look between them was so intense that Carson could actually feel a crackling in the air. Kerry must have felt it too as the color of her eyes darkened but Carson never looked away. That was the moment that it became clear to her—and most likely clear to Kerry as well—that their relationship had definitely taken a turn. Sure, Carson could pretend there wasn't an attraction between them, she could deny it, run from it, hide from it. She could be the one to change the course and steer them back down the road to friendship. She could turn away from this and leave Kerry alone, let Cody make his play for her affections.

But Carson wasn't going to do that. She didn't think Kerry would let her do that. Kerry showed no sign that she was running scared.

Mr. Burris called for Kerry, breaking the spell between them. She wasn't sure if it was relief or regret in Kerry's eyes as she stood. She took several steps away, then turned back to her.

"Thank you for breakfast, Carson."

Carson nodded, her gaze following Kerry as she joined Mr. Burris inside the bunkhouse. Carson let out a deep breath, just now aware that her pulse had been racing.

CHAPTER TWENTY-ONE

After her shower—which she'd drawn out as long as she could—and after drying her hair thoroughly, Kerry nervously made her way downstairs for dinner. She hadn't seen Carson since their impromptu breakfast picnic, and she wasn't entirely certain who had been avoiding whom. To say their conversation had rattled her would be an understatement. But was it the words or the looks? Or was it the electricity that seemed to pass between them so easily? She knew Carson felt it too. Her eyes just pulled her in and Kerry couldn't look away, couldn't—wouldn't—break the spell. Her heart had been pounding in her chest, and it was with perfect clarity that she saw them together...as lovers.

She nearly stumbled over the last step as the image remained in her mind, and she paused, trying to shake it. She was so lost in these thoughts that she gasped as Mr. Cartwright's nurse appeared, carrying a plate and a bottle of water up the stairs.

Kerry simply nodded as the nurse passed by her without a word, her pace brisk. The encounter was enough to somewhat derail thoughts of Carson from her mind. She went in search of Martha.

"Smells wonderful," Kerry said, leaning over Martha's shoulder as she stirred the stew.

"I think it turned out great," Martha said. "The bread is warming."

Kerry took a glass and filled it with water. "I met the nurse on the stairs," she said. "That's only the second time I've seen her."

"Oh, she doesn't talk much. She made it clear she was only here for Mr. Cartwright. She wasn't here to socialize or make friends," she said. "Only comes down to collect meals. Of course, it's only for her now. He hasn't eaten in days."

"Have you seen him?"

"No. Not since they brought him back from the hospital. The nurse does everything for him, including changing his sheets. I just do the laundry and bring it back up."

"Carson seems to think it'll be any day now," she said.

"Yes. Chance told me that when he left. It must be a terrible feeling riding away, knowing your father will most likely die while you're gone," Martha said. "They were all close."

"Were they?" Kerry really hadn't gotten that impression at all. Or maybe since he'd been sick for so long, they'd just accepted his dying and had the chance to prepare for it.

"Well, he was a difficult man, abrasive with them sometimes, but he was still their father," she said. "They were always respectful to him."

Kerry didn't say anything, but she knew that respecting someone and deeply loving them were two completely different things. When Carson had told the story of her mother dying, the pain and anguish in her voice, in her eyes, spoke of a truly loving relationship. She felt none of that between the brothers and their father.

"Have you seen Carson?" she asked as nonchalantly as she

could. Martha glanced at her, a smile on her face, as she covered the stew pot again. Kerry remembered their conversation from that morning and hoped Martha wouldn't bring that up again.

"She went upstairs earlier. You didn't see her?"

"No. Actually, I haven't seen her since breakfast," she said, hoping that would signal to Martha that they weren't spending all that much time together.

"Oh? I thought she had been with you all day. She wasn't around here. I just assumed she was at the bunkhouse."

"No. Maybe the stables. She's reconnected with Windstorm, her old horse," she said vaguely.

"What about Windstorm?"

Kerry turned, finding Carson leaning casually in the doorway. Kerry's eyes followed the length of her, noting clean jeans and moccasin loafers. When their eyes met, she had to catch her breath. It was still there. That look. She swallowed, struggling to find words. Finally Carson released her, her eyebrows rising slightly as she smiled. Kerry let out her breath, returning her smile shyly.

"Miss Kerry said she hadn't seen you all day," Martha said, picking up the conversation that had lagged. "She thought maybe you'd been at the stables."

"I was. Windstorm probably hasn't been brushed so much in years as the last two days," she said. "He loves it." She went to the stove and lifted the pot, sniffing appreciatively. "Smells wonderful, Martha. Stew?"

"And homemade bread," Martha said, taking the lid from Carson and shushing her away. "Everything is ready, so whenever you are."

"I'm starved," Carson said.

"That's because you missed lunch," Martha fussed. "I have sandwiches every day. You should come in at noon and get one."

Carson smiled at Kerry. "I guess you got one?"

"Yes. Egg salad today."

Kerry went to the cabinet for bowls, but Martha took them from her. "Put that down, young lady. That is my job. I'll serve you in the dining room."

"You don't have to serve us, Martha. With the guys gone, this could be a nice break for you," she said.

"Thank you, but I don't need a break. I've enjoyed being able to cook things the boys aren't too fond of. That's enough break for me."

"Come on," Carson said. "Let's check out their wine stash and see if we can find a nice bottle for dinner."

After much debate—neither of them being experts on wine—they settled on a cabernet sauvignon. But Martha, playing up to her role, took the bottle from them and firmly told them to sit while she served them. To both of their surprise, the dining room was dimly lit with two candles flickering between them. Kerry really thought Martha was enjoying herself a bit too much and suspected that Martha was simply satisfying her curiosity about what was happening between the two women. Kerry glanced up, finding Carson's eyes on her. She held her gaze—how could she not? To say she was in a dangerous, foreign place would be an understatement. But she was feeling no panic, no fear. Only uncertainty.

"Did you make progress on the bunkhouse?" Carson asked.

Kerry nodded, taking a sip from her wine. "They've got it all out. Tomorrow they start with the new plumbing."

"And how long will it all take?"

"I'm guessing two months. They have plumbing to do for the two new bathrooms. That'll be first. Then frames for the new bedrooms. I still haven't decided on the floors yet."

"Here you go, ladies," Martha said as she brought in the serving tray. She placed the freshly baked bread between them along with pats of butter, then gave them both a steaming bowl of the beef stew. "Enjoy."

"Thank you," they said in unison, then smiled at each other. Kerry mentally rolled her eyes, amused at how *corny* she suddenly felt.

Their dinner conversation was sparse, forced and they both seemed to be searching for a topic that was impersonal...and safe. Kerry had so many questions to ask, so many things she wanted to know about Carson but she kept them to herself. Personal questions always seemed to lead them in a direction that she wasn't certain she was ready to go. Not yet. Carson seemed to sense this as she, too, talked abstractly, never bringing the conversation back to them.

That didn't mean the tension in the room lessened any. If anything, it grew thicker as they danced around the subject. Their glances lingered as the silence stretched out, both, finally, at a loss for words.

Carson pushed her bowl away and took her wineglass. "Do you want to talk, Kerry?"

Kerry's eyes flew to hers, surprised that Carson would be so bold. What would they talk about? This attraction that Kerry couldn't seem to find a place for? Or perhaps the heat that flowed so easily between them? Or maybe Kerry could give a boring litany of her past boyfriends to try and reiterate that she wasn't in the least attracted to this beautiful woman sitting across from her. But in the end, she shook her head. No, she wasn't ready to talk.

"I really need to work on the website," she said. "In fact, I should probably head up now." She finished her last sip of wine then stood. She paused before leaving, their eyes again seeking, finding each other. Carson's were filled with questions and Kerry nearly gave in. Yes, they needed to talk. But she was still too afraid to broach the subject, too scared to say it out loud, to bring voice to it all. So she nodded, then hurried from the room.

She nearly ran up the stairs as if she could run from her feelings, leaving them behind with Carson, but she could not. She closed the door to her bedroom and leaned against it. How could there be more tension, not less, when they hadn't said a word about what was happening between them?

Kerry closed her eyes, for a moment wishing the brothers were back. At least there would be some kind of buffer then, instead of them being totally alone.

Though alone they were, at least for another four days. She knew they wouldn't last four days without talking about it. She doubted they could make even one more.

Carson sat alone in the study, twirling the glass of scotch between her hands. Dinner had been a tedious affair—she'd seen the confusion in Kerry's eyes. She knew Kerry was struggling with what was happening. She thought maybe they could talk about it but knew now that it was a silly offer. To talk about it would make it real, it would mean Kerry acknowledged the attraction between them. No, Kerry obviously wasn't ready for that. Kerry would rather still pretend it didn't exist when they both knew it did.

Subconsciously, Carson wondered if she didn't want the same thing. Pretending to have only a platonic interest in each other might prove to be the wisest choice, if not the most difficult.

She leaned back in the chair and closed her eyes, trying to recall another time when a woman was able to capture her senses like Kerry had. She wasn't surprised that she couldn't remember any. She knew there had been none. She always thought it was because she wasn't interested in anything but sex. She didn't want any attachments, emotional or otherwise. It had been effortless, really. Never once was she tempted to prolong an affair because her heart was involved. It simply never was.

Yet here she was, feeling an emotional connection with Kerry and she wasn't running scared. Not yet. The fact that Kerry had never been with a woman before should have been enough to halt her in her tracks. Add to that Cody's interest, Carson knew she should leave well enough alone.

She also knew that wasn't possible. It was too strong between them. Kerry knew it. She knew it. And it wouldn't surprise her if even Martha knew it.

Tomorrow, they would talk. She would get Kerry alone. She would make her talk.

CHAPTER TWENTY-TWO

With intentions of getting up earlier and perhaps joining Kerry for breakfast, Carson found herself still in bed when the sun broke through the pane of her window, hitting her in the face. She didn't need to look at her watch to know she had missed Kerry. She rolled over, staring at the ceiling, thinking maybe it was a good thing she had overslept. She doubted Kerry would be in the mood to talk first thing in the morning.

She lingered through her shower, no longer feeling the need to hurry. In fact, by the time she finished in the bathroom she'd nearly convinced herself that there really was no need to have that talk with Kerry. Maybe it was best to just let nature takes its course, let things go where they may.

Let Kerry talk if she wanted to. No need to force her into it.

Probably not the wisest decision she'd ever made, but it certainly lightened her mood. She grabbed a fresh-baked muffin from a plate in the kitchen to go with her coffee. She heard Martha in the laundry room whistling along with a song on the radio. For a moment, Carson was taken back, picturing her mother doing the exact same thing, although singing, not whistling. It was a thought that made her smile and she was surprised that the edges of it were no longer bathed in sadness. Before, thoughts of her mother would rarely bring a smile. That, too, had changed since she'd been back. She was able to get past her grief and remember the goodness of those memories.

"Oh, Miss Carson, I didn't hear you come down," Martha said, her arms laden with folded towels. "You found the muffins?"

"Yes. Very good. You like to bake?"

"I like to make breads and such. Not big on cakes." She headed out, then stopped as she turned back to Carson. "I heard on the radio that we'll get a strong storm tonight. You think the guys will be okay?"

"Yes. That's why they left Sunday. Chance wanted to make the next valley before the storm hit. They'll ride it out there then head up again once the threat of lightning is over," she said.

"Good. Oh, and Miss Kerry is out at the bunkhouse." She smiled. "I guess you already figured that out."

Carson nearly laughed at Martha's attempt to be subtle. But her suspicions were answered. Martha wasn't dumb.

After her second cup of coffee, she made her way down to the stables. Windstorm was waiting for her, his low whinny making her laugh.

"Didn't take you long to get spoiled," she said. She hopped into the pen and stood still. He, like before, circled her, his large head bumping against her as he sniffed out the carrot in her back pocket. He pulled it out deftly, crunching it loudly between his teeth. Carson wondered how long it would be before Martha knew she'd been stealing from her vegetable stash.

She rubbed his neck as she looked out over the valley, seeing low clouds building to the west. If she wanted to get a ride in today she'd better do it early.

"How about it, Windstorm? You feel up for a ride?"

She led him into a stall then eyed the mare Kerry had ridden the other day. Maybe she'd steal her away for an hour or so. Surely Mr. Burris would be thankful. So she saddled up both horses and led them to the bunkhouse where the constant banging of the last two days had ceased.

Kerry was inside, sitting alone as she studied what Carson assumed were the remodeling plans. She looked up when she felt Carson watching her.

"Hey," she said, smiling immediately.

Carson motioned out the door. "Come ride with me."

She noticed the hesitation and thought Kerry would decline but she nodded.

"Let me just tell Mr. Burris."

Carson went outside to wait, feeling a touch of apprehension, when really, she had no reason to be nervous. They would take a quick ride through the valley, maybe see if the old trail was still there to the Conley's ranch. There was nothing to be nervous about.

"I think I should be offended," Kerry said when she joined her.

"How so?"

"Mr. Burris smiled and his eyes lit up when I said I was leaving."

"Have you been badgering him?"

Kerry climbed onto the saddle, leaning over to pat the mare on the neck. "I wouldn't call it badgering. I'm simply making sure he does everything as planned," she said.

"In other words, you're underfoot," Carson stated with a laugh. "Yeah, he's probably doing cartwheels now that I've stolen you away."

"Is that what you're doing?" Kerry asked. "Stealing me away?"

While their tone was teasing, playful, there was an underlying seriousness in their words. Carson didn't shy away from it.

"Yes," she answered simply.

The horses fidgeted, ready to run, but Carson held back, watching, waiting to see if Kerry understood what she was saying.

Kerry finally nodded. "Okay. Then let's go."

With those few words, the tension faded completely between them. Carson felt everything settle around her, freeing her, and she laughed with delight as Windstorm took off, heading into the valley.

Kerry's mare caught up to them as Carson reined Windstorm in, slowing their pace, easing into a slow canter and finally to an easy walk.

"How did the valley get its name?" Kerry asked.

"Elk Valley? Probably from the winter herds that call it home," she said. "When the snows hit, the elk leave the high country, wintering down here. The valley is full of them. They start heading up again in late spring," she said. "They're still around though. I spotted some past the lake the other day."

"Where are you taking me today?"

"I thought I'd see if the old trail to the Conley ranch was still there. It's a great ride," she said. "It crosses two little trout streams and goes through the foothills before hitting their property."

"And is your family still friendly with them? You mentioned once that your father had a falling out with them."

"I don't have a clue," Carson said. "Chase never mentioned it. I'd think that Justin is running the ranch now. His father was older, already in his sixties when we were in high school."

She pulled Windstorm to a halt, reaching out to stop Kerry. Up the mountain a ways, four cow elk and their calves were grazing. She wished she'd thought to bring the binoculars that were hanging in the stables. She slid out of her saddle, motioning for Kerry to do the same.

"Do you see them?" she asked quietly.

"No. Where?"

"Elk and calves, about halfway up the mountain," she said. "Here." She pulled Kerry in front of her, holding her close. "Follow my arm," she whispered as she pointed to the spot. "Do you see them now?"

"No."

"Why not?"

"Because my eyes are closed," Kerry murmured.

Carson was aware of how close they were when she felt the

heat of Kerry's body. She stood still, letting the moment happen as it may. Kerry leaned back against her, pressing their bodies together. Carson felt her breasts smashed against Kerry's back, but she didn't move away. It was the first true intimacy between them, and Carson let it sink in, knowing that it was Kerry who had initiated it.

She finally lowered her arm, placing her hands at Kerry's waist. Kerry's hands covered hers, pulling them around her from behind and holding them tightly against her stomach. They stood that way for long moments and Carson felt Kerry's thundering heartbeat, a rhythm that matched her own.

She took a deep breath, closing her eyes, letting the sensation of Kerry's body being pressed to hers envelop her. Then Kerry shifted, turning so that their eyes met. In her own way, Kerry was offering herself to Carson. Carson leaned closer, wanting so badly to kiss her. But something stopped her. If they did this, if they kissed, then everything would change. There would be no going back. Despite the desire in Kerry's eyes she still wasn't certain Kerry understood the magnitude of this.

So she pulled away, clearing her throat before speaking. "We should...we should get going," she said. Then, as if needing an excuse, she looked to the sky. "Clouds are coming in. We better head back to the barn. We don't want to get caught in the storm."

She climbed in the saddle and turned Windstorm back toward the ranch, thoughts of the Conley trail forgotten. She glanced behind her, seeing a confused look on Kerry's face. She should say something, she should explain, but no words would come. They rode back, Kerry a few paces behind her, but Carson couldn't stand the silence any longer.

She pulled Windstorm to a stop and turned him around, riding next to Kerry and facing her. Without thinking, she leaned closer and grabbed her, kissing her hard, possessively. Her lips softened when she heard Kerry's tiny moan and her mouth lingered for long seconds as Kerry kissed her back.

"That's what I want to do to you," she said as she pulled away. "That's just the beginning of what I want to do. That's why I stopped earlier."

She turned then, kicking Windstorm into a trot, riding—and running—away from Kerry.

She'd just taken the saddle off when Kerry rode the mare into the barn. She slid from the saddle, her eyes avoiding Carson's. Carson didn't offer to help with Kerry's saddle. She thought it was safer with two horses separating them. They proceeded to brush down their mounts but again the silence was wearing on her.

"Kerry, look, I'm sorry. I—"

"Please don't say it."

"I had no right to do that."

Kerry put her brush down and stood in front of Carson. "I'm not young and naive, Carson. I'm not blind to what's happening between us. Scared, maybe, but not blind."

No, Carson knew she wasn't. But she still wasn't prepared to go there. "When I told Cody that I was too old to chase after straight women, I meant that. If you're curious, I'm not going to be that person, Kerry. I can't."

"This feeling," Kerry said, touching her chest, "has nothing to do with the fact that you're a woman."

"Of course it does," Carson countered. "It has everything to do with it."

Kerry stared at her, that confusion again clouding her eyes. Finally she nodded. "You're right. It does have everything to do with it. That's why—"

"That's why you're scared," Carson finished for her.

As they stood there, the confusion in Kerry's eyes ebbed, replaced by what Carson could only call a craving—a yearning. It was a look she couldn't resist. She knew she shouldn't...God, she knew it...but she just couldn't stop herself. She dropped the brush she'd been holding, reaching out, her hand tangling in Kerry's hair, pulling her closer.

She kissed her...not the hard, possessive kiss of earlier. No, this one was soft and tender, moving over a mouth that opened for her. She wasn't sure if the moan she heard was hers or Kerry's—it didn't matter which. She felt Kerry's body melting against her as Kerry clung to her, their bodies touching from head to toe. She deepened the kiss, parting Kerry's lips with her tongue. Kerry moved with her, their passion flaring as their tongues brushed together.

But of course she knew it would happen, knew Kerry would push her away. And she did, eyes wide with wonder. Kerry took a step back, away from her, the want and need in her eyes replaced with panic. She moved away, shaking her head slowly as she turned and fled.

Carson let her go. What else could she do? It had been wrong, yes. She knew it. Kerry obviously wasn't ready. That didn't matter though. She couldn't stop it from happening. Kerry had wanted their kiss as much as she had. She wasn't going to take the blame for that.

She picked up the brush she'd dropped, continuing to groom Windstorm, telling herself it would all work itself out. It had to. For the first time in her life, she wasn't going through the motions with someone. For the first time, she felt her heart opening to another person. Here, at her childhood home, where the line between love and pain remained blurred, she felt a ray of hope, a glimmer of the future, and it wasn't filled with grief and remorse for what could have been. It was filled with a promise of happiness, of completeness. It was filled with a sense of *home*, something she thought she'd never have again.

She didn't think about the way Kerry had run from her. She didn't think about the panic she saw in Kerry's eyes. She saw the passion, the need, the desire…she felt Kerry's fingers digging into her arm as they kissed. She felt the promise of more to come.

She would give Kerry all the time she needed. She had to. Because for the first time, she craved what she'd only dreamed of.

Love.

CHAPTER TWENTY-THREE

Kerry sat on her bed, watching the clock as it ticked closer and closer to seven. The dinner hour. Unlike Carson, she couldn't just disappear and skip it. Not after what had happened earlier.

She closed her eyes, admitting to herself that she was still reeling from their kiss. The shower hadn't helped in the least. The kiss was everything she'd imagined it would be and so much more. That was what frightened her. Carson's kiss turned her inside out, made her knees weak, made her cling to her for fear she'd fall. Carson's kiss made her want so much more, made her want to tear at her clothes, made her want to beg Carson for her touch upon her skin.

And that kiss aroused her more than she'd ever been. She had been shocked as she felt a throbbing need between her legs, shocked at the wetness there. And she was absolutely stunned to know that she was on the verge of begging Carson to touch her ...*there*.

That was what made her stop, made her pull out of Carson's arms. The realization that she was powerless to resist her, that it felt so incredibly right to press her body tight against Carson—that's what made her stop. She'd lost control. She'd lost total control in a matter of seconds. And it scared the hell out of her, the ease at which Carson was able to render her so helpless. So she pulled away, forsaking what her body wanted, needed, and letting her mind regain some control again.

Then she fled, her body throbbing with a new desire—a new want and need she didn't understand. How could she be so attracted to Carson, a woman, and not feel even the tiniest of sparks for one of her handsome brothers? How did it come to this? How could her body feel so alive in Carson's presence?

And how could she want something so badly, something she knew absolutely nothing about? How could she want another woman this much?

She rubbed her forehead as if warding off a headache when really all she was trying to do was to stop the direction of her thoughts. She finally stood, knowing she must go downstairs. She'd heard Carson leave her room earlier so she knew she'd be waiting. She wondered if Carson was going to want to talk. It was the last thing she wanted, but her only alternative was to run and hide.

She heard Martha and Carson talking in the kitchen and she went in, acting as nonchalant as possible when she felt anything but that. Her nerves were raw and she nearly collapsed when Carson looked at her, when Carson's gaze dropped ever so slightly to her lips.

"Smells wonderful," she said, her words sounding forced, she knew. In fact, she wasn't even certain she smelled anything. Food was the last thing on her mind.

"It's a chicken casserole that the brothers would hate, but I thought you girls would enjoy it." She ushered them toward the dining room. "I picked out a bottle of wine too. Go sit. I'll bring dinner in."

Once alone, Kerry twisted her hands together, her eyes landing everywhere except on Carson. Like last night, the lighting was dim. Two candles separated them and Kerry wondered if Martha had any idea of the romantic mood she was setting.

"Kerry...relax."

Her eyes flew up. "Relax?"

"Should I apologize?"

Should she? Kerry shook her head. "No."

"You can—"

"Here we go," Martha said as she carried in the serving tray. Two plates were steaming with a medley of chicken and pasta and vegetables. Carson stood up, taking the wine from Martha as it teetered dangerously on the tray.

"This looks delicious, Martha," Kerry said. Yes, it did. She had no appetite, but it certainly looked delicious.

"Thank you, Miss Kerry. It's an old recipe that I haven't made in years. I hope you girls like it."

"I'm sure we will," Carson said. "Thank you."

Martha smiled and turned to go and Kerry was certain she'd caught a twinkle in her eyes as she left them.

Kerry picked up her fork, her gaze remaining fixed on her plate. She chanced a quick glance up but Carson, too, was staring at her food. Kerry sighed. This was ridiculous, this...this silence between them. She pushed her food around, finally taking a bite. It was excellent, yet she had to force it down. She took a sip of wine, hoping it would relax her. The sound of thunder rolled in the distance, and she assumed the late spring storm would be upon them soon.

"Don't be afraid of me."

The words were spoken quietly and Kerry looked up, meeting Carson's eyes head on. There was a hint of regret there and she put her fork down and leaned her elbows on the table. Of all the things she wanted to see in Carson's eyes, regret wasn't one of them.

"I'm not afraid of you, Carson. I'm afraid of *this*," she said, motioning between them. "I'm scared to death," she whispered.

"Don't be. You control everything, Kerry. Whatever happens or doesn't happen, it's up to you."

"Is it really? I seem to have *no* control when I'm around you," she said with a slight smile.

Carson nodded and her lips twitched with a smile too, but she said nothing. Kerry went back to her meal, the silence not quite as uncomfortable as before, although her appetite had not returned. Carson, too, seemed to have little interest in her food.

"We need to clean our plates," Kerry said. When Carson's eyebrows shot up, she explained, "Martha will think we didn't enjoy her cooking."

"And we most definitely enjoy her cooking." Carson reached across the table and added more wine to Kerry's glass. "What do you think she's trying to accomplish with these candles?"

Kerry laughed. "She does set a romantic table, doesn't she." A loud clap of thunder sounded, startling her. "Are the horses okay?" she asked.

"Yes. I don't know what the common practice is, but I left the stables open so they could go in. Except for Windstorm and your mare. I actually closed them up in their stalls."

"I like the mare I ride. She's gentle."

"Yes, especially for being so young. She's only three."

"What's her name?"

"Ginger," Carson said. "Such a unique name for a horse," she added with a smirk.

Kerry took another bite, glad the conversation had returned somewhat to normal. Perhaps she would be able to clean her plate after all. Again thunder, the lull between them getting shorter.

"I like storms," she said. "I like to watch the lightning."

"I used to go sit in the hayloft when a storm rolled in," Carson said. "The view of the valley, with the mountains in the background, was a perfect spot to catch the lightning show."

"And were you alone in the hayloft?"

Carson laughed. "Yes. I'll have to show it to you sometime," she said.

Kerry knew she was teasing but still, her words sent a hot chill across her body. She was saved from replying when Martha came in.

"I'm sorry to interrupt," she said. "Miss Carson, the nurse

is here. She says your father is asking for you. When you finish dinner, she wanted to know if you'd come up."

"Okay, sure." When Martha left, Carson let out a heavy sigh. "Just how I want to end my day," she said.

"Maybe it's time," Kerry said. "Maybe he's ready to talk."

"No matter how ready we are to talk, it always ends in an argument," Carson said. "Always." She stood, moving the chair back against the table. She leaned on it, her eyes lingering. "Do we need to talk about it, Kerry?"

"Will that change anything?"

Again, Carson's gaze dropped to her lips. "I don't think so."

"Me either."

Carson nodded, then left, leaving Kerry alone as the candles flickered and the thunder continued to rumble.

CHAPTER TWENTY-FOUR

Carson stood in her father's doorway, noticing that the incessant coughing had stopped. For a minute she wondered if he'd died.

"Come in," the nurse said, getting up from her perch beside him to offer it to Carson.

She walked closer, still not certain he was alive until his eyes fluttered open. She stood still, waiting for him to focus on her.

"You came," he said, his voice nothing more than a hoarse whisper.

She nodded. "You wanted to see me?"

He turned his head into the pillow, and she wondered how much trying to talk drained his energy.

"I was wrong," he whispered. "It was wrong what I did."

She contained the sarcastic retort she wanted to reply with, instead she agreed with him. "Yeah. You were wrong to send me away."

"I was...I was hurting."

"Okay, so we're going to go back down that road?" She leaned closer. "I was hurting too."

"I'm sorry, Carson. I only added to your hurt. I'm sorry. I was wrong."

Her eyes widened in surprise. Those were the last words she ever thought she'd hear him say, deathbed or not. His hand opened, beckoning her. She stared at it, almost afraid to touch him. Finally she did, placing hers in his open palm. He tried to close his fingers but couldn't so she wrapped hers around his and squeezed.

"Can you forgive me?" he asked. "I need you to forgive me."

It was the moment of truth for her. She'd been over this scenario a thousand times—him asking her to forgive him. Her answer was always the same. No. She knew in her heart it wouldn't be any different this time. She couldn't forgive him. There were too many lost years, too many memories that were now tainted.

But as this once strong, proud man was reduced to an invalid, reduced to begging for forgiveness in his last hours, she didn't have the heart to tell him the truth. She leaned closer, still squeezing his hand.

"Yes. I forgive you," she said softly. As soon as she said the words, she was glad she'd chosen to lie. His eyes lost the hardness that she always associated with him. Weakly, he squeezed her fingers.

"Thank you," he whispered.

His eyes slipped closed as his hand went limp and she glanced quickly at the nurse. "I think he—"

"No. Not yet," she said as she moved Carson out of the way. "But it won't be long now. I don't think he'll make the night."

The nurse sat down beside him again and took his hand, gently patting it. "He's been in so much pain," she said absently.

Carson only nodded, not knowing what else to say. She

watched them for a bit longer, the nurse still holding his hand, the lightning casting an eerie glow on the valley outside his window. She left then, stopping at the door for one last look, silently saying her goodbye.

Kerry climbed the stairs slowly, listening for voices. She heard none. She doubted Carson stayed long with her father. The few times she'd gone to visit him it had ended quickly and usually with raised voices. In the hallway, the door to her father's room was closed but Carson's was open.

She stopped in the doorway, finding Carson standing in the dark near the window, the blinds pulled back, lightning flashing across the sky. Carson must have felt her presence. She turned her head, glancing at Kerry, then turned back to the window. Even with the muted shadows, Kerry could see that she'd been crying. She debated whether she should ask permission to enter but realized that was why Carson had left the door open.

She walked up beside her, keeping quiet. They both watched the lightning show, the silence broken only by the clap of thunder.

"He said he was sorry," Carson said at last. "He asked me to forgive him."

"Did you?"

"I told him I did."

Kerry glanced at her. "But?"

Carson took a deep breath, turning to look at her. "I don't know if I can ever forgive him. He's in there dying and I...I don't feel anything," she said, her voice nearly a whisper. "I should feel something, shouldn't I?"

"You have to care about someone—love them—to feel a deep sorrow at their passing."

"He's been dead to me for so many years, Kerry, I just can't conjure up any...any grief, any sorrow. It's just not there."

"And you feel guilty for that?"

Carson shook her head. "No. I'm not going to feel guilty." She gave a bitter laugh. "And I feel guilty for not feeling guilty.

But I've already paid the price. I'm not going to burden myself any more because of him."

Each time lightning flashed, Kerry could see the tear stains on Carson's face. They weren't tears for her father. Most likely they were tears for all she'd lost...and all she'd never have again. And yes, despite Carson's words, Kerry could tell she did feel guilty. She couldn't help herself as she reached out, her fingers lightly touching Carson's face, brushing over the tears. She watched Carson's eyes slip closed, and she could swear she felt a tremor under her hand.

"You shouldn't be in here, Kerry," Carson said, her voice a low murmur, as if she were thinking the words, not saying them out loud.

"But I am here."

Those eyes opened again, finding hers. "I need you tonight."

The words were whispered so quietly, so sincerely, Kerry could offer no other answer than the one she gave.

"Yes."

She walked with a confidence she wasn't feeling. She turned on the small lamp in the corner, then closed the door and leaned against it. She took a deep breath, knowing the rest was up to her. She could leave and they could have another day where they danced around this, where they fought this, where they pretended there wasn't this heat between them. But she didn't want to go another day. Carson needed her tonight. She reached behind her and locked the door as Carson stood at the window, watching her...waiting. She wasn't sure what gave her the courage to take the handful of steps necessary to reach her again. Truth was, she was scared to death.

"Kerry? If you want—"

Kerry tried to smile. "No. It's just...I don't know what I'm doing," she said. "I don't even know what I'm thinking. I don't know what's—" She stopped, realizing she was offering disclaimers for what was about to happen. "No, that's not true," she said. "I *do* know what I'm doing. I want...I want to be with you," she finished in a whisper. "I want to make love with you." She took a deep breath, admitting the one thing that frightened her the most. "I want this very much."

Despite Carson's plea that she needed her, Kerry knew that Carson would never initiate this. She wanted Kerry to be sure. And she was. So she answered the unasked question that she saw in those eyes.

"I'm sure, Carson."

Carson finally moved, as if having been given permission to touch. It was almost with wonder that she lightly moved her fingers across Kerry's cheek and into her hair, brushing it away from her face. There was a look—a need—there that she hadn't seen before. Not with Carson. Not with anyone.

"I haven't wanted—" Carson started, then stopped, as if considering her words. "It's been a very long time since I've wanted to make love with someone." She brushed her thumb across Kerry's mouth, causing Kerry's lips to part. "I want that with you," she whispered. "I want that so much."

Kerry's eyes slipped closed as Carson pulled her closer. Soft lips were gentle on hers, taking their time. But knowing she could give herself freely, knowing what was about to happen ignited the fire so quickly, there was no time to douse it. Their kisses turned ardent, moans mingling as their bodies touched. Kerry couldn't remember a time when she was ever aroused this quickly. The fact that she was with another woman had no bearing. She relished the feelings Carson brought out in her and her mouth opened fully, their tongues mating in a sensual dance as her hands clutched Carson's waist.

She thought she wouldn't know what to do. She thought she would be afraid to touch like this, to be touched by a woman. But she stopped thinking and let her body lead the way. She tugged at Carson's clothes, wanting to feel skin, *needing* to feel skin. They pulled apart and Carson did her bidding, tossing her shirt and bra aside. Kerry stood in awe as she blatantly stared at Carson, her breasts small, her nipples rock hard. Unconsciously, Kerry wet her lips, then her eyes flew to Carson's, embarrassed for staring.

But Carson's eyes were gentle and she smiled. "It's okay to look...to touch."

"I'm scared," she said, then laughed nervously. "I mean—"

"I understand."

Carson took her hand, slowly bringing it up to her breast. Kerry's breath caught as her hand hovered inches away. She was about to touch another woman, she was about to make love with another woman and there was no panic, no second thoughts. Her body hummed with life, and she recognized the want and desire for what it was. She was sexually attracted to Carson and she wanted this. She'd probably always wanted this.

She covered Carson's breast with her hand, her eyes closing again as a slow moan escaped. Carson's skin was so soft, yet her nipple so hard against her palm. She looked up, meeting Carson's smoky eyes. It was with a near desperation that she moved closer, her mouth finding Carson's again. Gentleness fled, along with her hesitancy, replaced with a fire she couldn't quite comprehend. She didn't resist as Carson's hands unbuttoned her blouse. In fact, she wanted to beg Carson to hurry, to rip it open, and she helped her along, letting the garment fall to the floor before reaching for Carson's jeans.

The storm raged outside, lightning flashed and thunder shook the windows as Kerry lay down on the bed, pulling Carson with her. She relished the feel of skin on skin, of Carson's weight pressing into her. Carson's mouth left hers, nibbling gently along her throat as her hand slid along the length of her body. Kerry closed her eyes, unrecognizable sounds coming from her as Carson's lips traveled across her skin. It should have felt foreign to her, but it didn't. Carson's touch was familiar, as if she'd felt it a thousand times before.

What wasn't familiar was the aching desire she had. When Carson found her breasts, when her tongue wet a circle around her nipple, Kerry moaned loudly, her body arching. Carson took her nipple, suckling it gently and Kerry found her hips moving, seeking relief. She opened her legs wider, her hands at Carson's hips pulling her hard against her.

Carson leaned up, her weight on her hands. Their eyes met, Carson silently asking one more time if she were sure.

"Yes," she whispered.

Carson lowered herself again, her mouth going back to her breast, her hand moving excruciatingly slow, her fingers gliding across her skin. Kerry moaned in frustration, wanting Carson to hurry, to touch her...to release her. She could feel how wet she was, could feel the pulsating ache between her legs.

"Please, Carson, don't tease me."

Carson's lips moved to her mouth. "Slow," she murmured.

"No. Please not slow," she countered, her hands again gripping Carson's hips to pull her tight against her. "*God*, please touch me." She was begging, but she didn't care. "*Yes*," she hissed when Carson's fingers finally parted her. Her hips jerked and she moaned as Carson touched her for the first time, her fingers circling her throbbing clit. Kerry's fingers dug into Carson as she gasped for breath, then moaned loudly when Carson's knee spread her thighs even farther.

A mouth at her breast again, she arched her hips as Carson filled her, her fingers going deep inside. Kerry met her thrust, her hips moving wildly against Carson's hand as Carson still devoured her nipple, her teeth and tongue tugging at it, sending Kerry's arousal to new heights.

She was panting, her hips undulating, meeting each stroke of Carson's. Carson straddled her thigh, and Kerry moaned again when she felt Carson's wetness coat her leg. Carson's hips moved in rhythm to Kerry, her lips leaving Kerry's breast, finding her mouth instead. Kerry opened to her, drawing her tongue inside. Carson was in perfect sync, her tongue making love to her mouth much as her fingers were her body.

Kerry felt a thundering roar in her ears and wasn't certain if it was from the raging storm outside or the one inside. She was near orgasm, and she so wanted Carson to join her. She moved her hand, slipping it between her thigh and Carson, touching Carson.

"Oh...*God*," she moaned, Carson's slick wetness greeting her fingers.

"Yes, just like that," Carson gasped as she, too, moaned at the contact. Grinding now against Kerry's offered hand, Carson's body rocked against her, both panting, struggling to breathe.

The wonder of it all was too much as Kerry's senses were on overload. A blinding light—was it lightning? Kerry wasn't sure as her body exploded. She screamed out her pleasure and Carson was there to catch it, her mouth covering hers. Two, three more strokes of Carson's hips and she too climaxed, the sound muffled against Kerry's mouth.

She collapsed, her weight on Kerry now, and Kerry kissed her softly, her arms pulling Carson even closer to her. She felt her heart rate slowing, going back to normal, and she was finally able to string thoughts together coherently. She held another woman in her arms—a woman she'd just made love with—and there was no awkwardness, no sense of embarrassment, no feeling that it was wrong. They'd been moving in this direction since the very first time they met. When Carson had looked at her that first day, Kerry now admitted she felt an acute attraction, one that she hadn't even given conscious thought to at the time.

But day after day it grew, and she could no longer ignore it. That's why she had come into Carson's room tonight. Not to see if she was okay after her visit with her father. That had only been an excuse. No, what she really wanted was this. To be with Carson in the most intimate of ways, to make love with her, to try to make some sense of what she was feeling.

"Are you okay?" Carson whispered as she finally lifted her head.

Kerry nodded and reached up, caressing Carson's face. "Yes. I'm fine. Better than fine," she added.

"I thought maybe—"

"No." She leaned up, kissing Carson hard. "Whatever you're thinking...no."

Carson smiled then. "Yeah?" She rolled them over, Kerry now on top of her. "Now what am I thinking?"

Kerry grinned. "I don't know what you're thinking, but I definitely know what I'm thinking," she murmured, not shy as her mouth found Carson's again. She felt Carson's legs part and she settled between them, the dampness of their arousal still evident. She pulled her mouth from her lips, moving lower. She bent her head, going on pure instinct as her mouth closed over an erect nipple. She moaned, the hardness of it surprising her. She bathed the nipple, finally drawing it into her mouth, hearing Carson's breath catch as she suckled it.

"Feels so good," Carson whispered, her hands threading through Kerry's hair, holding her close.

Kerry raised her head, meeting Carson's hot gaze. "Show me everything," she said. "I want everything with you."

Carson nodded. "Yes. Everything."

CHAPTER TWENTY-FIVE

The sun hit her face, and she turned away from the window, finding Kerry still snuggled close against her. Carson watched her, feeling...well, feeling content for once. So many mornings when there was someone sharing her bed, she simply wanted them to be gone. The night of pleasure had ended and she wanted to be alone. There would be no courtship, no time for small talk. It was a night of sex, nothing more than a physical connection. Chances were there would be no repeat. In fact, repeats were rare.

This morning, it all felt different. Kerry had been full of wonder, full of awe. She didn't shy away from anything, and their night together was one Carson would not soon forget.

They had made love until they were both sated, both too

tired for anything but blissful sleep. There was never any discussion that Kerry would leave her bed, that she would slink back to her own room. No, Kerry had snuggled against her and Carson held her, secretly pleased that Kerry even wanted to stay. Part of her feared that once Kerry's curiosity was satisfied, she would flee.

"What are you thinking?" Kerry mumbled sleepily.

Carson smiled. Kerry hadn't opened her eyes, yet she must have felt Carson observing her.

"I was thinking how nice it is to have you still in my bed," she answered honestly.

Kerry's eyes blinked open. She propped herself up on her elbow, the sheet slipping down to her waist, her breasts exposed. Carson wasn't shy about staring. In fact, she wasn't shy about touching either. Kerry leaned closer, kissing her, the taste of sex still on her lips and Carson's desire flamed again.

Kerry slowly pulled Carson down on top of her, her thighs parting, her hands needy as they cupped Carson's hips, pressing their lower bodies together.

The storm had passed, the sun was high, the morning was getting away from them, yet Kerry wanted to make love again. Carson didn't care that Martha would miss them, that Mr. Burris and his crew would miss them. All she concerned herself with was Kerry's desire for her...and fulfilling that desire.

"Carson," Kerry murmured. "It feels so good like this," she whispered.

Like this was Carson pressing their centers together, their wetness merging. She pushed Kerry's legs even farther apart, arching into her, their clits rubbing together. Kerry gasped at the contact, her fingers digging into Carson's side. Carson started a slow, rocking motion, grinding against Kerry, listening as Kerry panted in her ear. She moved, finding Kerry's mouth—her tongue—kissing her passionately.

Kerry matched her intensity, their hips moving faster now. She was surprised at how quickly it built, how quickly she was ready. She couldn't hold back a second longer and she gave in to her orgasm, feeling Kerry do the same as she clung to her, their breaths mingling.

"It's never been like this," Kerry said between breaths. "I've never *wanted* like this."

Carson dipped her head, capturing a nipple. How did she respond to that? Did she confess this was new to her too? Did she tell Kerry about the numerous women she'd had meaningless sex with? Did she tell Kerry how very different this was for her?

A quiet knock on her door saved her from answering. She rolled away from Kerry, smiling as Kerry made no move to get out of her bed. She simply pulled the sheet over her, watching as Carson searched for clothes.

"Coming," she said, pulling on her robe. She opened the door hesitantly, knowing she looked—and smelled—like sex. She was expecting Martha and was surprised to find her father's nurse there instead.

"I'm sorry," she said abruptly. "Your father passed."

Carson nodded and the nurse turned and left without another word. There was no sense of loss for Carson, no sorrow. There wasn't the emptiness she felt at her mother's death. For that, she felt a twinge of guilt. He was her father, after all.

"Carson?"

She turned, wondering if there was need to pretend to feel some grief at his passing. But no, not with Kerry. She wouldn't have to pretend with Kerry.

"He died."

Kerry nodded, then slid from the bed, looking for her own clothes. "Do you know who to call?"

"Yes. Chance left me instructions. He'll be buried here at the ranch."

Kerry's eyebrows shot up. "Your mother—"

"Yes. She's here too." Carson shrugged. "I just haven't been up to visiting her yet," she admitted as she openly stared as Kerry moved around her bedroom.

Kerry slipped on her shirt, glancing at Carson. "I have no idea where my panties are."

Carson smiled at this, finally moving away from the door. She took Kerry's hands, stopping her searching. "Come here," she said, pulling her close. "Last night was fantastic. You're not sorry, are you?"

"No. No, not sorry. Not at all."

"Confused?" Carson guessed.

"A little, yes." Kerry kissed her, then pulled back quickly, as if afraid their desire would flame again. "But we can talk later. You need to—"

"I know."

When Kerry left her room later, she heard Carson and the nurse talking. The door to Mr. Cartwright's room was open, but she didn't dare intrude. She went downstairs instead, but there was no sign of breakfast and Martha appeared to be getting ready to make lunch. Kerry's eyes flew to the clock on the wall, wondering just how long they'd lingered in bed. Thankfully, it was only nine thirty.

She found she was blushing profusely as Martha eyed her. She poured coffee, trying to ignore the look she was getting. She had no idea how Martha would take the events of last night, but she didn't think she would be shocked by them.

"Slept in, did you?" Martha finally asked.

Kerry sipped her coffee and nodded. "Yes. Very tired," she said.

"Yes. What with the storm and all, must have been hard sleeping. I know it was for me."

Kerry blushed anew and looked away. "I suppose the nurse told you about Mr. Cartwright?"

"Yes. A blessing, really. Poor man has been suffering for weeks now." Martha went to refill her own coffee cup. "How did Miss Carson take it?"

"You must know by now that there was no love between them," she said.

Martha nodded. "Yes. Sad. But why did she come back then?"

"I think she wanted to reconcile with him. I don't know if she would admit that or not, but I think that was the real reason," Kerry said. Carson may say for closure, but Kerry really suspected that Carson *wanted* to reconcile, she just was not able to. Perhaps if her father had been more receptive to it. But he hadn't been.

"Is she going to make the arrangements?"

"Chance left her instructions. I think the arrangements were already made."

Martha stared at her again, and Kerry grew uncomfortable under her watchful eyes. She was startled when Martha patted her hand.

"Are you okay this morning?"

Her question was spoken quietly. Kerry didn't pretend that she didn't know what Martha was referring to.

"I...I think so, yes," she said. "This is new for me," she admitted. "I'm—"

"You don't have to explain. Not to me." She moved away then, back to her cutting board. "Cody, however, will probably be surprised."

Kerry did feel the need to explain. She didn't want Martha to think she'd just fallen into bed with Carson without so much as a thought given to the consequences.

"Martha, I'm thirty-four years old, never once close to marriage," she said. "I blamed my choice of career, the constant travel. Truth is, I just never met anyone who I was attracted to. Insanely attracted to."

"And now you have?"

"Yes. And it isn't Cody."

"Well, it's certainly none of my business," Martha said. "But, well, it's been quite fun to watch you two," she said with a smile.

"And fun to plan your romantic dinner settings?"

"Yes. But when the guys come back, you'll need to be careful," she warned. "Even though they are men, I doubt you'll be able to hide this. It's written all over your face."

Kerry blushed again. "I'll try to be careful," she said as she put her coffee cup down. "I better go see how Mr. Burris is doing."

She walked to the bunkhouse, even though it was nearly a half-mile from the ranch house. She needed the time to think. No, she didn't regret the night—or the morning—but they'd not considered what they would do once the brothers returned. She stopped suddenly, wishing they'd had time to talk. Was she being presumptuous to assume that she and Carson would have more nights like the one they'd just shared? Or was that it? One night together?

No. Even though she had no experience with this, it wasn't going to be just one night. There was too much attraction, too much heat between them. Even when she dared to dream about meeting someone who set her on fire, she never thought it would be a woman, and she never thought she'd spend an entire night making love, drifting in and out of sleep, only to wake, to touch, to love again.

Her face felt flushed as she continued to the bunkhouse. Was she really the same woman who had begged Carson to touch her? Had she really cried when Carson brought her to orgasm for the first time with her mouth? Had she really held Carson down, her own mouth seeking—and finding—her most secret spots? Was she the one who had begged Carson to take her just one more time, even when her body was spent?

Yes to all of those and more. She didn't need to analyze it, she didn't need to make sense of it. What had happened was inevitable.

CHAPTER TWENTY-SIX

Carson sat in a chair by the window, feeling terribly out of place as she watched them preparing to take her father's body. She felt like an outsider. Chance should have been here. They *all* should have been here. Why did they leave this chore to her? She had no part in the family, yet here she was, watching the proceedings without emotion, without any sentiment.

The men murmured quietly to each other as they lifted the body onto the gurney. The nurse was busily packing her things, her glance going often to her father, then occasionally to Carson. Carson was convinced it was an accusatory glance but she wasn't certain why. Yes, they'd quarreled each time she'd come to visit him, but not last night. No, last night she'd lied and told him she'd forgiven him. She let him die in peace.

She, however, felt no such peace at his passing. She hadn't reconciled things with him, she didn't get the closure she knew she needed. And of course, now she never would.

"Miss Cartwright? We're ready to take him." Harry Hanes, the same man who had buried her mother, walked over and held his hand out to her. "Again, my condolences."

"Thank you," she said, shaking his hand lightly. "My brothers should be back in a couple of days. Chance will call you."

"Of course. Is there anything else we can do?"

"No. We'll be fine. Thank you."

He nodded politely, then ushered the others from the room, leaving her alone with the nurse. She sighed, her gaze going out the window and to the lake. It was a sunny, warm day, hinting of summer. After last night's storm and rain, everything looked fresh and new, the grass a little greener this morning.

"I'll be taking my leave soon. I just have my clothing to pack."

Carson turned from the window, nodding at the nurse. "Is there any paperwork to finalize? Do we owe you anything? I'm not sure what arrangement you had with them," she said.

"No. That's all taken care of." She didn't move, and Carson thought there was something else the nurse wanted to say, but she finally just nodded and turned to leave.

"Thank you for taking care of him," Carson said, feeling she needed to offer some appreciation.

The nurse stopped, looking back at her. "I don't know anything about the circumstances of your estrangement, but I do think he was genuinely sorry for his part of it."

"Do you?" Carson shook her head. "I think he wanted to be sorry but just couldn't bring himself to do it. He didn't want to take any blame." Carson stood up, not feeling the need to explain any of this to the nurse. "Thank you again," she said dismissively.

The nurse took her cue and left without another word. Carson knew she'd been rude but really, how dare this stranger try to patch up the broken pieces of their relationship?

She shoved her hands into her pockets, standing again at the window looking out. Was she wrong to hold on to her anger?

Wouldn't it all have been a lot simpler if she could have forgiven him? Truth was, she didn't want to forgive him. It was almost like there would be emptiness inside of her if her anger, if her sense of abandonment, of rejection, left her. She'd devoted so much energy to hating him. If she gave that up now, what would she have? Would she regain some of the happiness that she'd lost in her youth? Would the bitterness fade? Could she learn to love?

Not surprisingly, Kerry's face popped into her mind, and she felt an involuntary smile on her lips. She didn't deny how good it felt to give of herself last night. To truly give. In the past, it was only a sexual act. She never allowed it to turn emotional. In her circle of friends—acquaintances—she'd slept with nearly all of them. That was the reputation she carried with her. They all knew it would be nothing more than sex. It was all Carson wanted, all she needed. She'd learned that from Rebecca.

That's why it surprised her that she wanted more with Kerry. Kerry was nothing like the women she socialized with. Kerry was *real*. Carson had let her guard down, she'd let it become emotional between them. And when they'd made love, she didn't hold anything back. She let Kerry see it all—her desire, her need, her longing for the physical and emotional connection she felt with her. Kerry didn't shy away from it, she embraced it.

And none of that sent Kerry running. Quite the opposite. She'd taken everything Carson offered and gave it back with the same fervor. Oh, no doubt Kerry needed to talk about it. She was probably questioning her sanity right about now. That's what really scared her the most. Would Kerry come to her senses? Would she think she'd made a huge mistake and keep her distance? What about Cody?

Carson took a deep breath and slowly exhaled. So many questions and none she had answers for. She turned away from the window, her eyes lighting on the empty bed. Again, no sense of loss and a twinge of guilt— but she could not summon up any grief.

CHAPTER TWENTY-SEVEN

Kerry fidgeted with her laptop, barely able to concentrate on what Mr. Burris was asking her. She was torn between doing her job and the consuming need she had to see Carson. She knew Carson was alone now, knew they'd left with her father's body. What was Carson doing, thinking? Did she feel lost? Did she need comfort?

No. Not because of his death. As Carson had said many times, she felt no sorrow or grief. But loneliness? Yes, Kerry thought. It hovered around Carson. She wondered if that wasn't part of her allure. She appeared aloof and indifferent, but it was only a pretense. She'd let her facade slip with Kerry, showing her the woman behind the mask. Kerry doubted she did that with many people. Had the mask slipped back into place today?

"So? The extra large shower liner?"

Kerry blinked several times, forgetting that Mr. Burris was waiting for her. She glanced at her laptop, happy to see she'd at least gotten as far as pulling up the plans.

"I think so. That only takes a foot away from floor space. Let's go with it," she said, giving him a quick, apologetic smile. "Sorry. I'm not focused today."

"It'll take us a couple of days to get the plumbing run, if you've got something else to take care of," he said, offering her a reprieve. "With Mr. Cartwright and all," he added.

"I may actually head back to the ranch house to see if there's something I can do." She held up her phone. "You've got my number."

She closed her laptop, leaving it in the kitchen. Now, she wished she'd driven instead of walked. She'd just started up the path when she saw Carson strolling down the road toward her. Or toward the stables. Carson seemed to find solace there with Windstorm. So she waited, leaning against the same tree where they'd shared breakfast. She was nervous and wasn't sure why. Was she afraid Carson would walk past her? Was she afraid the closeness they'd established would be diminished somehow?

But as Carson got closer, close enough to read her eyes, Kerry's fears were laid to rest. She felt her pulse increase but she didn't move, presenting a relaxed demeanor as she rested against the tree.

Carson stopped in front of her, and Kerry saw the questions in her eyes. Of course there would be. She didn't know why it hadn't occurred to her earlier that Carson must have her own fears. Kerry shoved off the tree, stepping close to Carson, letting her hand find Carson's.

"Okay?" she asked, knowing the question was ambiguous.

Carson nodded. "You?"

Kerry squeezed her hand and gave a slight smile. "Did you think I was going to run and hide?"

"That occurred to me, yes." Carson glanced quickly at the bunkhouse then back at her. "Is this a good time? Do you want to talk?"

"Mr. Burris has all but kicked me out, so yes, it's a good time."

Carson tugged on her hand, leading her to the stables. "We'll have privacy there," Carson explained.

They were silent as they walked, but Carson did not release her hand. Their fingers were entwined, and Kerry was content with the light contact, thinking it didn't feel strange at all to be holding hands with Carson.

It was warmer in the barn, the sweet smell of hay overshadowing the scent from the stables. The horses were out in the pasture, and they stood there together, the quiet surrounding them. At that moment Kerry wasn't sure there was anything to talk about. The air was thick between them, crackling with an energy that still surprised her. She could see Carson's pulse in her neck, its rapid pace telling Kerry that their closeness wasn't only affecting her. But there was something in Carson's eyes that wasn't there last night—a wariness, guardedness. Carson always exuded such confidence and Kerry wondered what she could be worried about. Maybe it was her. Now that it's the light of day, Carson could be worried that Kerry may be just a curious straight woman after all.

Well, Kerry knew of only one way to ease Carson's doubts.

"Can we talk later?" she asked playfully. At Carson's raised eyebrows, she smiled. "Why don't you show me your hayloft?"

Carson smiled too, that wariness leaving her eyes. "You mean my teenage lair?"

"Is that what you called it?"

"Yes. I lured Cody's unsuspecting girlfriends to it, then pounced," Carson teased. She took a deep breath, her smile fading. "Seriously, are you okay? I mean, for you, last night was—"

"New? Different?" Kerry nodded. "Yes. In so many ways. It was also the most intimate lovemaking I have ever shared with someone." Kerry moved away, debating how much she should confide in Carson. She felt a closeness with her, more so now, but the fact that they'd slept together changed things between them. There wasn't much a person could hide after being as intimate as they had been. "I think maybe your first assumption about me was true."

She watched Carson, seeing doubt cloud her eyes again. Kerry understood what she was thinking and shook her head.

"No. No, not that I'm just a curious straight woman." She went to her, taking her hand. "When you first met me, you assumed I was a lesbian. I denied it. Carson, you weren't the first person to say that to me. But I always denied it. The level of comfort I felt around women, well, I didn't associate it with physical desire, certainly not sexual. It just never was a consideration of mine." She paused, daring to meet Carson's eyes, not knowing what all she was revealing. "It was different with you from the start. I was drawn to you in a way I didn't understand, and I didn't want to fight it. I couldn't. And being with you last night, making love with you, it felt so right. It still does. These feelings don't seem alien to me."

Her words finally had the desired effect as the shadows of doubt left Carson's eyes. She could tell Carson was relieved.

Carson cleared her throat. "Then I should confess something as well. I've slept with a lot of women, Kerry. When I was younger, it was nothing more than a game. Rebecca, the woman I told you about, taught me how to play it. She taught me how to keep it physical only, never emotional."

Carson moved away, pretending to be interested in the bridles hanging on the center post. Kerry kept quiet, letting Carson gather her thoughts before she continued.

"It was easy for me at first," Carson said. "I was still bruised inside from my mother's death, from losing my home. I didn't want an emotional attachment with anyone. I didn't want to be close to anyone, I didn't want to love anyone. Love brought pain and I'd had enough of that." She turned back to Kerry, her eyes reflective now. "I've lived a rather solitary life, moving about from place to place, calling a sterile apartment in Manhattan home. The last few years, I haven't had much physical contact with anyone, really. I got tired of that game, yet I still never met anyone who I wanted to give more to, more than the physical part of me. But then, I hadn't yet met you."

Kerry's heart was pounding as the meaning of Carson's words sunk in. Before she could speak, Carson moved closer, her hand cupping Kerry's face, her gaze dropping to her lips.

"I haven't let anyone have any power over me, any control," she said softly. "Yet here I am, scared to death of this thing between us. It's new for me too, Kerry."

Kerry turned her face, her lips grazing Carson's palm. "Don't be scared," she whispered. "I don't want either of us to be scared of these feelings."

They stood close together, their bodies nearly touching, close enough for Kerry to feel the heat. Carson's hand slid from Kerry's face to her neck, slipping under her hair. Kerry didn't hesitate, her mouth meeting Carson's, opening to her, inviting her in. Again, she was amazed at how quickly their passion ignited, how swiftly the fire spread between them.

She was gasping for breath, but she wasn't shy. She tugged Carson's shirt from her jeans, her fingers moving over warm, soft skin. She impatiently shoved her bra aside, her hands cupping both her breasts, Carson's moan sending a thrill through her.

"Kerry, not here," Carson murmured against her lips but she made no move to pull away.

"Too late," Kerry said as she rolled Carson's nipples between her fingers. Yes, it was too late. She couldn't stop, didn't want to stop.

But Carson stilled her hands, her mouth still on Kerry's. She smiled against her lips. "Come on then. Let me show you the loft."

CHAPTER TWENTY-EIGHT

"And she just left without a word?" Kerry asked.

"Yes. Just packed her things and left. Of course, it wasn't like she socialized any while she was here," Martha said of the nurse. "Stir that for me, Miss Kerry," she said, pointing at the pot on the stove.

Kerry opened the lid on the soup that had been simmering, dutifully stirring as Martha had requested.

"Is Miss Carson okay?"

Kerry nodded, not wanting to look at Martha for fear she'd see right through her. They'd spent the better part of two hours in the hayloft and Kerry had been as worthless as a slug the rest of the afternoon.

"I didn't expect her reaction to his death to be anything

other than it is," she said. "There was still too much bitterness. They never did clear the air about it all," Kerry added.

"Yes. I suppose the brothers will take it much harder. Especially Chance. He seemed to be the closest to him."

"I'm sure they'll grieve, but Martha, really, they've known this day was coming for so long. I think when you're prepared mentally for death, then you've already done your grieving."

"I suppose that's true. But even living here as long as I have, I still don't understand the family or their relationships. And now with Miss Carson back..."

"I know. I don't understand it either," she said as she put the lid back on the pot. She leaned against the counter, waiting, knowing Martha had more to say. Her eyes were very watchful.

"Are you okay, Miss Kerry?"

Kerry smiled. "Yes."

"Because if you needed to talk or anything, well, I'll be happy to listen."

"You mean because of Carson?"

"Yes. I know I'm not worldly or anything like that and I probably wouldn't have any good advice for you, but sometimes, when things are..." she paused, smiling. "I should just mind my own business, shouldn't I?"

Kerry smiled affectionately at her, wondering if her own mother would take this new development in her life as easily as Martha had.

"I like her an awful lot," Kerry admitted. "But when the guys come back, when Cody comes back, then, well, I have no idea how things will be."

"I don't know anything about this, and I won't even pretend that I do," Martha said. "But to see the way you two look at each other, well, let's just say you'd have to be blind not to see the...well, the...the attraction there," she finished and Kerry was surprised by the blush on Martha's face.

"I know," she said. "And it'll be hard to hide it. We obviously couldn't hide it from each other either."

"They will probably be back tomorrow," Martha cautioned.

"Yes. Carson thinks so. The storm hit at night so that probably didn't set them back a day like they'd feared."

"Well, then should I plan on an early dinner?"

Kerry frowned, then added her own blush to the mix as Martha's meaning became clear.

"How about leftovers?"

They both turned, finding Carson leaning against the wall watching them. Kerry wondered how long she'd been eavesdropping.

"That chicken casserole from the other night sounds good," Carson continued, her gaze moving between both of them. "Because yes, it will be an early night."

Kerry and Martha sported matching blushes as Martha busied herself with emptying the dishwasher and Kerry was left staring at Carson.

She walked closer, her voice low, the words for Carson's ears only. "You're assuming I'll have the energy after this afternoon?"

"The hayloft was only an appetizer," Carson countered, a lazy smile on her face.

"You do realize I got no work done today."

"And that's okay," Carson said. "They'll be back tomorrow afternoon, most likely."

Which meant they would not have the opportunity to be alone again. Not at night, anyway. The thought thrilled her to know that tonight they would go to bed together. There would be no pretending, no avoiding the inevitable. Tonight they'd go to bed as lovers. And they would be alone. She glanced at the clock on the wall, wondering how early she could persuade Martha to serve dinner.

Carson must have read her thoughts. She took her hand and pulled her out of the kitchen, holding her against the wall. Kerry's hands slid around her neck, bringing her mouth to hers. God, would she ever tire of this? She moaned into Carson's mouth, forgetting where they were as her hands moved to Carson's breasts.

Carson stilled her movements and Kerry felt Carson smile against her lips. She pulled back, seeing her desire mirrored in Carson's eyes.

"Should we be afraid?" Kerry whispered.

"Afraid?"

"I obviously can't be trusted," she said with a smile. "I can't seem to keep my hands to myself."

"Does that make you afraid?"

"That I want you this much? No. It makes me afraid that I won't be able to *hide* how much I want you."

"We'll deal with that when they get back. Tonight, it's just us." Carson stepped away from her. "Now, how about a walk to the bunkhouse? We'll check the progress and you can feel like you did some work then."

Kerry nodded. "Okay." She squeezed her hand. "Let me tell Martha. Dinner at six?"

"Dinner at six," Carson agreed.

CHAPTER TWENTY-NINE

After pushing her food around on her plate, Kerry felt positively wanton as she climbed the stairs with Carson. It was still daylight, yet here they were, retiring for the evening. Oh, they'd tried to make it somewhat normal. They'd gone to the study and had brandy. Even then, their conversation had been forced. Innocent glances, touches, belied any pretense they may have had. Carson had finally set their glasses aside, pulling Kerry to her feet. They'd stood close together for long seconds, just watching each other. Their kiss, while nearly chaste to begin, turned passionate as their hands roamed freely.

"Bed?" Carson had murmured before they went too far.

"Yes. Yes, please."

Now, their fingers were entwined as they paused at the top of the stairs. Carson's glance went to her father's closed door and Kerry wondered what she was thinking.

"I think he would have liked you," Carson said, surprising her. She smiled then. "Of course, he would have liked you much better for Cody than for me."

"Do you want to talk, Carson? I mean, about him, about—"

"No. There's nothing really to say. I regret that we weren't able to reconcile," she said. "I think maybe I didn't really want to."

"Tell me why."

"If we reconciled, then I would lose the resentment, the anger, the hatred I had," Carson said. "Then I would be empty. What would I have left?"

"Oh, sweetheart, you wouldn't be empty. You would be free. He wouldn't have a hold on you anymore." Kerry was surprised how vulnerable Carson looked at that moment. She wasn't sure what to say to her to ease her conscience.

"Yes, he has had a hold on me," Carson admitted. "It was always there. When I was young, I wasn't good enough, I wasn't *girl* enough, I wasn't smart enough. I had the wrong friends, I wore the wrong clothes."

"But your mother—"

"She took up for me, yes. She was the one person who could talk back to him. He didn't always listen but at least she had her say. She knew how much I wanted to be a part of the ranch. She begged him to let me ride with the guys and the herd."

"But you never did?"

"No. I was relegated to the background. I think that's why I don't have a relationship with my brothers."

"Chase—"

"Chase, sure. Twins. How could we not be close? But when I left, I had convinced myself that even Chase didn't miss me. No one missed me."

Kerry's heart was breaking for the lost young woman Carson must have been back then. For all her bravado now, she still harbored those same insecurities.

"Carson, no one can take away your pain." Kerry's hand slid

up her chest, resting between her breasts. "It's a part of you. It probably always will be," she said. "But look at you. You're a beautiful woman. You made a life for yourself. You can still laugh and smile. You can still love."

Carson looked at her with sad eyes. "I've been so lonely," she whispered. "I don't think I realized the extent of it until I came back home." She reached out, touching Kerry's face lightly with her fingertips. "I don't think I realized it until you."

Kerry frowned. "What do you mean?"

"I've never let anyone get close to me. I've never let anyone *inside*," Carson said. "I never wanted to give myself to someone before. I...I let you get close because, well, because you're real." Carson closed her eyes, her voice soft. "Does that make sense?"

Kerry took Carson's hand and kissed it gently. "Yes. It makes sense." And it did. From what Carson had told her, the women in her life were just bed partners, nothing more. She was thankful Carson didn't view her that way. While their relationship was certainly physical, Kerry hoped it went deeper than that. Carson had awakened a sexual side of her that Kerry didn't know existed. She had also awakened an emotional part, one where Kerry found herself opening her heart to Carson.

Carson's eyes were gentle on her now, the sadness nearly gone. "Are you still frightened by this?"

"No." She could say that without hesitation. She wasn't frightened by her feelings any longer. What scared her was the future. Was she getting in too deep? Was she falling in love with a woman? Were they just passing through each other's lives? Was this just a learning experience or was it more than that?

"But?"

Kerry smiled and leaned closer, letting her lips lightly touch Carson's. "But nothing," she murmured, letting her kiss deepen.

They were still in the hallway, neither making a move to go into Carson's bedroom. They were alone. They had nothing to hide. Not tonight.

She felt the wall press against her back as Carson held her there, her thigh nudging Kerry's legs apart. As always, their passion flared so quickly, there was no time to change course.

Kerry moaned as Carson's thigh pushed against her center, her hand stroking her breast, rubbing against her nipple.

She tore her mouth from Carson's, breathing hard as she leaned her head against the wall. Carson's mouth moved to her throat, nibbling and sucking her skin, making Kerry squirm with desire.

"God, Carson," she gasped, cupping Carson's hips and pulling her harder against her. They were both fully clothed yet she felt her orgasm building. She spread her legs farther, pressing her throbbing center against Carson's thigh, her hips moving, the friction setting her on fire.

"Yes. Like this," Carson said, her mouth at Kerry's ear. "Come for me like this."

One stroke of Carson's tongue inside her ear was all it took for her body to explode. She cried out, her body convulsing as she clung to Carson, the throbbing ache between her legs only partially squelched. Before she could catch her breath, Carson was inside her jeans, her fingers spreading her, entering her.

"God, *yes*," she whispered, finding Carson's mouth again, their kisses hard and wet. Her hips moved with each stroke of Carson's hand, the hallway filled with the sound of their lovemaking as Carson's hand, now wet, slapped against her with each thrust. Kerry pulled her mouth from Carson's, gasping for breath now, struggling to stand as her hips rocked wildly. Carson added another finger and Kerry groaned, her body giving way again as she climaxed for a second time.

"I've got you," Carson whispered as Kerry slumped against her, her legs too weak to stand.

"My God," she murmured, her breath still coming fast. "That was...that was amazing," she managed, the word seeming too small for what Carson had just done to her.

"Come on," she said, leading Kerry into her bedroom on wobbly legs.

Kerry's hands immediately went to work on Carson's clothing, their hands tangling as they each sought to remove the other's clothes. Kerry had a need she couldn't control, didn't want to control.

"I want you," she breathed, finally touching skin. "I *need* you," she clarified. "I want my mouth on you. I want to taste you, feel you come in my mouth," she whispered, urging Carson to the bed.

Carson groaned as Kerry knelt between her legs and Kerry didn't wait for a response. She lowered her mouth, greeted by Carson's wetness. She closed her eyes as she gathered Carson to her, holding her firmly by the hips as her mouth feasted, finding the throbbing bundle of nerves, her tongue licking, moving quickly.

"Jesus, Kerry," Carson groaned again. "Yes...don't stop," she gasped as she tried to press Kerry's face harder against her.

Kerry pulled back, not ready for it to end. Carson moaned in frustration as Kerry slowed her movements. With her tongue, she tasted the length of her, slipping inside as far as she could, moving with lightning strokes in and out, finally settling on her clit again, sucking it hard into her mouth. Carson's hips rose off the bed, and she grasped Kerry's hair with one hand. Kerry ignored the stinging pain, letting Carson grind against her mouth.

She could hear Carson gasping for breath, could literally feel her swell inside her mouth. She devoured her, starving for her taste, her lips and tongue working together, finally allowing Carson to reach orgasm.

Carson's guttural scream was too much and Kerry felt her own body climax again as she squeezed her legs together. She drank every ounce that Carson gave her, only stopping when Carson collapsed on the bed, her hand falling away from Kerry's hair.

Kerry climbed up the bed beside her, not even pausing to consider the act she'd just performed, executed with a proficiency and skill she couldn't possibly possess. How could she know? Last night, she'd been tentative in her lovemaking, unsure of what would please Carson. Tonight, she simply needed to share the most intimate part of lovemaking.

"Are you okay?"

Kerry let her eyes flutter open, meeting Carson's smoky gaze. "Are you going to ask me that every time we make love?"

"No. It's just—"

"That I wanted—needed—you like that?"

Carson nodded, her fingers lazily grazing Kerry's skin. "No one's...no one has needed me before."

"I don't believe that," Kerry said.

"I haven't ever let anyone need me," Carson admitted. "I couldn't ever be there for anyone. Not totally."

Kerry leaned up on an elbow, her gaze moving from Carson's breast to her face.

"Has that changed?"

"Yes. I want to be here when you need me. And I want you to need me."

Those words frightened her and she wasn't sure why. Was it because she *did* need Carson? Did she tell Carson that she'd never made love with the intensity that she had the last two days? Did Carson already know that? Did she tell Carson she was dangerously close to falling in love with her? Or did Carson already know that too?

"What are we going to do?" she whispered.

"You mean when the guys are back?"

"Yes."

"Well, if you want to get past your three-month window on the contract, then we need to hide this."

"How can we hide this, Carson? I can't even look at you without advertising it all over my face. Martha has told me as much."

"Cody thinks he has feelings for you," Carson said. "He told me he was going to tell you as soon as they get back."

Kerry groaned and lay back, covering her eyes with her arm. "God, say it isn't so."

Carson laughed quietly. "It is so. I told you if you weren't careful, he would propose marriage."

"What am I going to do?"

"We'll go back to avoiding each other whenever he's around."

"And then what? I can sneak into your room at night?"

Carson leaned over and kissed her. "Yes." She pulled back and grinned. "You couldn't have set your sights on Chase, could you? We wouldn't have anything to worry about then."

Kerry raised her eyebrows.

"He's gay."

"Chase? You're joking."

"No."

"Do the others know?"

Carson shook her head. "He just told me last week when we were on an evening walk."

"How does he stand it here then? I mean—"

"I know. He takes long weekends and meets *friends*," she said. "But still, it's a lonely life."

"Doesn't he want to get away?"

"Yes, actually. He says there's some property on the Idaho border that he wants to buy. Start his own ranch, breed horses. Use Windstorm as stud," Carson said. "I offered to help him, to buy it for him but..."

Kerry again raised her eyebrows again.

"You still think I'm here to collect inheritance?"

"No. But I realized I don't really know anything about you. You said you had an apartment in Manhattan. I'm assuming it costs more than my yearly salary," she said. "But I don't know what you do."

"That's just it. I don't do anything," Carson said. "One of my many faults," she added.

"Why do you consider that a fault?"

"Everyone should do something, shouldn't they?"

"Your grandmother?" Kerry guessed.

"Yes. She and my father couldn't stand each other. It was only natural he send me to her. Grammy Mae and her family owned a lot of land on the plains east of Denver. They made a fortune when the airport was built."

"That explains the comments Colt and Cody made that first day."

"I didn't have anything to do with her will. In fact, I had no idea I was the sole beneficiary. But it allowed me to escape."

"But you haven't been happy," Kerry stated. It wasn't a question, just an observation.

"No. Never."

"Then what do you want to do with your life that might make you happy?"

Carson smiled, her hand moving higher to brush under Kerry's breast, but she made no attempt to turn it into a seduction. She was simply touching her and Kerry enjoyed the lightness of it.

"I think if someone had asked me that question a month ago, I wouldn't have had an answer other than the status quo. I traveled a lot. I have a handful of friends. But being back here made me realize how much I've missed this. I don't necessarily mean here. This doesn't really feel like home anymore, but it feels familiar," she said. "But I think I might want to stay out here somewhere."

"Maybe you and Chase could get something together," she suggested.

"Oh yeah? Like play with horses?" She leaned closer, kissing Kerry softly. "Can I play with you too?"

A simple, teasing question, yet Kerry knew there was an undertone of seriousness about it. When her six months was up here—if she even made the six months—she had no idea where she'd go next. The potential client in Idaho? Or maybe hit some of the contacts she'd made while with Randall? She had no idea.

She decided to ignore Carson's question behind the question and keep her answer light and teasing as well. She dipped her head, her mouth grazing across Carson's nipple.

"I'll play with you anytime, anywhere," she murmured. She looked up, meeting Carson's gaze, seeing a bit of her insecurities slip back into place. It was the wrong response, obviously. But God, what did she tell her? That she was in danger of falling in love with her? But she had no chance to change her answer. Carson pushed her back against the bed, settling her weight on top of her.

"Let's play now."

Kerry woke, feeling the coldness of the bed, knowing Carson had been gone for some time. It was dark out and she sat up, looking around for a clock. She found none. She lay back down, still exhausted. There had been no more discussion last night, not with words, anyway. But there was a depth, a fervor in their lovemaking that Kerry knew they would be hard-pressed to match. She wasn't sure how it happened but they'd both ended up crying, the emotional give-and-take too much for them. She'd opened herself, letting Carson see everything. There were no words, no, but Carson had gathered her close, her gentle crying bringing on Kerry's own tears when their bodies were finally sated.

Carson, most likely, was embarrassed by her emotional outpouring. She'd clung to Kerry, much like a drowning woman might cling to her capsized boat, fingers holding tight, Carson's touch frantic on her skin. The next minute, she'd be in control again, her kisses nearly desperate, demanding things from Kerry that she didn't think she had the energy to give. But give she did, her body no longer hers to control. She had never had anyone need her as much as Carson had and she'd certainly never experienced lovemaking like they'd shared.

She had no idea when Carson had left their bed. She didn't remember falling asleep. Most likely, her body had simply collapsed from exhaustion. But she made herself move now, getting up, needing to find Carson. Her clothes were scattered about, but she spied Carson's robe and she slipped it on, walking barefoot out into the hallway and down the stairs.

The house was dark but she found her sitting in the study, the bottle of scotch out beside her. She leaned in the doorway, watching. Carson looked up, the shadows making it hard to read her eyes. Then she said the very words Kerry knew she would say.

"I'm sorry."

"What are you sorry for?" Kerry asked gently, not sure how much she could push Carson into answering.

"It was...it was too much," Carson said. "I had no right to—"

"If it was too much, I would have asked you to stop," Kerry said, interrupting her. "And you would have."

"Yes. But I'm just not used to this, I'm not used to needing someone like this, like I did tonight," she whispered. "It's frightening to know that I do."

Kerry moved into the room then, going behind Carson and

draping her arms across her shoulders. She bent down, kissing the top of her head, feeling Carson tremble from such a light touch.

"It's okay when we both need like this," she said softly. "I didn't want you to stop, Carson. And when I needed, you gave to me. Isn't that what it's all about?"

"Yes."

Kerry straightened, but did not move from behind her. She trailed her fingers through Carson's hair. "Tell me what's bothering you."

"I can't."

"Why?"

Carson gave a gentle laugh. "Because it's crazy."

Kerry's hand didn't still as it continued threading through Carson's hair. "Are you worried about your brothers coming back?"

Carson nodded.

"Worried that it'll be different? That *I'll* be different?" she guessed.

"Cody will want to talk. He...he thinks that there's something between you. And you have the threat of the contract. It would be easier for you to just—"

"Stop it right there," she said, finally moving, kneeling down in front of Carson's chair. "Is that what you're afraid of? That my curiosity has been satisfied? Jesus, Carson. After what we just shared, *that's* what you're thinking?" She stood quickly, her anger flaring. "You think this is some act? Some game I'm playing?" She tapped her chest. "I'm scared to death over what I'm feeling. Don't you dare belittle this by thinking that all I care about is the damn contract."

She spun on her heels, racing from the room and back up the stairs. She didn't want to be angry with Carson, not after the beautiful lovemaking they'd shared. It was just hard for her to fathom that this was new to Carson too. She was the worldly one. She was the one with experience. Not Kerry. Yet Carson could be so vulnerable, so insecure.

She paused, letting her thoughts sink in. "Jesus, you're an idiot," she whispered. Of course she was vulnerable. Of course her insecurities showed. She'd been told she wasn't loved, wasn't wanted by her father. She'd been banished from her home. She'd been on her own for twelve years. Twelve years of being alone, being lonely. She hadn't had love. She hadn't had a home.

Kerry shook her head. Carson appeared so confident on the outside, so impervious to others, yet she was so very vulnerable on the inside. She knew she had to apologize. She'd accused Carson of thinking things that Kerry now knew were not true. Carson didn't think Kerry was playing a game. She wasn't that good of an actress.

She dropped the clothes she had picked up from the floor and turned, startled to find Carson standing in the doorway. She cursed herself for the tears she saw in her eyes.

"I'm sorry," she whispered. She went to Carson, into her embrace. They held tight, both of them pulling the other close. "I'm sorry," she said again.

"Stop," Carson murmured. "It's just...I'm scared too, Kerry."

"I know." She pulled away, her eyes searching Carson's. "I know you're scared. You're scared I'm going to break your heart," she whispered, finally seeing the truth in Carson's eyes.

"Yes."

Kerry tried to smile. "Funny. I was thinking the very same thing about you."

CHAPTER THIRTY

Carson stared at her cell phone, startled by its ringing. A constant fixture before she'd come to the ranch—she'd simply plugged it in to charge and had forgotten about it. She picked it up now, seeing Rebecca's name. She grinned, realizing she had missed her friend.

"I've been gone nearly a month, you just now decide to check on me?"

"The proper thing would have been for you to let me know you're safe," Rebecca said. "I assume you are?"

"Yes. But I'm glad you called." She glanced at her opened door, knowing Kerry was at the bunkhouse, but she moved to close it anyway. "I need to run something by you," she said.

"Okay. Then don't keep me in suspense."

Carson went to the window, staring out down the winding road and the valley beyond. She took a deep breath, already knowing what Rebecca's reaction was going to be. "Do you think I'm capable of falling in love?"

Silence greeted her question and she could imagine Rebecca's mind racing.

"In love? I thought I taught you better than that," she said.

Carson noticed a strange hitch in her voice and she frowned. "Is that a yes or a no?"

"What have you done?"

"I met someone. She's a consultant here at the ranch. And—"

"And you've slept with her. Good. *That* I did teach you," Rebecca said with a laugh.

"That's just it. I didn't just sleep with her. I made love to her. That's a first for me."

"Oh dear God, are you serious? You really think—"

"Yeah. I do. Crazy, right?"

"I'll say. What's she like?"

"She's not like anyone I've ever met. She wouldn't fit in with our crowd, that's for sure."

"Then what's the attraction?"

"Maybe that's the attraction. She's nothing like the women I've been with before."

"Oh, Carson, do you have any idea what you're saying?"

"Yeah. It's different for me. It's also really different for her."

Silence again. Then, "Oh my God! She's *straight*?"

"No, she's not straight," Carson said. "She's just never been with a woman before."

"Carson, sweetheart, listen to what you're saying. That's a classic line. You must know she's only after your money."

Carson laughed, although she realized the nervousness of it. "She's not after my money. She doesn't know anything about my finances. She thought I came here to claim part of the inheritance."

"Oh, Carson, don't be naive. Women are manipulative. They'll tell you whatever you want to hear. You've got to be careful, Carson. Didn't I teach you *anything*?"

"Yes, you taught me plenty," she said. "But this is different, Rebecca."

She laughed and Carson wished she'd never brought it up. Carson was scared of what she was feeling and who better to bare her soul to than Rebecca. Her friend. But she should have known better. Rebecca would never understand. She wouldn't even try to. She'd preached to Carson for years how she didn't need love, she only needed the physical act to be satisfied. Carson had believed her for a while. Until the emptiness of it all outweighed the pleasure.

"Do you really need this, Carson? You said yourself, she's not going to fit in. What's she going to do around our friends here?"

"No. She won't fit in," she said quietly. But then, Carson didn't think she fit in either. She wondered if she had *ever* fit in. So she changed the subject. "So, you're back in Manhattan?" she asked.

"Yes. I spent three weeks in San Francisco. I thought maybe you'd come back after your little trip."

"No. Sorry."

"Well, I had a good time on my own. Just let me know when you'll be coming home. I'll have a party." Rebecca laughed, the sultry laugh Carson always associated with her. "With lots of ladies for appetizers, of course," she added.

"Yeah. Okay, sure. I'll be in touch."

Carson ended the call, her jaw clenched tight. A party? Not just a party. One of Rebecca's sex parties. That only added to her conviction of how truly empty her life has been, how she only pretended it was full by keeping busy, by jetting off to Europe on a whim, by trying to follow in Rebecca's footsteps...by attending her sex parties and feigning pleasure. She tossed the phone on the dresser and shoved her hands into her pockets, her gaze still fixed on the road outside the window. Her life didn't have to be empty. She'd bought into Rebecca's reasoning because she'd needed to. That was the only way she could survive.

Not any longer. She was tired of that life. Tired of the empty feeling she had night after night, no matter how many of those nights women shared her bed. Because she was different now.

She felt different. She wasn't the same woman who left Rebecca in San Francisco. She didn't want to be that woman ever again.

It occurred to her that her relationship with Rebecca was nothing more than superficial. Had it always been that way? She'd lived with her for two years before getting her own place, but their friends were mutual. Well, they were mostly Rebecca's friends, Rebecca's lovers. Carson had only collected Rebecca's castoffs. They spent time together often but their conversations only grazed the surface. She knew nothing of Rebecca's past, and until recently, Rebecca hadn't known much about Carson's. Hell, Rebecca hadn't even asked if her father was still alive. Most likely because she had forgotten the reason Carson was in Montana in the first place.

She turned from the window, her gaze settling on the bed. The covers were still rumpled, despite Kerry's attempt to straighten them. It was the most incredible night she'd ever spent with someone. It was so intense between them, so emotionally draining. She'd never *needed* like that before. She had no explanation for it.

Yes, she did.

But after Rebecca's reaction, Carson didn't want to give voice to it. Not yet.

She found Kerry sitting under the trees near the bunkhouse, her laptop balanced on her knees. She looked up when she heard Carson approach, a smile lighting her face immediately.

"Hey."

"Hey yourself," Carson said. She sat down beside her, folding her legs under her. "Busy?"

Kerry shook her head. "Distracted."

"Oh?"

"When do you think they'll be back?"

Carson shrugged. "Another couple of hours, I'd think."

"Is it terrible of me to say I don't want them to come back?"

Carson laughed. "Not terrible, no. Cody's not stupid. He'll get a clue eventually. And he won't be happy."

"Do you think I should talk to him? I mean, just be up front with him?"

"You're determined for them to void your contract, huh?"

"Like I told you last night, the contract is not my biggest concern," Kerry said. "If they void it, they void it. I'm more concerned with you and...well, all the drama that could happen when he finds out."

"Don't worry about me. My relationship with Cody is not going to improve or worsen. It is what it is." That much was true. Her relationship with all of her brothers wasn't going to be impacted by the fact that she and Kerry were sleeping together. "Let's just see how it goes, okay?"

Kerry took a deep breath. "I'm nervous, I don't mind saying." She reached across the short distance separating them, lightly rubbing Carson's thigh. "No matter what happens, I don't regret anything," she said. "I feel like a completely different person than the one who first came here. I feel like this is me, finally."

Carson covered her hand, pressing it hard against her leg. "I know what you mean. I've been pretending to be someone I'm not, pretending that I didn't need anyone. I'd convinced myself that I was happy, but I didn't really know what that word meant. Not as an adult, anyway." She wrapped her fingers around Kerry's, squeezing. "I never knew what it felt like to truly make love with someone. To really open myself up, to give more than just sex. I never knew what it was like to give emotionally, not just physically." She brought Kerry's hand to her mouth and kissed it gently. "I felt raw and exposed after we made love," she confessed. "I was terrified, really. I didn't know what to do. I didn't know where to put all these feelings I was having."

Kerry leaned closer—apparently unmindful of Mr. Burris or his crew—and kissed her softly on the lips, lingering for long seconds before pulling back.

"You don't have to be terrified of this, Carson. I just want to embrace these feelings, because it fills me up so," Kerry said, her eyes smiling into Carson's. "You've touched a place in my heart where no one else ever has. I can't explain it any more than you can, but it's there. So I don't want to be terrified of it."

Carson didn't want to be scared of the feelings. That didn't mean she wasn't. If she were completely confident, she would have told Kerry she'd fallen in love with her. But to say those words out loud frightened the hell out of her. And really, she didn't know why. She could see her feelings mirrored back at her, could see that in Kerry's eyes. Maybe Kerry was a little bit scared too.

So she changed the subject, her glance going to the bunkhouse. "How's it going?"

Kerry smiled quickly, acknowledging that the conversation had changed. "They're making good time. There's only four of them so I thought it would drag out, but they've got the plumbing all in and they'll start on the framing next."

"Another six weeks?"

"To be totally finished, floor and all, probably. I'm still debating on only one pier and using those extra funds for the deck and sitting area. I guess I should really run it by the guys," she said.

Carson nodded. "If you want it to pass, run it by Cody first," she said with a wink.

Kerry laughed. "I think I'll do a group pitch of that. No more one-on-ones," she said.

Carson got to her feet and offered her hand, tugging Kerry up beside her. They were close but refrained from touching.

"I think I'm going to take Windstorm out," she said. "Maybe ride up the mountain and see if I can meet them. Give them the heads-up on the old man," she added. "But I don't think it'll be a surprise."

"No. The service will be Sunday?"

"Maybe tomorrow. I saw the Hanes truck go out to the family plot," she said. "I gave him the letter like Chance asked so it must have had instructions about the gravesite. Hanes is the one who buried my mother."

"Who else is buried out there? I mean, I know your mother—"

"It goes back to my great-grandparents," Carson said. "My grandparents, obviously. There are two of my father's uncles and my father's brother," she said. "There are thirteen graves total, I believe. My great-grandparents lost two children when they were babies."

"That's kinda interesting," Kerry said. "I mean, having a family cemetery like that. There's so much history."

"It's also kinda creepy," Carson said with a laugh. "Especially when you're a kid and your brothers convince you of ghosts."

Kerry laughed too, bringing her closer to Carson. This time Carson didn't refrain from touching. It was the most natural thing in the world to wrap her arms around Kerry and hug her, their quiet laughter ceasing as soon as their bodies made contact.

"God," Kerry murmured, burrowing her face against Carson's neck. "How are we going to do this? I just want to touch you."

"It's going to be hard." She smiled and quickly kissed the top of Kerry's head. "Very, very hard." *Very hard.* But she untangled herself from Kerry, backing away. "Stables. I'm going to the stables."

Kerry nodded and pointed to the bunkhouse. "And I have supervising to do."

Carson walked away without looking back, knowing it was the last time they would be alone. Tonight, her brothers would be there. Dinner would be a group event again. It would be a very solemn and mournful affair, as they would most likely lament the passing of their father. Carson couldn't begrudge them that. She wondered which of them would take it the hardest. Chance, most likely. He had taken on the role of patriarch and was the closest to him. She would have thought it would be Colt since he was such a daddy's boy as a kid, but Carson didn't see that now. In fact, Colt, much like Chase, seemed almost indifferent to his impending death. She assumed much of their grieving would be forced, if only for Chance's benefit.

She paused before going into the stables, her gaze traveling across the green valley and up to the mountains in the distance. How close to home were they? It didn't matter. She would ride for an hour. If she didn't come upon them, she'd turn back to the ranch. If nothing else, it would give her a chance to organize her thoughts, formulate a plan. She didn't really think she and Kerry could keep their affair a secret but she had to try.

For Kerry's sake.

CHAPTER THIRTY-ONE

After racing through the valley, Carson pulled Windstorm to a fast trot, finally a slower walk as they hit the trail that would take them to the first pass. She bent low, affectionately rubbing his neck.

"You like to run, don't you, boy?"

She took a deep breath, the air cooler up here than it had been in the valley. She didn't think to bring a jacket, but she had an old sweatshirt tied to the back of the saddle. She would be riding in shadows soon and the temperature would dip. She slowed Windstorm again, taking the time to glance over her shoulder at the valley down below. It was a vibrant green, still bathed in sunlight, the shadows of the mountains starting to creep across it. The lake looked small from up this high, the bunkhouse and stables nothing more than dots on the landscape. She couldn't make out the ranch house as it was hidden by trees. Her gaze went back to the bunkhouse, wondering if Kerry had watched her ride away. She knew Kerry was nervous, but she didn't know what to do to ease her trepidation.

She gave Windstorm a gentle kick and they climbed higher, the forest now becoming thick with spruce and fir trees. She'd been on this trail before as a kid, riding up hours after the herd had passed through, pretending that she was a part of the process. Funny how those same feelings came back to her now, years later. Her mother knew she did it, her only words of caution that she make it back down before dark. One Saturday, she left before daylight, making it all the way to the first pass. She'd been thirteen, a few years before she got Windstorm, but the young gelding she'd ridden back then was full of energy, and they'd made it back to the stables as the sun set behind the mountains. It had been a day of adventure for her, her first full day out alone. That night at dinner, just Carson and her mother, she'd talked nonstop about her trip, and her mother had listened to her every word. They both knew that once her father and brothers returned, there would be no more mention of it.

After riding more than an hour, she was about ready to turn back, thinking the storm the other night must have set them back a day after all. But Windstorm's ears perked up and he gave a low whinny.

"What do you hear, boy?"

He shook his head and neck, his long white mane fanning out and Carson smoothed it down, her gaze following his farther up the trail. She heard the choppy steps of the horses long before she saw them—her brothers, Johnny Mac, the two full-time cowboys—Greg and Lucas—and the three seasonal cowboys they'd hired on this year. The mules that followed behind were carrying a lighter load than when they started out.

They all stopped when they saw her. Chance's and Cody's eyes wide. Chase was laughing delightfully, but it was Colt who surprised her.

"Holy shit, Carson, you're on Windstorm? Are you crazy?"

Carson laughed. "What? He's just a big baby. I can't believe you guys are all scared of him."

"That horse nearly broke my back when I tried to ride him," Johnny Mac said. "I nearly took my pistol after him."

Carson knew he was teasing but she took offense nonetheless. "You lay a hand on him and I'll take a pistol to you."

Chase nudged his horse closer, his grin still wide. "Show off," he murmured.

"He's as gentle as a lamb," she said.

"He's a beast. Low on the temperament scale, remember?" He nodded at her. "But you look good on him. Just like old times."

"What are you doing up here?" Chance asked.

"Yeah? Is Kerry okay?" Cody added.

Carson flicked her eyes at Chase, just barely avoiding a dramatic eye roll. "Yes, Kerry is fine. But...the old man passed away," she said bluntly.

"When?"

"Thursday morning."

"Did you call Hanes?" Chance asked.

"No, Chance. I left him up there. He's still in his room," she said sarcastically. "Of course I called Hanes."

Chance looked at the brothers, then Johnny Mac, who held one of the cattle dogs in his lap. Solemn faces, some. She was surprised there were no outward displays of grief. She had apparently misjudged their relationship with him.

"Well, it wasn't like we weren't expecting it," Chance said, as if trying to explain their lack of emotion at the news.

"He was in a lot of pain," Cody added.

Again, Colt was the one who surprised her. "Are we going to pretend we're heartbroken over this?" he asked. "He hasn't been the same since...well, since mom died," he said, glancing over at Carson. "He always treated you bad, but not us. Not until she died. Then he was cold and hard, even with us. He lost the few friends he still had after that." He kicked his horse, moving again down the trail. "I, for one, am glad it's over with."

Carson expected a rebuttal from Chance, at least, but none came. He, too, lightly gave his horse a kick and followed Colt, the others joining him.

"Damn, where did that come from?" she asked as she and Chase hung back.

"It's what we're all thinking, I guess. But hell, we never talk. I had no idea Colt felt that way."

They started down the mountain, a good ways behind the others. All the guys sported scruffy beards except Chase. He was clean-shaven. She pointed at his face. "You took a razor along? That's just wrong."

"I don't go for that rugged cowboy look," he said, rubbing his face. "So Windstorm let you ride him, huh?"

"Just like old times. I cried when I saw him," she admitted. "He remembered me. He went behind me like he used to, looking for a carrot."

"Oh, yeah. You used to hide them in your back pocket."

"The first time I got on him, I let him run. Man, that was great. You could practically see him smiling."

"I know he's missed that. We all tried to ride him after you left. He wouldn't tolerate anyone. Half the time he wouldn't even let us get a saddle on him. We finally just gave up."

She leaned forward, affectionately rubbing his neck. "I don't know why we bonded, but he's as gentle as a lamb with me."

"He always was."

Carson reached behind her for the water bottle she had tied to the saddle. "So, how was the storm?"

"Pretty bad. Even down low like we were, the lightning was close. We had a hell of a time keeping the herd together." He raised an eyebrow. "Everything okay here?"

"Of course. Why wouldn't it be?"

He laughed. "Come on, sis. We've made our small talk. You're hiding something. Are you going to make me guess?"

She felt a blush cross her face. "Is it obvious?"

"What? Just because you're glowing I shouldn't assume that you've had sex?"

"I'm not glowing," she said weakly, knowing it was true.

He laughed again. "Oh, yeah, you are. Are you going to tell Cody?"

"Hell no."

"Car, he's going to find out. It's going to be ugly."

"And it'll be just as ugly if we tell him outright."

"True." He glanced at her and grinned. "So? How did it happen? I want details."

"You're not getting details. But it just happened," she said. "I don't know how to explain it, Chase. She opened doors that I thought I'd shut tight, you know? The attraction was just too strong to fight." She glanced at him. "For both of us," she added.

"How does she feel about it? I mean, with Cody and all?"

"She's scared. She's scared about what he's going to do to me."

"Yeah. Like shoot you," Chase teased.

"I think I'm in love with her," Carson blurted out. "That's crazy, right? I mean—"

"Since you don't fall in love?"

"Yeah. That."

They were silent as they followed the others, then Chase laughed quietly. "So, did she move into your room yet?"

"I'm glad you're finding this amusing," she said, her smile matching his. Actually, she was just glad to be able to tell someone how she felt. Someone besides Rebecca.

"I'm just trying to figure out how you're going to pull this off."

"You think Cody is going to sneak up the stairs at night and do a bed check?"

"Wouldn't surprise me. Especially if he's suspicious. But—"

"Why does he think he has a hold on her? Why does he think he has any say in this?"

"You know, I think that of all of us, Cody is the only one who wanted that traditional marriage and family. We used to think Chance was the one, that he'd marry Marla and they'd live here and start a family. Don't know why that ended, of course, but I think maybe he didn't really want that. Then there's Colt. He doesn't date. Never really did." He grinned. "And you know my preference. So that leaves Cody to carry on the family name."

"And he thinks Kerry is just the one to do it? God, is he in for a shock."

"I think it would be more of a disappointment than a shock. I mean, come on, he's not blind. Surely he could tell there was an attraction between you and Kerry. Why else was he so adamant that you stay away from her?"

"Yes, he could tell. But I think he just assumed I was playing with her, playing with him. Just like high school. And she did present herself as straight," Carson added.

"But she's not?" Chase asked cautiously.

Carson shook her head. "Just because she'd never been with a woman before doesn't mean she was straight. Chase, this isn't just about sex. With me, that's all it ever was before. But not this time. It's much deeper than that. We have this amazing connection between us. It's like we were lovers before, in another life."

He laughed. "Good God, Carson, you're making me nauseous. Another life?"

She grinned. "What? Too romantic?"

"Oh, hell, maybe I'm just jealous," he said. "I'd like to meet someone, fall in love, build a life, a home. This," he said, waving his hand out to the valley below them, "isn't enough any longer. Getting away a few times a year isn't enough."

"Then get out, Chase. The old man's gone. Tell the guys you want to move on, start your own place."

"I know. It's just this is all I've known. It's scary to think about leaving and starting over."

"Not scary. Exciting," she said. "Challenging. Something fresh and new. Not scary."

"And what about you? What do you want?"

"I know what I don't want," she said. "I don't want to go back to Manhattan. I don't want to go back to that life. I think I belong out here." She glanced at him. "I don't mean here, as in the ranch, but out here with the wide open spaces, the mountains and valley. This feels right to me."

"But?"

"If I stayed out here somewhere I'd want Kerry with me. And that's something we've not talked about. She's just starting her own business. I don't know how we'd manage that. I don't know if she'd even want to." Were those words an excuse in case Kerry didn't feel the same? No. Because she knew. Kerry had fallen in love too. And God, it felt good to know that. No, it felt good to *believe* that. She had no doubts.

Not anymore.

CHAPTER THIRTY-TWO

Kerry knew he would seek her out. She knew that. And she thought she was prepared. Mr. Burris and his crew had already left and she was doing a walk-through in the bunkhouse. She'd glanced several times out the window, looking for them...looking for Carson. But when Cody burst into the bunkhouse, a big smile on his unshaven face, she wasn't prepared. She wasn't prepared for the bear hug he gave her. She wasn't prepared for his words.

"I missed you."

She shouldn't have been so annoyed at his exuberance, but she was. And she was annoyed at herself for letting it get this far in the first place. She took a step away from him as he tried to kiss her, his lips grazing her cheek instead of her mouth.

"You're back?" she asked, her voice sounding strange to her.

She made a show of looking behind him. "Where is everyone?"

"Still at the barn." He looked around the room, trying to hide his embarrassment over the botched kiss. "They've made progress," he said, taking a quick walk down the new hallway.

"Yes. Plumbing is finished. It'll take another week to finish with the electrical. Then they'll begin with the siding and we'll finally have rooms."

"You're doing a good job."

She smiled. "Well, Mr. Burris is doing a good job. I tend to get underfoot so he's always happy when Carson comes to occupy my time." The words slipped out honestly, but she saw the change in his expression immediately. At first she panicked, wanting to take the words back.

"Occupy your time?"

She was surprised by the sudden anger in his eyes and she should have been expecting it. "Yes. We've been out riding. She's showing me around the ranch, remember?"

"I told you to stay away from her," he said. "She's trouble."

Kerry matched his anger as she stepped closer to him. "You *told* me to stay away from her? Cody, why do you think you have the authority to tell me who—or not—to spend time with? I like your sister. We get along great. You obviously have issues with her but that's your business."

"Issues?"

"Or whatever you want to call it. I enjoy her company."

He grabbed her arm, his eyes accusing now. "What has she done?"

She pulled away from him, frightened by his actions. "What are you talking about?"

He pointed his finger at her. "You stay away from her."

She heard voices outside and knew the others were coming inside to inspect the progress as well. She faced him, wishing she could just tell him the truth. But she couldn't. She was actually afraid of his anger. Before she could reply to his directive, Colt and Chance walked in and she stepped away from him.

"Wow, look at this," Colt said, his smile nearly contagious. "They did a lot in a week."

"Yes. They had the old walls down in two days." Only then

did she realize she hadn't offered her condolences to any of them for the loss of their father. Judging by the looks on their faces, she could almost think Carson hadn't told them. She glanced at Cody, but went to Chance first, lightly touching his arm. "I'm sorry about your father," she said quietly.

He nodded. "Thank you. But it was time."

"Yeah," Colt said. "He laid up there six weeks waiting to die. I'm glad it's over."

"I wish you'd quit saying that," Cody said. "It's almost like you wanted him to die."

"Didn't you?"

"He was our father," Cody said loudly. "Not some stranger."

"I didn't mean it like that," Colt said. "I just mean he's been so sick, in pain, he wanted to die. He told us that when they brought him home from the hospital. Hell, none of us thought it would take six weeks."

"Let's don't argue," Chance said. "I'll call Hanes. We'll have the service tomorrow."

Colt nodded, then looked back at her. "Looks great, Kerry. But I'm ready for a shower and a shave," he said.

"Me too," Chance added. "And I'm looking forward to Martha's cooking."

"I think she's got a huge roast in the oven," Kerry said.

Colt and Chance left and Kerry hoped Cody would join them, but he stayed, presumably to continue their discussion. Before he could say anything, Carson and Chase were standing in the doorway. Kerry hoped her relief didn't show on her face as she smiled at them.

"Welcome back."

"It's good to be back." Chase, too, inspected the work on the bunkhouse. "It hardly looks like the same place," he said.

"They've been busy," she said, chancing a quick glance at Carson. Cody didn't miss a thing as he stepped between them.

"Now that I'm back, Carson, I can take over the chore of showing Kerry around the ranch," he said.

Carson raised an eyebrow. "It's certainly been no chore, Cody," she said. "We've had fun. Or at least I have."

Kerry saw the anger on Cody's face, but she didn't know

what to say to temper Carson's words. It was Chase who tried to lighten the mood.

"I guess you have had fun," he said. "Windstorm's probably making up for lost time."

"We've been all over," Carson said and Kerry was thankful she didn't continue to bait Cody. "Found the old trail to the Conley Ranch."

"Is it still there? I haven't been out that way in years," Chase said. He glanced at Kerry. "Did Car find you a nice mare to ride?"

"Ginger," Kerry said. "And she's very gentle."

"Well, I can take you out next time," Cody said again and Carson just shrugged.

Kerry didn't argue, but she had no intention of going anywhere with Cody. Again, it was Chase who intervened and Kerry suspected Carson must have told him about them.

"Come on, bro. We need a shower. We stink," he said. "I'm sure these ladies would appreciate that."

Kerry thought Cody would refuse, but, after sending Carson a threatening glance, he followed Chase. "I guess I'll see you back at the house then," he said as he turned to go.

Kerry felt Carson's eyes on her and she turned to her once the guys were up the path and away from them.

"Are you okay?"

Kerry shook her head. "He's so...so angry," she said.

Carson's eyebrows shot up. "You told him?"

"No. That's just it. He's angry at the possibility of it, I guess. Like he can sense something."

Carson reached for her, pulling her close. "Come here," she murmured, holding Kerry tight against her.

Kerry sunk into her body, her arms sliding around Carson's slender waist. She so wished they were still alone, wished they didn't have to hide. Part of her just wanted to run away with Carson and say to hell with the ranch, the conversion and the damn contract. But not exactly the most practical thing to do when starting your own business. But she hadn't counted on falling in love, certainly not with a woman.

"I want to tell him," she said. "I want to tell them all." She lifted her head. "If they void the contract, then they do, but I can't continue to do this."

"What did he do?"

"He tried to kiss me." Carson's jaw clenched, and Kerry smiled at Carson's obvious annoyance with her brother. "I managed to avoid it, but it's only going to escalate. I doubt my excuse of 'I'm not attracted to you' will work."

"He tried to *kiss* you?"

This time Kerry did laugh, seeing the fire of jealousy in Carson's eyes. "Carson, even if this thing between us hadn't happened, I still wouldn't be interested in Cody."

Carson relaxed and smiled. "No. That's because he's a guy."

Kerry let her fingers entwine with Carson's, holding hers tightly. "Does it bother you?" she asked. "That I haven't been with a woman before," she clarified.

"No. I just want you to be sure. And I know that's a lot to ask," she said. "How can you be sure? You've always dated men."

"Yes. But no matter what happens between you and me, I've at least realized that I've been dating the wrong gender," she said. She released Carson's hand, her fingers sliding up her arm to her shoulder, then across her chest, just brushing against her breasts. She heard Carson's surprised gasp, and it was enough to stir her desire. Kerry pushed into her, holding her against the wall, her lips moving up her neck, feeling Carson's rapid pulse beating. She moaned as her teeth nipped at her skin, feeling the power she had over Carson at that moment. Her hands were driving Carson wild, her lips and mouth making Carson squirm. And Kerry loved it.

"Kerry, we should maybe—"

"Shh," Kerry silenced her with her mouth, kissing her firmly, letting her know she had no intention of stopping. She should stop, of course. They shouldn't be doing this, not here. But Kerry's want and need won out, and she didn't mind saying the words out loud. "I want you."

Again, a gasp from Carson and then her hands were pulling Kerry closer, not pushing her away. Kerry stilled Carson's hands, firmly holding them at her side, meeting her eyes, seeing her desire mirrored there. Both their chests were heaving, trying to draw breath. "I want you," Kerry whispered again. She didn't wait for a reply. Her mouth found Carson's, her hands tugged Carson's shirt from her jeans, touching skin, her fingers moving across soft flesh, then she impatiently pushed her bra aside, cupping both her breasts.

"Kerry," Carson murmured, her body arching against Kerry's.

Kerry dipped her head, holding Carson's shirt and bra up as her lips closed around a nipple. She suckled it softly, then tugged at it, her teeth scraping against it. She heard Carson groan, and she let herself be pulled roughly against Carson as their bodies pressed together.

Their breathing was labored, the sound loud in the empty bunkhouse. She went back to Carson's mouth as her hands went to Carson's jeans, her fingers unbuttoning them quickly. She didn't hesitate as she slipped her hand inside. She wanted her. She wanted her like this—hard and fast. Carson was wet, ready for her. She shoved two fingers inside her, feeling Carson close around her. She pulled out, adding a third finger, relishing the loud moans coming from Carson. She used her hips to drive her fingers deeper into Carson, her mouth resting against Carson's neck as she struggled to breathe.

It was all still fresh and new—this want. She knew that whatever she needed, Carson would give her. Carson wouldn't say no. She wanted it just as badly. Her moans, the desperate grip she had on Kerry, told her as much.

"God, Kerry," Carson panted.

"Yes," Kerry whispered, saying the word that would answer any unasked questions, the word that would tell Carson she would agree to anything at that moment.

Carson's fingers dug almost painfully into her shoulders and Kerry drove her fingers deeper, harder, inside her. She used her thumb to graze her clit, stroking it with each thrust. Carson was close, her hips moving wildly with Kerry's. Kerry ignored the throbbing ache between her own legs as she brought Carson closer to orgasm.

"Let go," Kerry murmured, her lips moving to Carson's ear, her tongue snaking inside. "Let go," she said again, her fingers curling deliciously inside her, feeling Carson heed her command as her orgasm claimed her.

"*God*," Carson groaned, her body shuddering against Kerry, her wetness soaking her hand.

Kerry's fingers slipped out of her and she wrapped her arms around Carson's waist, resting against her, trying to catch her breath. But Carson didn't let her rest. In one motion, she unbuttoned her jeans and pulled them down, sliding her panties with them. Carson fell to her knees in front of Kerry and Kerry gasped when she felt Carson's breath on her damp thighs. Carson cupped her hips, bringing her forward to her waiting mouth.

"*Jesus*...Carson." Kerry braced herself against the wall as Carson shoved her legs farther apart. "*Carson*," she moaned when she felt Carson's tongue stroking her. Her hips rocked against Carson's face, increasing the friction between them. Then Carson's lips closed over her clit, sucking it into her mouth like her nipple. Kerry groaned loudly, the wet sucking sounds driving her over the edge quickly. She bit her lip to keep from screaming out.

Her gaze was unfocused as she looked at Carson, still on her knees, her mouth still buried against her. Kerry touched her hair, bringing Carson up. She kissed her, slower now, her need sated for the time being. They leaned together, their skin damp with sweat from their exertion, their breath slowly returning to normal.

"Thank you," she whispered. "I—"

"I know," Carson murmured. "I wanted that too."

Kerry tucked her face against Carson's neck, feeling her pulse finally slowing. She rubbed the spot with her tongue, then sighed.

"Can we stay like this forever?"

She felt Carson smile, felt her lips kiss her hair, felt her arms tighten against her.

"Yes. I'd like that very much."

CHAPTER THIRTY-TWO

Clouds were building to the west and Kerry assumed Martha's forecast of a storm was coming true. Her gaze turned back to the road, no longer able to see their trucks. They had left for their father's service and burial. She'd never met the man and didn't feel she had a place at the service, despite Cody's offer that she could accompany them. That alone made her decline, but Carson had already told her she shouldn't feel any obligation to attend.

She let out a deep breath as she leaned against the railing, her eyes again going to the thick clouds making their way across the valley. Dinner last night had been a tedious affair, and she wasn't sure how many more she could take. Cody sat next to her, of course, but Carson had been across the table and they'd found their eyes meeting often. Chase had tried to keep the conversation light and impersonal and Kerry was thankful. Even Colt seemed to sense the tension and made an effort to keep the conversation friendly, taking them down memory lane as he recanted tales from their younger years.

Inevitably, the conversation turned to Carson and her exploits, and before long, Angie Bonner's name was mentioned, causing the brothers to roar with laughter as Colt told the story of Cody catching Carson in the hayloft with his girlfriend. Kerry managed to contain her laughter, having heard the story from Carson in a very different context. Cody did not find any humor in it, his face red with anger and perhaps embarrassment. It was then that Kerry wished she could run and hide.

"That's what I'm talking about," Cody told her. "She uses people for whatever suits her. That's why you need to stay away from her. You can't trust her."

"Come on, Cody. That was a long time ago," Chase reasoned.

"And you think she's changed?" Cody stared across the table at Carson. "Was it fun for you? Seducing Angie? You probably scarred her for life."

"You think I seduced her? I was sixteen. What did I know about it?"

"You obviously knew enough," Cody said loudly. "I can't believe you forced yourself on her like that."

Carson laughed then, and Kerry knew she'd taken all she was going to. Kerry's gaze focused on Chase, not Carson, as she silently asked him to intervene.

"I didn't force her, Cody. She begged me. The first time was just a quickie behind the stables, but it was enough for her to know I could give her what you obviously couldn't," Carson said.

Kerry leaned away from Cody as she could literally feel the heat of his anger.

"The first time?" he asked, his voice tense.

There was silence around the table as all eyes went to Carson. Kerry realized Carson was completely unfazed by it all as her lips twitched in a smile.

"What? You think the day you caught us in the hayloft was the only time?"

Cody stood so quickly, he knocked his chair down. "You goddamn bitch," he spat. "I should—"

"Sit down," Chance yelled as he got to his feet. "Sit down and shut up. Our father just died and this is what we do? Have a family argument? That was fifteen years ago, Cody. Get over it."

But Cody didn't sit down. He glanced quickly at Kerry, then turned and stormed from the room, leaving behind only silence. Colt was the one to finally break it.

"That was awkward."

"Kinda funny though," Chase said with a short laugh.

"Quit baiting him," Chance said to Carson.

"Me? I didn't bring it up."

Chance had turned to Kerry then. "I'm sorry you had to witness all that," he said, his apology sincere.

After dinner, Kerry had escaped to the kitchen to help Martha clean up despite her protests. There was simply too much tension, and she didn't want to join them in their father's study for drinks.

She'd gone to bed before the others, never seeing Cody again. She went to sleep hoping Carson would wake her when she came up. It was the early morning hours before Kerry stirred, pleasantly surprised to find a warm body wrapped around hers. Carson was sleeping soundly and Kerry only snuggled closer to her warmth. When she woke later, she was alone and wondered if she'd dreamed it all. But she'd rolled over, clutching the pillow to her, smelling Carson's unique scent and knew it had been no dream.

The midday sun was now overhead, blue sky still dominating, at least for a few more hours. Mr. Hanes had called earlier, letting the brothers know he was on his way with their father's body. The service would be short, Carson had said, with no one in attendance except them and perhaps Johnny Mac. They would bury him close to their mother in a spot their father had picked out years ago. It would be Carson's first visit to the family plot since the day of her mother's funeral.

That was another reason she had declined to attend. She

didn't know how Carson would handle it, and Kerry knew if Carson got emotional, if she cried, then Kerry would want to comfort her and the ease with which Carson would slip into her arms would surely give away their secret. She could only imagine another scene like the one last night.

"Are you okay, Miss Kerry?"

Kerry turned, finding Martha watching her. She nodded, then accepted the glass of iced tea Martha held.

"Thank you. And yes, I'm fine."

"Have you talked to Cody yet?"

"No. And after last night's episode at dinner, I don't think we will," she said. She took a sip of tea, meeting Martha's eyes questioningly. "This thing with me and Carson, you don't seem bothered by it," she said. "I'm surprised."

"Why? Because I'm a simple woman from a tiny town in the middle of nowhere?"

Kerry smiled. "Something like that, yes."

"I found out the hard way how short life can be," Martha said. "I lost my husband and my only child one night in a storm. They hit a tree. They were killed instantly. I never looked for love again after that." She shrugged. "I've been living here, taking care of the boys since they lost their own mother. The first few years, I worked just to try to forget," she said. "I never thought I'd make this my home. But I think you were right when you suspected they weren't all close. I think they just pretended sometimes. There hasn't been any love here. Not really. Not until recently," she said with a smile. "I hope I'm not out of line to say this, but when you and Miss Carson look at each other, I see so much love. It just fills the room around you."

Kerry reached over and squeezed her arm. "Thank you. And no, you're not out of line," she said quietly. "Like I told you before, this is new for me. Not just the fact that Carson is a woman, but...well—"

"Being in love?" Martha guessed.

Kerry felt a blush cross her face as she looked away. "Yes. Being in love is new too."

"Honey, don't shy away from it. Grab it and hold on to it. It can be taken away so quickly sometimes."

Kerry squeezed her arm again. "I'm sorry about your family."

"It was a late spring storm, full of wind and lightning and cold rain," Martha said. "Probably much like the one we'll have tonight. Every time a storm blows in, I think of the accident. I think of what could have been. My Beverly was only sixteen. She had her whole life in front of her." She sighed. "But accidents happen, don't they."

Kerry watched Martha's eyes swimming in sadness, but the older woman forced a smile to her face anyway. Kerry returned it with a slight nod as Martha turned and left her. Kerry let her gaze slip back to the valley, then to the sky where the clouds were continuing to build. Off in the distance, she heard the first faint rumble of thunder.

Carson stared across at the somber faces of her brothers. Somber, yes, but not riddled with grief. Not like when their mother died. She wondered what Mr. Hanes thought of the whole thing. Here they were, five siblings and Johnny Mac, her father's oldest friend—and hired hand—standing around a casket that cost a small fortune, waiting for someone to speak a few words.

Chance finally cleared his throat, his hands nervously twisting his cowboy hat around.

"Our father died right where he was born—here at the ranch. I think we're all sorry to see him pass, but thankful his fight is over." He looked up, his gaze fixed on Carson. "He had regrets, I'm sure," he said. "He was a proud man, never one to admit his mistakes."

Carson nodded, surprised to feel her eyes damp. Not because of her father, but just for the fact that Chance had acknowledged the rift between them.

"He joins our beloved mother," he continued and Carson looked at her grave for the first time, seeing the beautiful headstone but unable to read the words there. She squeezed her eyes shut, wishing Kerry were there beside her. Kerry would hold her hand tightly, would keep her grounded. Instead, she linked her own hands together, squeezing her fingers until they hurt.

"He joins his parents and his brother and his grandparents. All of them worked this land at some time, worked it just as we work it today," Chance said. "Because of them, this is ours." He looked up and Carson was surprised at the hint of a smile on his face. "For better or worse," he finished in a murmur and Colt joined him in a quiet laugh. Chase, too, looked amused. Cody, however, stood off by himself, his face expressionless.

Chance put his hat back on, signaling the end. "May they all rest in peace." He glanced at the crew standing discreetly away from them. "Thank you, Mr. Hanes," he said with a nod. He headed to his truck and Colt and Cody followed. Johnny Mac lingered a second longer, then he too turned to go.

Carson felt Chase come up beside her and he took her hand. "Come on. Let's go see her."

Carson nodded, letting Chase lead her the short distance to her mother's grave. She realized then how haphazardly their family cemetery was laid out.

"Why isn't he buried closer to her?"

"He would have had to cut through the roots of that spruce tree. The old man planted that tree after mom died. You know how much she liked spruce."

"Yeah. I remember. She planted enough of them around the house."

"He picked this spot out himself," Chase said. "It's creepy."

"What?"

"Picking out a spot to be buried."

Carson smiled. "Yeah. Where's your spot?"

Chase laughed. "Not here. I've been stuck on this ranch long enough. When I find my little slice of heaven, I think I want to be cremated and, you know, scattered."

Carson leaned closer, resting her head on his shoulder. "There were no tears, Chase. Not a one. What's up with that?"

"Some things you just can't fake."

She sighed, knowing it was true. "Do you come up here to see her much?"

"A few times a year. The old man came up here at least once

a week. He'd sit over there," he said, motioning to where the casket sat, "and talk to her."

"It's funny," she said. "While I was gone, I missed her so much. I couldn't bear to think of her. I would be overcome with grief. Now that I'm back here, I don't miss her as much. It's like, like I can almost feel her still, you know."

"Being back among familiar things, places," he said quietly. "Maybe you don't miss her because you've allowed yourself to think about her, talk about her. You've let your memories come back."

She nodded. "Yes. I shut my memories out for so long. I didn't want to remember. It just brought pain."

"And now?"

"Now the memories bring a smile, happiness. I have fond memories of my childhood. Mostly," she said.

"So coming back was a good thing?"

"Yes. It was the best thing. Thank you for making me."

"You're welcome."

She leaned closer and kissed his cheek. "Thank you for reaching out to me. If you hadn't, I would still be that bitter, lonely person I had turned into. It's like you freed me of that, Chase."

"And Kerry?"

Carson smiled. "And Kerry. God, I wouldn't have met her. I wouldn't know what it was like to be touched by her, to be loved by her. It's amazing how life's turns take you places, isn't it?"

"Yeah, it is." He tugged her hand, leading her back to his truck. They both nodded at Mr. Hanes and Carson assumed they wanted to finish up. "I hate to bring this up again, but what about Cody? You've got to tell him."

"Tell him? You saw how crazy he got last night. Can you imagine what he'll do when he finds out Kerry and I are sleeping together?"

"Kerry needs to tell him. He'll take it better coming from her. You, he might shoot."

Carson closed the door and glanced back at the cemetery, watching as her father's casket was unceremoniously lowered into the ground. The finality of it hit her then and she realized she would never have the chance to reconcile with him. She sighed. Did she need it? He said he was sorry. He said he was wrong. Was that enough?

"You okay?"

"Yeah," she said quickly. "I'm fine. It's just...it's over now."

"Maybe it's time, Car. It's time you let go of it all."

"I think maybe I already have."

CHAPTER THIRTY-THREE

Kerry visibly jumped as the loud crack of thunder rattled the windows. Dark clouds had long ago obscured the sun, making the late afternoon seem like dusk. She found Martha staring out the kitchen window, watching the clouds and rain swirl around them. She stood next to her, finally reaching out to lightly rub the older woman's arm.

"They were coming home from a school play," she said. "Beverly loved to sing and dance, to act. He went alone to it. I had a bad case of the flu. I was in bed with fever." She turned to Kerry, her eyes sad. "Storm came out of nowhere really. Like this. Sunny one minute, thunder and lightning the next." She sighed. "The house was dark and I was lying in bed, watching the show, thinking how beautiful it was. I had no idea I would lose my family that night to that very same storm."

Kerry didn't offer words of condolences or sorrow. She knew they weren't needed and weren't really appropriate. Martha was just remembering, something she most likely always did silently. Having Kerry beside her allowed her to give voice to her memories. So she squeezed her arm affectionately instead as she remained silent.

Finally Martha stirred, a sad smile on her face. "Thank you," she whispered.

A bright flash of lightning and clap of thunder moved them away from the window. Kerry's eyes went down the road to the stables.

"They're not back yet, are they?"

"No. But the boys will be careful, don't worry. This lightning may have them stuck inside though."

Chase, Colt and Carson had hurried down to the stables to secure the horses. They thought they'd have time but in an instant, the storm was upon them. Kerry now wished she'd gone along, but Cody's wary eyes had stopped her. She didn't want to cause a scene so she'd stayed behind, offering to help Martha in the kitchen to avoid being alone with Cody. He seemed to sense her hesitation and left her, going back into his own room while Chance said he had some paperwork to tend to.

It had been at least thirty minutes since they'd driven off and Kerry was getting worried. With lightning all around them, she hoped they weren't out in the pasture trying to corral the horses. Hopefully they'd gotten to them in time and were just waiting out the storm in the stables. That thought didn't ease her worry as she went back to the window, trying to see through the rain-splattered pane.

At first, she thought it was just lightning, but it lingered and grew. Her eyes widened as she realized it was a fire.

"Oh my God! Martha, come look."

"What is it?"

"Looks like fire."

"Oh, dear Lord, it's not the barn, is it?"

Kerry's heart caught in her throat, and without thinking she ran out the kitchen door, ignoring Martha's call for her to come back inside. The wind and rain hit her, but she didn't care as she ran blindly down the road, her only thought, that of Carson's safety.

When a streak of lightning sizzled overhead she instinctively ducked, closing her eyes as thunder boomed all around her. She stumbled and fell, vaguely aware of voices calling to her from the house. The rain felt like ice as it pelted her face but she ran on, squinting through the downpour to keep from falling. As she got closer, she saw that it wasn't the barn that was on fire—it was the bunkhouse. Her relief was short-lived as she saw figures running between the barn and bunkhouse.

She ran too, then screamed as lightning hit one of the pines—their picnic pine—and split it in two.

"Carson!" she yelled, brushing the rain from her face, trying to find her. "Carson!" she yelled again, the wind carrying the sound of her voice away. The barn door stood open and she ran toward the light, amazed that they still had power.

"Jesus Christ, Kerry," Carson said as she grabbed her. "What the hell are you doing out here?"

"The fire, I thought it was the barn," she said between gasps of breath. "I thought you were hurt—"

"Lightning hit the bunkhouse. There's nothing we can do."

"I'm sorry. God, I was just so worried about you."

They stared at each other, both soaking wet. Then Carson pulled her into a tight hug and Kerry clung to her, her body trembling now as her adrenaline ebbed.

"Don't ever do that again," Carson said quietly into her ear. "The lightning, you could have been killed."

"I didn't think. I'm sorry," she said again. She pulled out of her arms, looking at the amused faces of Chase and Colt. She blushed profusely as she was totally embarrassed, but Carson didn't release her hand when she tried to move away. "I guess denying this and saying we're just friends isn't going to work?"

Colt shook his head and laughed as he glanced at Chase. "Like we didn't see this coming from a mile away."

What none of them saw coming was Cody, the rain dripping down his face not enough to hide his rage as his eyes locked on their clasped hands.

"You goddamn bitch," he yelled, forcefully pushing Kerry

out of the way as his hands landed on Carson. "I could kill you right now."

Kerry tumbled backward, falling away from Carson. She screamed as Cody swung, knocking Carson to her knees. Chase jumped in front of his next punch, taking the hit squarely in the nose.

"Stop it," Kerry screamed, frantically crawling over to where Carson lay. Blood trickled out of the corner of her mouth, and she was blinking at her as if trying to clear her head. She held her hand up to Cody as he bent over them. "Stop it!"

Stepping into the barn, Chance helped Colt grab Cody's flailing arms. Chance pushed Cody back against the wall, his face as red as Cody's.

"Don't be goddamn stupid," he said loudly as Cody tried to get away.

Cody's eyes blazed at Carson. "Are you happy now? I liked her. I *wanted* her. I wanted to marry her! Why is it every time I like somebody, you have to take them away from me? It's nothing but a goddamn game to you. That's all it's ever been."

Carson sat up, rubbing her cheek. "You're wrong. It's never been a game."

"Bullshit!"

Kerry stood up then, standing between them. "Why do you think this is all Carson? Why do you think I didn't have a part in this? Me? It has nothing to do with you, nothing to do with Carson. It's me," she said, tapping her chest.

Cody shook his head. "No, I don't believe that."

"I'm sorry, but it's true."

"Fine." He jerked his arm out of Colt's hold. "Then I want you off the ranch. First thing in the morning." He pointed at Carson. "And you, I never want to see your ass again. Both of you, I want you out of here."

"That's not how we make decisions around here," Chance said.

"Well we don't have a bunkhouse anymore," Colt said. "There goes our guest ranch idea."

"Insurance will cover that," Chance said. "Let's don't—"

"You can talk all you want to, but I want them gone," Cody

said. He stomped back outside into the storm and no one tried to stop him.

Kerry helped Carson to her feet then extended a hand to Chase. He had a steady stream of blood running out of his nose.

"I'm sorry. I'm so sorry," she said.

"It's okay. A broken nose will make me look a little rugged, don't you think?"

She smiled at him, then turned to the others. "I'm really sorry. This is my fault. I never should have—"

"Don't apologize," Chance said. "It's not your fault." He glanced at Carson and raised an eyebrow. "You okay?"

"It's not the first time he's hit me," she admitted.

"But it'll be the last."

"Yeah, yeah. I'll get out of here. You won't have to see me again," Carson said. Kerry whipped her head around, her brow furrowed. Surely Chance wasn't just kicking Carson off the ranch?

"That's not what I meant. Cody has always had anger issues. Hell, the old man should have gotten him some help when he threw you out of the hayloft and broke your arm."

Colt laughed. "I'd have thrown her out too if she was fucking my girlfriend."

Carson winced. "Must you be so crass?"

Colt glanced at Kerry. "Sorry. That was rude of me."

"Well, when you're sixteen, I guess that's all you're doing is fucking, isn't it?" Kerry said with a smile.

Carson groaned. "Can we get off of this subject, please? We do have a fire outside, you know."

"A fire that will have to burn itself out," Chance said. He went to the barn door, the storm moving away from them now as the lightning flashed across the valley. "The rain will help, but I doubt we can salvage anything." He glanced over at Colt and motioned him to follow. "Let's go check it out."

Colt put his hat on, then paused on his way out. "Welcome home, sis," he said with a smile. "It's just like old times, ain't it?"

Kerry guided Carson over to sit on a bale of hay. "Colt seems to have warmed up to you," she said. "Here, you too," she said as she sat Chase down beside Carson. "Hold your head back."

"Yeah, what's up with Colt?" Carson asked.

"Cody was an ass the whole trip. We all got sick of it. Ragging on you, planning his marriage proposal to Kerry. He even—"

"Marriage?" Kerry shook her head. "Seriously?"

"Seriously," he said. "There are some towels over there," he said, pointing to a closed cabinet. "Can't vouch for how clean they are."

"Thanks for taking the hit for me," Carson said. "I owe you."

"Like Chance said, he's not going to hit you anymore."

Kerry found the towels, pulling one that was still neatly folded from the bottom of the stack. She turned the water on at the faucet to dampen the towel then took it to Chase, holding it against his nose.

"The horses, were they okay?" she said, glancing at Carson.

"Yeah. We only had two of the young foals who tried to take flight, but we got them all."

"I need to get a towel for you too," she said, wiping at the blood near her lip.

"I'm fine, Kerry. Really. He just grazed me."

Kerry took her hand and squeezed it. "What did you mean when you said it wasn't the first time he'd hit you? There were other times besides the hayloft?"

"Oh, Cody's always had a temper. I seemed to be the one he took it out on."

"But he hit you?"

"The problem was, she never told anybody," Chase said, "so we didn't know. The one time Chance saw him hit her, he bloodied Cody's lip."

"Yeah. The only time Chance stood up for me," Carson said. "But Cody left me alone after that. Until the hayloft incident."

It wasn't the time to get into it now, but the fact that Cody had used her as a punching bag disturbed her greatly and Carson's acceptance of it even more so. Of course, the Carson she knew today would never put up with that. Maybe as kids, there was a certain pecking order and Carson had been at the bottom. Carson's confusion over her sexuality and her father's insistence that she would have no part in the ranch probably all played a part. Low self-esteem would have caused her to think she deserved Cody's wrath.

"Hey."

She looked up, meeting Carson's eyes. She tried to hide her thoughts but obviously didn't do a very good job.

"You're trying to analyze it, aren't you?"

She nodded.

"Don't, Kerry. Don't try to find blame or fault. That was a long time ago."

"But he's your brother. You don't hit—"

"No. You don't." Carson stood then, signaling an end to the conversation. "Let's take a look at the bunkhouse. Chase? You up for it?"

"Yeah. The bleeding stopped."

"You should probably see a doctor," Kerry said.

"It'll be okay," Chase said. "It's probably not really broken."

Judging by the bruising that was already evident, Kerry wasn't convinced, but it wasn't her place to argue. She took Carson's hand, letting her lead the way outside. Chance and Colt stood nearby, watching the smoldering embers. Thankfully, the fire had started on the remodeled end. Since it had been gutted, there was little to fuel the flames. The rock siding deterred the fire from spreading. The original log structure, built generations ago, only had minimal damage, other than the roof. Apparently, the torrential rain had helped to douse the flames.

"What do you think?" Carson asked Chance.

"A miracle those old logs didn't burn," he said. "If you guys are willing, let's bring some hoses out and soak it. We can maybe salvage the main part after all."

They spent what seemed like hours spraying water on the bunkhouse logs, the wind igniting embers as fast as they could put them out. Kerry was exhausted, but kept up the effort, not wanting to lag behind. They were all soaking wet by the time Chance signaled for them to stop.

"I think this is the best we can do. The wind has died down finally."

"We look like drowned rats," Kerry said with a laugh.

"And smell like it," Chase said. "Not that I can smell much," he added, pointing to his nose.

"I think Kerry is right," Carson said. "You should probably have a doctor look at that."

"Oh, hell, I wouldn't give Cody the satisfaction," he said.

"I can't believe he didn't come down to help with the fire," Kerry said as she rolled up the hose she was using.

"Cody just spent the last week telling us that he was going to marry you," Chance said. "So when he saw that you and Carson had...well, the last thing he wants is to see any of us right now."

"I can't believe he thought we were going to get married. I mean, there's been *nothing* romantic between us," she said.

"Cody hasn't had a lot of experience in that area, so in his mind, there was something between you two."

Kerry glanced at Carson. "I should go talk to him."

"No. Not alone. You just saw what he did," Carson said.

"He won't hurt me," Kerry insisted. "He deserves an explanation."

CHAPTER THIRTY-FOUR

After assuring Martha she would "never do anything that stupid again" and after a long, hot shower, Kerry made her way through the downstairs hallways and into Cody's suite. After her first knock was met with silence, she knocked again.

"Cody? Can we talk?"

"Go away. I told you I didn't want to see you again."

She sighed and bent her head back, staring at the ceiling. Men can be such girls sometimes. So she tried again.

"Cody, please? I need to explain." Her request was met with more silence, then she heard movement in the room. He opened the door, his eyes still hard and angry.

"You don't need to explain," he said. "I know how Carson is."

"But you don't know how I am," she said. "May I come in?"

He hesitated and she thought he would refuse, but he finally stepped aside. She had never been in any of the brother's rooms before and was surprised at just how big they were. She entered into a nearly full-sized living room, a large TV on one wall muted now, but the picture was crystal clear. Through an opened door she glanced into his bedroom, the bed unmade, and discarded jeans were on the floor.

"What do you want, Kerry?"

She turned around and faced him, surprised by the coldness of his voice. She took a deep breath, not knowing where to start.

"I guess first I should apologize for letting it go as far as it did. I wanted to like you that way, Cody. Really, I did." *Was that a lie?* Yes, maybe a little. "But you have to know that there's just nothing here," she said, motioning between them. "I can't make myself feel things that you want me to feel."

"But that's not true," he said. "There *is* something between us."

She shook her head. "There's not. I'm sorry, but I'm just not attracted to you."

"So what? Are you gay? Or are you just another one of Carson's playthings?"

Okay, so that hurt a little, she admitted. Carson had already told her she'd had a lot of lovers. How many of them were Cody's girlfriends? But that was a conversation to be had between her and Carson, not Cody.

"What's between Carson and me has nothing to do with this, Cody. Even if there was no Carson I still wouldn't have feelings for you. I'm sorry."

"But you do for her?"

She met his eyes, thinking she really should lie at this point, but she couldn't. Not about this.

"Yes, I do. And I won't apologize for it."

He gave a bitter laugh. "You'll end up just like the others. Carson doesn't have feelings. She uses people, that's all. She's selfish."

"You haven't seen her since she was eighteen years old," Kerry reminded him. "I doubt you know her at all."

"And you think you do?" He laughed again. "What do you think will happen? She's going back to New York or wherever it is she calls home. You think she's going to invite you to go with her?" He shook his head. "No. You're just a little plaything for her while she's here."

For the first time, Kerry felt the uncertainty of their situation. What would they do? Where would they go? Was Cody right? Would Carson go back to New York? She turned away from him, not wanting him to see the doubt in her eyes.

"You really should see a doctor," Carson said as she handed Chase the icepack. "I'd hate to see that perfect nose of yours disfigured."

"That was crazy, wasn't it?"

"Yeah. The whole day's been crazy."

"Did Kerry really go talk to him?"

"Yes."

"Aren't you worried?"

"What? That he'll get violent with her?"

"No. I don't think he'd hit her. But you never know what he's going to say to her."

"He can say what he wants. Kerry already knows everything."

"You really like her, huh?"

"I'm in love with her." Carson grinned. "God, it feels good to say that."

"I wouldn't know," Chase said. "Maybe someday."

Carson poured scotch into their glasses, then handed one to him. "Here. This'll make you feel better." She pulled the leather chair closer to his and mimicked his position—feet propped up on their father's desk.

"Let's hope Chance doesn't catch us," Chase murmured.

"What? Feet on the desk?"

"That, and having our after-dinner drinks *before* dinner."

"Too many rules," she said. "And after the day we've had." She glanced at him, smiling as they touched glasses. "You know, I've been thinking," she said. "Why don't we buy that piece of land you've got your eyes on. We'll buy it together."

"What? Seriously?"

"Yes. We can start over. We can take Windstorm and Ginger and those young fillies you like. And that mare you've been breeding. We can have our own place."

"Leave the ranch?"

"Yes. You said yourself, you were ready."

"Saying it and doing it are two different things," he said.

"Yeah. But we're not getting any younger. Why wait?"

"You think you'd be happy living way out here? Away from the city?"

"I belong out here," she said. "And I think Kerry would love it too."

Chase smiled and sipped from his drink. "It's two thousand acres, got a nice little trout stream running through it. A valley, nothing big like this but enough for grazing. It's in the foothills," he said. "You can ride up into the mountains from there and into public land. It's just perfect."

"How many times have you been out there?"

"Just once officially," he said with a grin. "I may have trespassed a time or two."

"So? You want to do it?"

"I don't know. It's a lot of money, Car."

"I've got the money, Chase. I really want to do this with you."

"Okay. How about we call him up and go look at it? You may hate it."

"Or I may love it." She tapped her glass to his again. "Thank you."

She had already decided if he said no that she would find someplace of her own. For her and Kerry. Provided, of course, that Kerry was willing. Even if Kerry wasn't ready, she still didn't want to go back East. There was nothing in her apartment in Manhattan that she couldn't leave behind. Even saying goodbye to Rebecca wouldn't be difficult. Rebecca represented everything she hated about her life. She credited Rebecca with helping her when she needed it the most, for taking her in, for teaching her about life. But there were so many things she missed out on by following Rebecca's lifestyle. Rebecca was content with her sex parties and her one-night companions. Carson no longer was.

CHAPTER THIRTY-FIVE

Kerry stood still, watching as Carson closed and locked her bedroom door. The last thing she wanted was another scene with Cody.

"Are you sure this is okay?"

"Yes. There's nothing to hide anymore." Carson gave her a tired smile. "And after everything that happened today, I don't really care."

Kerry moved then, going to her and slipping into her arms. She was exhausted, and she could tell Carson was too. After the emotional scene with Cody, then the fire, they were all drained. Dinner had been short and quiet with all of them excusing themselves early. Cody hadn't bothered to join them at all, which wasn't a surprise.

"It's been a crazy day," she said. She kissed Carson lightly, mindful of her split lip. "We finally get to sleep together and now you're injured and we're both tired and I...I'm going to start my period just any minute now."

Carson laughed tiredly. "I just want to hold you. I don't have the energy for anything else."

She pulled her shirt and bra off, leaving Kerry staring at her. Yes, she was tired—emotionally and physically. Yet the sight of Carson sent a thrill through her, making her heart beat a little faster. Before she had time to consider it all, Carson was tugging at her shirt and Kerry obediently held her arms up, letting Carson remove it. Carson's hand slipped behind her and unclasped her bra. She moaned when Carson's hand brushed her nipple.

"You're so beautiful," Carson whispered, lowering her mouth to Kerry's.

"I thought you were tired," Kerry said against her lips.

"I'm exhausted."

Kerry reached for her jeans, unbuttoning them as she kissed her. "Let me help you with these then."

Carson smiled against her mouth. "Are you trying to seduce me?"

"Of course not. We're exhausted, remember?"

Despite their playfulness at getting undressed, they were too tired to take it any further. Kerry snuggled against Carson, draping her arm across Carson's waist. She sighed contentedly, glad the day was finally over.

"Kerry?"

"Hmm?"

"I talked to Chase earlier about maybe buying a little ranch with him. North of here, on the Idaho border."

"Really?" Kerry's heart beat nervously as she tried to read between the lines, tried to understand what Carson was saying.

"Yeah. And if we do it, we're going to need a consultant, you know. Someone to design the house, maybe do the guest ranch thing there."

Kerry sat up, trying to read Carson's eyes in the darkness. "What are you saying?"

"I'm saying if you don't feel comfortable coming with me like this, as lovers, then maybe you'd come as a consultant."

Kerry closed her eyes and hid her smile. Carson's insecurities popped up at the strangest times. Like now, with both of them naked and in each other's arms and she's questioning Kerry's intentions. Well, there was only one way to ease her fears.

"Carson, you do know that I'm in love with you, right? I would go with you anywhere...like this." She felt the tension leave Carson's body and she bent down, finding Carson's mouth, touching it gently. "Did you think I wouldn't?"

"I was afraid it was too soon. This is new for you, and you just started your business. I didn't know if you'd take a chance on me...on us."

"It's not taking a chance, Carson." She smiled. "I was afraid you were going to leave. Leave without me."

"Oh, God...no, Kerry." Carson pulled her back down beside her, her injured lips moving softly across her face. "I couldn't leave. I would be leaving my heart behind."

Kerry nodded, relieved. "Tell me," she whispered. "Please."

She didn't have to explain. Carson knew what she meant. Carson also didn't have to say the words for Kerry to know, but she needed to hear them.

Carson touched her face, her thumb raking softly across her lips. "I love you, Kerry. I want to start over out here, build a home, a life. With you." Her lips moved gently across Kerry's. "Do you want that too?"

"Yes. Yes, I want that," she said, opening her mouth to Carson, forgetting all about being tired as Carson's tongue touched hers.

CHAPTER THIRTY-SIX

It was cold, but Carson was enjoying the view too much to suggest they go inside. Their fingers were linked together as they sat side-by-side on the porch, their view of the valley unobstructed. It wasn't the vastness of Elk Valley, but it was plenty big for what they wanted. The summer green was gone, replaced by the dry, brown grass of early winter but the horses still grazed—Windstorm and his mares. Chase would go down later to the stables, before dark, to put them inside for the night.

"There's a storm coming in," she said.

Kerry rolled her head lazily to the side, meeting her eyes. "Yeah? How much?"

"Ten inches."

"I guess winter is really here then."

They were quiet again, their gazes again lingering across the valley.

"I love you."

Carson smiled as she glanced at Kerry. Those words were said at night when they were making love, yes, but it was times like this, when they sat quietly, that she loved to hear them the most. Kerry didn't expect a reply and she didn't give one.

"It's just perfect, isn't it?"

Carson laughed. "You say that every time we sit out here."

"Well, it is. I can't believe it's been a year."

"I know. And I can't believe we're going to have *guests* coming in the summer."

"The guest ranch was your idea," Kerry reminded her. "Besides, I think Chase is looking forward to becoming tour guide."

Carson motioned down the valley as the two men came into view. "How soon do you think it'll be before Gerald moves in?"

Kerry laughed. "Are we taking bets?"

"I say before Christmas."

"Well, I like him. He's good for Chase. They have so much in common."

"Yeah. And it'll be interesting when Chance and Colt come to visit."

"Do you think he'll tell them?"

"I think so. There's no need for him to hide it. Besides, how else will we explain having a guy here?"

Kerry ran her thumb across Carson's hand absently. "Do you think Cody will ever come out here?"

"I don't know. He's got a lot of resentment. I doubt he'll get over it anytime soon." Carson glanced at her and raised an eyebrow. "What about your parents?"

Kerry sighed. "Oh, I think they'll come around eventually. It was just a shock to them, that's all."

Carson knew how much it bothered Kerry that there was still this rift between them. Kerry had been so certain that her parents would be accepting that it threw her when they weren't. In fairness to them, it had been a complete surprise when Kerry not only came out to them as a lesbian, but had her lover in tow as well. It had been a stressful evening, Carson trying to fade to the background as Kerry and her parents talked about it, about her. She only intervened when their words became hurtful and accusing, when their words caused Kerry's tears. But Kerry never backed down or shied away from their questions. Carson remembered the tears as Kerry had clutched her hand tightly. "Mom, I just want you to be happy for me. For the first time, I'm in love with someone. I...I love her so much."

But it didn't come that easy for her parents, and they'd left there without their blessings. Kerry had been upset by the visit and that night, she'd clung to Carson, making love with as much intensity as their first time together.

"I think I'm going to invite them to come up for the holidays. What do you think?"

Carson nodded. "I think that's a great idea."

"Maybe if they spent time with us and saw how happy we are, well, maybe they'd accept this then."

"I hope so. I hate that because of me your relationship with them has deteriorated."

"No, Carson. It's not you. It's just that I'm their only child. They wanted a son-in-law and grandkids, you know." She laughed. "Maybe they would accept Chase as a son-in-law." She wiggled her eyebrows. "He would make a great sperm donor, wouldn't he?"

Carson's eyes widened. "Kerry?" She swallowed hard. "You want...you want a baby?"

Kerry squeezed her hand. "I would want your baby," she said softly. "Maybe someday, if you wanted, and if Chase was willing, then maybe we can talk about it."

Carson was floored. It was a conversation they'd touched on only once and she was convinced she *never* wanted kids. "God, seriously?"

Kerry frowned. "No. Of course not. Not if you don't want to, Carson. I just thought—"

"No, no. I do. I mean, I think that would be wonderful." She leaned back and closed her eyes. "A baby," she whispered.

"Carson?"

"I love you. To know that you'd want a baby with me, well, I'm...I don't know what to say."

"You don't have to say anything, sweetheart. I love you. We're going to have a good life out here. I would love to have a family with you."

Carson didn't say anything. She was near tears as it was. *But a baby? God, how cool was that?*

"Carson?"

She turned her head, not trying to hide her tears from Kerry.

"Are you okay?"

Carson nodded. "Happy. I'm just very, very happy."

"You make me happy too."

Carson wasn't sure how long they sat there. Long enough for the cold to settle around them, the sun to set. They watched as Chase and Gerald made their way to the stables to tend to the horses. Carson finally stirred, bringing Kerry's hand to her mouth and kissing it gently.

"They'll be up here soon. We should get dinner finished."

"I'll do it. Why don't you get a fire going?"

They settled into their routine—Kerry setting the table in the dining room while Carson brought wood in for their evening fire. They didn't stick to the rigid seven o'clock dinner hour that Martha had set at the ranch, instead gathering when everyone was ready. When Gerald visited, it was usually later but no one minded. Tonight, Kerry had fixed Martha's beef stew, sans her homemade bread. Kerry had not perfected that yet.

After dinner, they would settle around the fire and Chase would pour brandy for them and they'd talk or watch TV. And later, as the evening wore on, Chase and Gerald would shyly slip away to their suite of rooms, leaving Kerry and Carson to watch the fire die down to embers.

Then Carson—or Kerry—would suggest bed, and they'd slowly make their way to their own rooms, pausing to kiss and touch, making promises of more to come. It was a familiar routine, one she'd grown to love. After so many years of being alone, of having no one, she embraced this simple act of togetherness.

"Sweetheart?"

Carson looked up, realizing she was still squatting by the unlit fire. She felt a blush cross her face.

"Sorry. I was just...thinking."

Kerry raised an eyebrow expectantly.

Carson smiled. "I love you. I love you very much."

Kerry's expression softened. She returned her smile, then blew her a kiss as she retreated back into the kitchen.

Carson struck the match and held it to the kindling, watching as it caught. Outside the wind picked up, and she glanced out the window, seeing the first big flakes of the snowstorm that was upon them. Soon, the door burst open and Chase and Gerald hurried in, snow clinging to their hair and clothes.

"Great! You have a fire," Gerald said, pausing to kiss her cheek before holding his hands out to the warmth.

"Storm just hit," Chase said unnecessarily. "Sorry we're late." He glanced at Gerald. "Fishing and you know, the time got away from us."

Carson laughed. "Fishing...right." She was rewarded with two sets of blushing faces. "God, you guys are worse than teenagers," she teased.

"You should talk," Chase said. "Like we haven't seen you two sneaking off to the stables."

It was Carson's turn to blush as Chase playfully bumped her shoulder.

"I'm going to grab a hot shower," Gerald said. "Or are you guys ready for dinner?"

"No, no. Go ahead," Carson said. "No rush." She smiled as Chase's eyes lingered on him as he walked away. It was good to see her brother so at ease now. At first, whenever Gerald visited, Chase was very much guarded. When Chase looked back at her, she gave him a quick hug. "He's a keeper."

"You think so? Because I like him a lot."

"I know. It shows."

Kerry walked over with two glasses of wine, handing one to Carson. "You want me to get you one?" she asked Chase.

"No. I'll wait for dinner." He glanced over his shoulder to where Gerald had disappeared, then looked quickly back at them. "Listen, there's something I wanted to talk to you about."

"What is it?" Kerry asked.

"Well, you know Gerald spends a lot of time here," he said. "I was wondering how you felt about him moving in here."

Kerry laughed. "We were betting on Christmas as the move-in date." She moved closer to Carson and slid an arm around her waist. "We both love him," she said. "I think it would be wonderful if he lived here."

"You do?" Chase looked at Carson. "You, too, sis?"

"Yes. He fits in nicely with our little family."

Relief shone on his face as he grinned. "Thanks. That means a lot."

"You better hurry if you plan to catch him in the shower," Kerry teased, causing an embarrassed Chase to flee. "God, he's so cute."

They both jumped as a gust of wind rattled the windowpanes. Heavy snow danced around, blowing in all directions, the light reflecting off each flake as they landed on the deck outside.

"Storm's picking up," Carson murmured, her gaze still fixed on the swirling snowflakes.

"I love storms," Kerry said, leaning over to kiss Carson. "In fact, I think we have time to welcome this new storm in." She kissed her again, her tongue tracing her lips. "The guys are in the shower," she said softly. "Let's sneak away. They'll never miss us."

Carson opened her mouth, letting Kerry inside, moaning as Kerry's tongue touched hers. She gave in to Kerry's desire, quickly setting their wineglasses down and leading Kerry to the other end of the house and their rooms. She barely had the door closed before Kerry had her pinned against it.

"I love you so much," Kerry whispered. "I love touching you, making you tremble," she said as her hands boldly cupped Carson's breasts. "I love making you want me, I love...making you wet," she murmured as her mouth covered Carson's again.

Carson groaned—powerless—as Kerry slipped her thigh between Carson's legs. Their desire always flared so quickly, there was no dousing the flame.

As the first winter storm of the season settled over them, the wind howling outside, flinging snow against the windows,

Kerry's warm hands chased the chill away, her whispered words fading in the quiet room, the only sound, their rapid breathing and stifled moans as they gave in to the love they shared.

No, they couldn't extinguish the flame. Not now.

Not ever.

Publications from
Bella Books, Inc.
Women. Books. Even Better Together.
P.O. Box 10543
Tallahassee, FL 32302
Phone: 800-729-4992
www.bellabooks.com

DEADLY INTERSECTIONS by Ann Roberts. Everyone is lying, including her own father and her girlfriend. Leaving matters to the professionals is supposed to be easier! Third in series with *PAID IN FULL* and *WHITE OFFERINGS*.
978-1-59493-224-3

SUBSTITUTE FOR LOVE by Karin Kallmaker. No substitutes, ever again! But then Holly's heart, body and soul are captured by Reyna... Reyna with no last name and a secret life that hides a terrible bargain, one written in family blood.
978-1-931513-62-3

MAKING UP FOR LOST TIME by Karin Kallmaker. Take one Next Home Network Star and add one Little White Lie to equal mayhem in little Mendocino and a recipe for sizzling romance. This lighthearted, steamy story is a feast for the senses in a kitchen that is way too hot.
978-1-931513-61-6

2ND FIDDLE by Kate Calloway. Cassidy James's first case left her with a broken heart. At least this new case is fighting the good fight, and she can throw all her passion and energy into it.
978-1-59493-200-7

HUNTING THE WITCH by Ellen Hart. The woman she loves — used to love — offers her help, and Jane Lawless finds it hard to say no. She needs TLC for recent injuries and who better than a doctor? But Julia's jittery demeanor awakens Jane's curiosity. And Jane has never been able to resist a mystery. #9 in series and Lammy-winner.
978-1-59493-206-9

FAÇADES by Alex Marcoux. Everything Anastasia ever wanted — she has it. Sidney is the woman who helped her get it. But keeping it will require a price — the unnamed passion that simmers between them.
978-1-59493-239-7

ELENA UNDONE by Nicole Conn. The risks. The passion. The devastating choices. The ultimate rewards. Nicole Conn rocked the lesbian cinema world with *Claire of the Moon* and has rocked it again with *Elena Undone*. This is the book that tells it all...
978-1-59493-254-0

WHISPERS IN THE WIND by Frankie J. Jones. It began as a camping trip, then a simple hike. Dixon Hayes and Elizabeth Colter uncover an intriguing cave on their hike, changing their world, perhaps irrevocably.
978-1-59493-037-9

WEDDING BELL BLUES by Julia Watts. She'll do anything to save what's left of her family. Anything. It didn't seem like a bad plan...at first. Hailed by readers as Lammy-winner Julia Watts' funniest novel.
978-1-59493-199-4

WILDFIRE by Lynn James. From the moment botanist Devon McKinney meets ranger Elaine Thomas the chemistry is undeniable. Sharing—and protecting—a mountain for the length of their short assignments leads to unexpected passion in this sizzling romance by newcomer Lynn James.
978-1-59493-191-8

LEAVING L.A. by Kate Christie. Eleanor Chapin is on the way to the rest of her life when Tessa Flanagan offers her a lucrative summer job caring for Tessa's daughter Laya. It's only temporary and everyone expects Eleanor to be leaving L.A...
978-1-59493-221-2

SOMETHING TO BELIEVE by Robbi McCoy. When Lauren and Cassie meet on a once-in-a-lifetime river journey through China their feelings are innocent...at first. Ten years later, nothing—and everything—has changed. From Golden Crown winner Robbi McCoy.
978-1-59493-214-4

DEVIL'S ROCK by Gerri Hill. Deputy Andrea Sullivan and Agent Cameron Ross vow to bring a killer to justice. The killer has other plans. Gerri Hill pens another intriguing blend of mystery and romance in this page-turning thriller.
978-1-59493-218-2

SHADOW POINT by Amy Briant. Madison McPeake has just been not-quite fired, told her brother is dead and discovered she has to pick up a five-year old niece she's never met. After she makes it to Shadow Point it seems like someone—or something—doesn't want her to leave. Romance sizzles in this ghost story from Amy Briant.
978-1-59493-216-8

JUKEBOX by Gina Daggett. Debutantes in love. With each other. Two young women chafe at the constraints of parents and society with a friendship that could be more, if they can break free. Gina Daggett is best known as "Lipstick" of the columnist duo Lipstick & Dipstick.
978-1-59493-212-0

BLIND BET by Tracey Richardson. The stakes are high when Ellen Turcotte and Courtney Langford meet at the blackjack tables. Lady Luck has been smiling on Courtney but Ellen is a wild card she may not be able to handle.
978-1-59493-211-3